Tales from The Warming:

Envisioning the Human Impact of the Climate Crisis

Lorin R. Robinson

Published by Open Books

Cover image "dead tree" by Jimmy B

Learn more about the artist at www.flickr.com/photos/96828128@N02/

ISBN-10: 0998427470/ISBN-13: 978-0998427478

To unborn generations
who will suffer the sins
of their forebears.

CONTENTS

STARTING OVER   200
Greenland
July 20, 2059

INTRODUCTION

Recent polls indicate that 70 percent of Americans believe global warming is real and that the phenomenon's existence is supported by solid evidence. But only nine percent rank the warming as their biggest worry. Polling data also puts the warming at the bottom of the list of American's environmental concerns. Further, 57 percent do not expect it to threaten their ways of life.

Why, after decades of red flags waived by the scientific community, has it taken this long for the majority of the general public to agree that the planet is warming and that human-generated greenhouse gases are primarily responsible? And why, despite almost daily reminders of warming-induced changes already affecting the planet and its inhabitants—human and otherwise—do the majority of Americans seem unconcerned about what will probably be its civilization-changing impact?

In the coming years, doctoral students in a number of fields will, no doubt, attempt to answer this question in their theses. What they will find, and explain in great detail, is that there were multiple reasons for this apparent apathy—reasons that reside both in our heads and in the social, economic and political environment in which we live.

For at least a partial explanation, one need go no further than the tried and true Theory of Cognitive Dissonance. In 1957, sociologist Leon Festinger delineated what now seems to be a fairly simple explanation for why it's so difficult to change people's minds or warn them of potential dangers. We all, he said, use built-in mental defense mechanisms to protect us from information we believe to be threatening or that runs contrary to our existing beliefs. The tools? Selective Exposure, Selective Perception and Selective Retention. In other words, if we can avoid aversive information, we choose not to expose ourselves to it; if we happen to be exposed to aversive information, we change it to fit our preconceived notions; if we are unable to do either, we simply forget it more rapidly than we forget information that's not scary or with which we agree.

The nature of the warming itself also has contributed to people's seeming inability to accept its existence and to consider its negative long-term impact.

There's a simple analogy. Have you heard the recipe for boiling a live frog? If you toss a frog in a pot of boiling water, it will hop out and keep on hopping. But if you put it in a pot of lukewarm water and slowly turn up the heat, it will boil before it realizes what's happened.

The warming is like that slowly heated pot of water. It's insidious, slow-moving. It has crept up on us. Every slight change in the planet's temperature becomes the "new normal" and is accepted as such. More drought and shrinking water supplies? The new normal. Increases in ocean levels? The new normal. Increasingly violent weather? The new normal.

I hesitate to stretch the analogy further. But, while we are not yet boiling, the regrettable fact is that, where the warming is concerned, we have passed the point of no return. It's baked in. It's irreversible.

2

Why is such pessimism warranted? If asked, a chemist will tell you that the CO_2 molecule is extremely robust. That means CO_2 molecules in the atmosphere take a long time to disintegrate—up to 90 years, depending on temperature and pressure. So, every molecule that goes up some smokestack or out some exhaust pipe today will, potentially, be up there causing trouble into the next century. Thus, if we stopped burning all fossil fuels today and converted tomorrow to solar, wind, nuclear, hydroelectric and thermal energy sources, the warming would continue.

Certainly its negative effects could be lessened if the world—particularly the heavily industrialized and industrializing nations—would kick the fossil fuel habit. But, despite all recent promises to the contrary, there's little evidence of significant reduction in greenhouse gas emissions. The Paris climate talks in late 2015, for example, failed to generate reduction pledges of sufficient size from the 196 attending nations to keep the global temperature increase under 2° C (3.6° F)—the maximum increase allowed, we are told, if the planet is to dodge the worst-case warming scenarios.

Instead, we continue to dump approximately 40 billion tons of CO_2 into the atmosphere annually. That figure, to make it more digestible, or indigestible, comes out at 1,268 tons per second. In September, 2016, the global concentration of atmospheric CO_2 officially exceeded 400 ppm, the highest it's been in 800,000 years. It was a very different planet back then. The seas were 100 feet higher and the average global temperature 11° F warmer than today.

Geopolitical considerations bring into question the likelihood that all—even many—nations will rally around a global solution. Approximately 150 countries are defined as developing. With justification, these nations blame the developed, industrialized world for trashing the atmosphere.

The warming puts poorer nations in a double bind. They are being asked to curb their greenhouse gas emissions by converting to more expensive alternative energies. But, without the economic growth that comes from burning cheap fossil fuels, they cannot afford the conversion to non-fossil fuels, nor can they afford the costly clean up and mitigation efforts necessary to deal with the growing crisis.

Ironic that, while building our civilization using cheap and readily available fossil fuels, we also have built in the potential for its destruction.

At the 2009 climate talks in Copenhagen, poor countries were promised $100 billion a year by 2020 to help wean themselves from the fossil-fuel habit while they continue to work to develop economically. These funds— from first-world taxpayers and the private sector—were to be placed in the UN's Green Climate Fund.

And how is the first world doing with that pledge? To date only $10 billion has made its way into the fund's coffers.

Here's one final factor that can help explain why we've taken so long to accept the reality of the warming and either ignored or refused to accept its implications.

Consider the active efforts by the petrochemical, coal and utility industries to discredit not only the science but the scientists behind the warnings of the impending climate crisis (Michael Mann, *The Hockey Stick and the Climate Wars*, 2012). They have spent uncounted millions in advertising, public relations, support of pseudoscience and lobbying in an effort to convince the public that the warming isn't real. Failing that, their focus shifted to blaming a "natural warming cycle" as the culprit instead of greenhouse gas emissions. Failing that, now we're being told that the forecast negative impacts are exaggerated.

This campaign of outright lies and disinformation is reminiscent of that perpetrated by the tobacco industry in its successful 50-year defense of smoking as was clearly delineated in the 2014 documentary, *The Merchants of Doubt*. Only, in this case, the deceit has been far more harmful. It has misled and confused the public, substantially slowing society's reaction to a potentially civilization-changing crisis.

Taking a rational approach to the warming was dealt another major blow with the election in 2016 of Donald Trump as President of the United States. His position on the warming may best be summed up by one of his incessant tweets: "The concept of global warming was created by and for the Chinese in order to make U.S. manufacturing non-competitive."

Trump has vowed to dismantle the U.S. commitment to the Paris climate change agreement, signaling his desire for America not to cooperate with global efforts to rein in CO_2 pollution. Trump, like many Republicans, slavishly adheres to the notion that efforts to control and mitigate the effects of the warming will require more "big government" and cause serious injury to our vaunted and largely mythical system of "free enterprise."

The irony is that by the end of the century—if Trump, like-minded politicians and corporate polluters succeed in continuing to block serious efforts to deal with the developing catastrophe—there will likely be no government, big or otherwise, and no enterprise, free or otherwise, as the world is inundated by its oceans, desiccated by high temperatures and battered by severe weather.

Why have I chosen to write a collection of short stories—of fiction—about what I call "the warming?" Anyone familiar with the literature of global warming can't help but notice that the majority of books and articles written about it are non-fiction—or what, in some cases, purport to be non-fiction. Obviously, these efforts have not rallied the public around the need both to reduce greenhouse gas emissions and to start preparing to mitigate the coming effects of the warming.

Science sometimes can be its own worst enemy. Couching its warnings in scientific jargon, statistics, charts and graphs can render readers comatose. Because writing about implications, "what ifs", is outside the realm of objective science, people are left struggling to understand why they should care. They can't relate what they're reading and hearing to their own realities.

Fiction that's based on near-worst case or worst-case warming scenarios proposed by climate and earth scientists, however, can bridge the gap. The stories in this collection are thought exercises in which I examine the human impact of the climate crisis. They are speculative fiction or, perhaps, they could be included in the recently named new genre—climate fiction.

Each story concerns a different challenge thrust upon us by the warming. The stories take readers all over the world and over time to witness people's struggles to deal with these new realities. Some of the stories put people in harm's way; others focus more on human creativity in mitigating the effects of the warming.

Perhaps novelist, poet and playwright Doris Lessing said it best: "There's no doubt that fiction makes a better job of the truth."

KILIMANJARO
TANZANIA
FEBRUARY, 2022

"There, ahead, all he could see, as wide as all the world, great, high, and unbelievably white in the sun, was the square top of Kilimanjaro. And then he knew that there was where he was going."
—Ernest Hemingway, "The Snows of Kilimanjaro"

Kent Whitaker repeated his new mantra under his breath: "Just put one foot in front of the other; one foot in front of the other; one foot in front...."

Back in the day when he was a regular at the health club it was: "That which doesn't kill you makes you stronger." A cliché, yes. But it had worked for him.

A glance at the altimeter on his wrist told him he had just passed 14,200 feet. Last time he'd been this high was six years ago when he and some college buddies scaled Mt. Rainier, which tops out at 14,400. He was just a kid then and ripped as hell. Now?

Not for the first time he asked himself: "What am I

doing climbing Mt. Kilimanjaro?" His legs felt like rubber. His muscles were on fire. His body screamed for oxygen.

One foot in front....

Joseph, his Tanzanian guide, led the way, a spring in his step. He was at least twice Kent's age, and carrying about twice the weight. He was sure Joseph was strolling leisurely for his benefit. Well, Kent thought, he does do this every couple of weeks. Still....

They'd been at it for about six hours, leaving from Horombo, a group of A-frame huts at 11,000 feet, after two days of acclimation. The only good news was that they were nearing Kibo Hut where they'd spend the night before pushing on to the summit.

Kent was on assignment for the Environmental News Network where he'd been a staff reporter for a few months. ENN specializes in coverage of global warming "events" and news. The Kilimanjaro assignment was his own misbegotten idea.

Around the world, ice fields and glaciers were melting at an alarming rate. Probably the best known was the Kilimanjaro ice cap with its outflow glaciers, "The Snows of Kilimanjaro," Hemingway's famous short story. Satellite images had for years shown Kilimanjaro's once massive ice cap shrinking to the point that it was barely visible. Climbers also reported that very little was left.

Why not, Kent wondered, time an expedition to be present when the last of the ice melts? He was moved by the melancholic nature of the event. It would mark the end of an epoch; a harbinger of the probable fate of glaciers worldwide.

So he did the research, made a proposal and was rewarded with the assignment. It would not, however, be an "expedition." All the budget would permit was a guide, required anyway by the Kilimanjaro National Park, and one "bearer." Yes, *Bwana*, Kent had thought. He would have to control expenses by getting in and out as quickly as possible and by keeping outfitting costs to a minimum.

He remembered the visit from Audrey, the uptight office manager, after he'd picked up the satcam.

"Please be careful with that," she admonished, sounding like his mother. "They're in short supply around here."

Kent knew he should simply have promised to guard it with his life. Instead he wondered aloud if it weren't covered by insurance should something happen.

"Yes," she said, icily. "But the deductible is $2,500. You going to pay that?"

He shut up.

So here he was, satcam strapped to his back. It wasn't that heavy, but the case was awkwardly shaped and, no matter what adjustments he made, it dug in somewhere. He didn't dare give it to Joseph, even though it would probably be safer with him.

Of the six officially sanctioned trails up the 16,000-foot mountain—actually 19,300-feet above sea level—Kent had taken the *Marangu* or "Coca Cola" trail because it was advertised as the fastest and easiest. Designated "medium" difficulty, it had several huts along the way and, with the one extra day at Horombo for acclimation, could be accomplished in five days. Its unofficial name stemmed from the fact that vendors used to sell Cokes at huts strung along the trail.

But the Cokes were gone as were many of the climbers.

The loss of the famous snows were a factor, and the worsening global economy had also reduced the number of adventurers willing or able to spend about $15,000 for the experience. Most who used to come would also extend their trips for wildlife safaris to Ngorongoro Crater and the fabled Serengeti, adding substantially to the expense.

Not only was cost a factor, continued poaching in East Africa's national parks had decimated the elephant and rhino populations to the point that sightings, particularly of rhinos, were becoming rare. Despite incontrovertible evidence that rhino horn is not an aphrodisiac, the Chinese couldn't get enough. And ivory? Who in this day and age, Kent wondered, would condone killing an elephant to make piano keys and billiard balls?

Poverty and poaching, he knew, went together.

The Tanzanian government was also a major contributor to its own declining tourism. In 2016, ignoring the global outcry, it completed a road bisecting the northern half of the 5,700 square-mile Serengeti, disrupting the greatest animal migration on earth. From time immemorial, two million wildebeest, zebra and antelope made a complete circle of the park each year seeking fresh grass and water.

Now the migration was in disarray and animals were dying.

Why did the government put its $5 billion annual tourism industry in jeopardy? It had colluded with China and the governments of land-locked Uganda and South Sudan, both with huge oil reserves, to allow its transportation across Tanzania to be loaded on tankers bound for the People's Republic.

The sanctity of the Serengeti was sacrificed for much-needed revenue. The irony is, with the depressed market for crude and resulting reduced flow from its neighbors, Tanzania was barely recovering road construction costs.

How much farther can it be to Kibo, Kent wondered? One foot in front....

It was late afternoon when they—well, he—staggered into Kibo Hut. The blocky stone house was situated on a barren alpine desert. Their destination, Uhuru Peak, rose above the rocky plain, a 3,500-foot ascent. Kent was glad Kilimanjaro wasn't a technical climb. If he'd had to deal with carabiners, crampons, pitons, ropes and all the rest, he knew he wouldn't have made it. Not that he was there yet.

A few climbers were already claiming their bunks. The hut had a capacity of 60, but was almost empty. Climbers on the way up would rise around midnight for the 7-8 hour ascent. Most climbers—and only about 40 percent actually make it—stay at the summit for less than an hour and descend the same day.

Kent would wait to depart until close to sunrise. He'd sent his bearer—actually Joseph's daughter—on ahead to set up a simple camp at the summit and lug up more of the all-important oxygen bottles. She was also tasked with locating what was left of the ice, assuming they weren't already too late. The plan was to stay tomorrow night, do the satfeed in the morning and then head down.

Kent had been surprised—concerned might be a better word—when Joseph told him that Josephine would be with them. It was easy to tell he'd had plenty of practice defending his daughter's role.

"When you meet her, you'll understand. She's bigger and stronger than me and was a long-distance runner in school."

She was also taller than Kent—long, lean and probably without an ounce of fat. As she maneuvered the 80-pound pack frame onto her shoulders, she gave Kent a big white-toothed grin.

"See you at the top!" She headed up the trail and, obviously, wouldn't need to stop at Horombo for acclimation. Kent appreciated the view of her long legs and tight butt until she disappeared around a bend.

———

After a trip to the outside facilities, Kent threw his bag on a lower bunk and rummaged around his pack for dinner—a couple of energy bars, chocolate and Diamox to prevent altitude sickness—chased with two bottles of water.

Seeing that Kent was in some distress, Joseph brought over an oxygen bottle and invited him to take a big hit.

"Keep it for tonight," he said. "Help you sleep."

Minus just his boots, Kent climbed into the bag. His only companion was batteries for the satcam. He'd been wearing them next to his skin, using body heat to help keep them from losing their charge in the freezing temperatures. The satcam had solar back up, but the summit could be heavily overcast, limiting its effectiveness.

Despite his exhaustion, sleep wouldn't come. Every time he drifted off, he'd suddenly come fully awake, gasping for breath. It was almost as if his autonomic nervous system, at least the part that controlled breathing, had shut down. He'd take a hit on the O_2 and try again, with no success.

So he lay in the total blackness listening to Joseph's soft snoring from a nearby bunk. His brain was the only "muscle" not shut down by the day's exertions. Bizarre and random thoughts flitted through his consciousness. He wondered if the altitude were playing games with his synapses, sending neurons down new and unexplored paths.

I'd better think about something specific, Kent told himself, to get my head under control. But what? How about how the hell you ended up here?

With some thought, it came to him that he was lying wide awake at over 14,000 feet on the side of Mt. Kilimanjaro for three seemingly disparate but converging reasons. First, he had been blown away in high school sophomore lit by Hemingway's "Old Man and the Sea." After that, he'd read everything the man had written, including what was arguably his best short story, "The Snows of You-Know-Where."

Kent strongly suspected his fascination with Hemingway, at least in part, led to the second life-changing decision—to become a journalist.

And third in the trifecta was mountain climbing in college. He and three like-minded friends formed an unsanctioned climbing club and vowed to make one major climb each year of school. And they did: California's Mt. Shasta at 14,100 feet; Mt. Rainier, towering 14,400 feet over Seattle; two trips to Rocky Mountain National Park to scale Flattop Mountain at 12,300 on the Continental Divide and Long's Peak at 14,200.

They'd become pretty good. But then life intervened. Graduation, jobs, spouses and kids for some. Vows to continue the yearly tradition went unfulfilled. Kent's last climb was Long's Peak in his senior year.

So, if it weren't for any one of these three things, he'd probably be at his desk right now at ENN's Chicago headquarters. Or selling real estate.

Another suck on the O_2 to no avail. As sleep snuck up he again seemed to stop breathing. Now what? What about the broadcast?

He didn't need to worry about a script. He'd written it before he left the office. Of course, there'd be no teleprompter, but Kent was comfortable adlibbing or going extemporaneous.

For some reason, his mind skipped from the coming broadcast to his first day at ENN. Senior Editor Jeff McElheny took him to lunch at a deli across from ENN's shabby headquarters on Dearborn. Their conversation was frequently interrupted by the Blue-Line El rumbling above the street.

His boss was only a few years Kent's elder, but seemed much older. He had an edge to him and—maybe he was just having a bad day—seemed cranky.

"So, what are you doing at ENN?" McElheny asked. Kent almost expected him to finish the question with "kid," like some stereotypically hard-bitten old editor. McElheny hadn't been involved in the initial interviews. He hoped they wouldn't be covering the same ground.

"I've been looking for the chance to specialize in environmental reporting. Obviously, it's a very important category of news considering what's going on in the world."

Kent was going to continue, but McElheny cut him off. "Did you say 'news'?"

Kent nodded.

"Well, I have a news flash for you. We don't do news at ENN. We do entertainment with which we hope to attract an audience of sufficient size to attract advertisers in sufficient numbers to keep the lights on and our paychecks coming.

"In fact, no one in broadcasting has done news for decades. Not since local TV stations in the '70s discovered that money—and lots of it—could be made by selling it like entertainment. The format came to be known as 'Happy News'."

The speech was starting to sound like one McElheny regularly delivered to new staff members.

"So, Kent, what's your job at ENN?" he asked, rhetorically. "It's to try to entertain an audience so we can occasionally afford to sneak in some information of importance.

"And how are we doing with that?" McElheny asked, again rhetorically. "Not well. No matter how hard we try, our news just isn't happy. Finding a happy environmental story these days is like finding a virgin in a whorehouse. People, you know, tend to confuse the messenger with the bad news.

"In short, we're not making any money and our backers are getting tired. I don't want to give you the impression that we're about to fold. But things are tight and we need you to help us turn things around.

"You up for that?"

Neither of them had touched the lunches that arrived during his lecture. Kent said he'd do the best he could and picked up his now cold burger.

He must have slept some, because, next thing he knew,

Joseph was gently shaking his shoulder. "Time to get going," he said, face bathed in the sickly green-yellow of a glow stick.

Kent tried to move, but it felt as if *rigor mortis* had set in. His muscles were saying: "Leave us alone. Let us die in peace." He was finally able to roll out and put on his boots. Returning from the latrine, he found that Joseph had rolled up his bag. He also had a luke-warm cup of instant coffee waiting. He'd fired up the small spirit stove.

Joseph, who had been pretty taciturn to that point, decided it was time for a pep talk. "We're close to the point where we have only half the oxygen available at sea level. So, it's going to be very slow going. I know you've done some climbing. Do you know the 'kili-shuffle'?"

Kent shook his head.

"It's a way of walking used by high-altitude trekkers. You take a few small, slow steps; stop, breathe in, breathe out; breathe in, breathe out; then move again. It's also very helpful on this stretch because it's steep in parts and there's lots of scree—very tricky footing."

With that good news they left the hut, head lamps illuminating the slowly lightening trail.

Later, Kent would have virtually no memory of the next eight hours as they "shuffled" toward their seemingly unattainable goal. He did remember looking occasionally at the summit and wondering why it never seemed to get any closer.

Climbing poles helped but, more than once, he went down, sliding on the sharp, loose scree—lacerating his gloves and knees of his padded pants. Each time, Joseph patiently pulled him to his feet, offering oxygen and water.

Then suddenly, miraculously, around 2 p.m., they were standing in front of a weather-beaten sign congratulating them for summiting Kilimanjaro's Uhuru Peak. He thought he should feel something—just a little exultation. But his mind and body were numb. Maybe later.

Josephine was waiting for them, looking very little worse for the wear. She gave Kent a hug, and then led them several hundred yards to camp, a single bright-yellow tent that shown like a beacon against the dingy gray landscape. She had hot coffee ready and a variety of energy and chocolate bars.

As they ate, she spread Kent's bag in the tent. The weather, she said, had been good. Overnight it hit around 0°F. She checked her wrist and announced a temperature of 22°F. "Pretty nice for daytime. I think we'll be good in the morning."

She told Kent to rest. When he was ready, they'd take a look nearby at the last ice she could find.

She led them about 100 yards over the moon-like landscape to a large oblong puddle. The water was trapped in a cleft of some depth between two outcroppings. The sun no longer shone on the puddle. With the temperature starting to plunge, a thin layer of ice, feathery and translucent, was forming.

"This is it. All that's left of the mighty snows of Kilimanjaro. I walked the whole area," she said with a trace of sadness.

Kent surveyed the site, looking for a good spot for the satcam and for him. It was obvious he couldn't do a stand upper and get the pool in the picture. There was a ledge along one side where he could sit. The camera could be positioned across the pool on pretty level ground. The sun would just have risen behind the camera, providing good front lighting. The transmission was scheduled for 9 a.m. local time.

With a nine-hour difference—backwards—there was no way to time the live segment for a large audience. It would be midnight in Chicago. Still, the segment would be recorded for broadcast throughout the day's news cycle.

Back in camp Kent checked the satcam. The batteries held an adequate charge, but he would deploy the solar panels as a backup. He taped the batteries to his waist again, but in a different location to avoid getting a rash.

Josephine warmed a celebratory dinner on the spirit stove—*mshikaki*, a traditional marinated beef dish she'd prepared and carried up with the rest of the supplies and equipment. Kent wasn't hungry, but, in appreciation, ate with what gusto he could manage. She seemed pleased.

Night was coming. The sunset was spectacular, painting the western sky over the Serengeti in a riot of reds and burnt orange. As Kent crawled into the bag, he realized that tomorrow's telecast would probably be anticlimactic.

Set up in the morning was quick.

The satcam was designed to be pretty dummy proof. He could go through the motions by heart. Flip the on-switch, aim the satellite dish to the appropriate sky quadrant, rotate it until a "beep" indicates alignment with the satellite, call the control room on the satphone to be sure somebody's home, confirm the connection, set up the shot, put on the wireless mic, get in front of the camera for video and audio checks.

Kent made his way to ledge and looked into the camera. As he did, he realized that this was probably the closest an ENN satcam had ever been to the satellite.

"Kent, you don't look so good," Brad, the board man, said in his earbud. "Are you that green, or is the color balance screwed?"

"What you see is what you get, smart ass," Kent fired back with as much good humor as he could muster.

"Seriously," Brad said. "We're all glad you made it. Audio and video levels look good. We go to commercial in about 30 and I'll put Terry on with us. We've got a great opener planned. Going to zoom in on your location by satellite while Terry introduces you. How far are you located from what we assume is a yellow tent?"

"About 100 yards northeast," Kent replied.

"Terry, I've got Kent," Brad said.

"Way to go hotshot. There was some betting around the office as to whether you'd make it. Looks like I won a few bucks.

"Here's the deal. We go live on the hour in about four. Brad told you about the opener? I'll intro you over the satellite picture as it zooms to your location. Okay? Incidentally, don't want to spook you, but McElheny actually came in for this. Word is CNN's going to pick it up. We also offered it to Fox but never heard back. Those guys still don't believe the warming is for real. Good luck!" And he was off.

"Here's live audio," Brad said. "On in less than three."

Kent listened to Terry summarize a just-released report on the atmospheric carbon dioxide level. It was over 500 ppm and the rate of accumulation did not seem to be slowing, reflecting continued inadequate efforts at emission reduction.

"Now," he heard, "ENN is taking you live to the top of Tanzania's Mt. Kilimanjaro where reporter Kent Whitaker climbed to witness what appears to be the demise of its famous snows. Kent, is that you sitting by the small pool?"

"It is," Kent replied after the brief lag. "And if I were at this spot in 1922 instead of 2022, I'd be sitting on top of a 20-square mile ice cap that graced this majestic 19,300-foot mountain for at least 12,000 years. But—over the last 100 years—the famous snows of Kilimanjaro have vanished. In front of me is all that's left—this pool covered with a thin coating of ice that will melt just as soon as the sun's rays reach it later this morning. It will refreeze in tonight's sub-freezing temperatures, but, through continued evaporation, this pool and the ice will soon disappear.

"Will there be more snow for Kilimanjaro? Yes. This is the dry season. Later in the year—primarily April and May—the snows will again fall on the mountain. But, because of changed climatic conditions, they will not stay. This massive peak—the highest in Africa and the world's largest free-standing mountain—sits just south of the equator. So it's enduring warmer temperatures than other bodies of ice and snow in the Arctic, Antarctic and temperate regions.

"The vanishing of Kilimanjaro's ice cap could be a harbinger of what's to come for most if not all of the world's other major ice fields and glaciers. Warming-induced temperature increases and decreases in precipitation in many regions are contributing to their demise as they have here in Tanzania.

"Sixty years ago, Tanzania—then known as Tanganyika—gained independence from Great Britain. In celebration, the country renamed the highest peak on Kilimanjaro *Uhuru*, which means "freedom" in Swahili. It's doubtful that anyone then could have known that—in just six decades—Kilimanjaro would know another kind of freedom. Freedom from its iconic cap of ice and snow.

"This is Kent Whitaker reporting live from Uhuru Peak, Mt. Kilimanjaro, Tanzania."

"Thanks for that amazing report, Kent. Have a safe journey down," Terry closed.

In a few seconds, he heard McElheny in his ear. "Great job, Kent. One of the best things we've done in a long time."

"Thanks, boss. I'm just trying to help keep the lights on."

EXODUS
VIATUPU, TUVALU, POLYNESIA
NOVEMBER, 2027

"Up to this time the vast Heaven has still ever remained separated from his spouse the Earth. Yet their mutual love continues—the soft warm sighs of her loving bosom still ever rise up to him, ascending from the woody mountains and valleys and men can see these mists; and the vast Heaven, as he mourns through the long nights of his separation from his beloved, drops frequent tears upon her bosom, and, men seeing these, term them dew-drops."
—From "KONGA TAMA A RANGI," the Polynesian tradition relating to the origin of the human race

*J*ust after sunrise, Solomone Lomu climbed the well-trodden path to Viatupu's highest elevation, 45 feet above the two-square mile atoll. Sunrise had been glorious. A low bank of clouds split the rising sun into orange halves. Its rays turned the slowly undulating ocean to burnished gold.

An auspicious omen for this sad day.

How ironic, he thought, that the day of exodus followed *Fiafia*, Happy Day, celebrated on November 25 since 1887—the date the islanders made final payment on a $13,000 debt to a venal *haole* trader who had encouraged them to buy on credit and then demanded payment in full, or he would take the island.

Two New Zealand Navy transports were anchored to the west in deep water some distance from the reef. A steady train of converted amphibians motored in and out through crashing surf carrying Viatupuans to the waiting vessels. The navy had chosen not to use Asau's wharf. It was more efficient for the amphibs to run up on Olosau beach and open their maws onto the sand.

Below him, along the beach north of Asau, families knotted together. Everyone was allowed two pieces of luggage. Men and women carried old suitcases or boxes. Most kids had backpacks. Each family had been allowed to ship some household goods.

Loading operations had begun early. And, though he wasn't close, Solomone could see that many of the adults suffered from the aftermath of last night's *Fiafia*. The navy actually had arrived a day earlier than expected, but agreed to give the islanders an extra day for the celebration—the last that 827 of Viatupu's some 1,000 inhabitants would enjoy.

Remnants of the huge bonfire still smoldered on the beach. The party, both bitter and sweet, had stretched into the early morning hours. Countless roasted pigs had been devoured; gallons of toddy—fermented coconut milk— had been imbibed. Many had danced until they could no longer stand. And, if one had cared to look, couples could be seen all night melting into the jungle darkness beyond the firelight's reach.

Solomone was the island's *ulu-aliki*, high chief. Although

the title was hereditary and ceremonial, he did have some influence over the *te sina o fenua*, Viatupu's council of elders, more commonly known by the translation—"gray hairs of the land."

Solomone was one of the few islanders with a college degree. After completing high school at the Island's Motofuoa Secondary School, where he now taught, he received a scholarship to attend the University of the South Pacific on Fiji. Considering all the problems facing Tuvalu, his country, and Viatupu, Solomone knew he should have studied something that would help— agriculture, fisheries, marine science. But he didn't have a scientific bent. Instead he developed a deep and abiding love for literature.

He watched as the line of islanders slowly snaked toward the landing site. The process would probably take all day. Some islanders who were staying picked through piles of clothing, furnishings and household items émigrés couldn't take and were leaving behind for them.

A few years earlier, Solomone had been first to talk about the need to abandon the island, home of his people for thousands of years. Others, too, knew it was inevitable, but, as high chief, he felt it was his duty to lead the people to this realization.

Everything that could possibly be wrong was wrong.

It was well known that the submerged mountain upon which the atoll sat was slowly subsiding. This was true, as well, for the seven other inhabited islands that comprised Tuvalu. For millennia this had not been a problem. But the warming of the Earth and its oceans was killing the coral. They could no longer grow as much or as fast as necessary to keep the island above water in the long term.

The rising ocean level was also taking its toll. In recent

decades, Viatupu had lost one-half square mile of beach front. As the island's coral reef gradually became more deeply submerged, it could no longer provide as much protection from wave action that scoured its beaches. And, at times of particularly high tide, Asau's wharf was almost submerged.

It's fortunate, Solomone thought, that this area of the Southern Pacific is not prone to cyclones. A serious blow could wash everything off the face of Viatupu.

But, in the short term, fresh water was the major problem. The island's several freshwater aquifers just below the thin layer of soil and vegetation had been contaminated by rising salt water percolating through the coral base. The water was no longer potable and the wells had been shut down. Island residents now relied on catch water.

But catch water was undependable, sufficient during the winter wet season, but in short supply in summer. Changing weather patterns also had reduced the amount of rainfall. On a couple of occasions, water had to be imported, a very expensive proposition made possible only with help from the central government on Funafuti.

Discussions about the subject at council meetings had been unusually argumentative. Many members were simply not willing to accept the necessity for evacuation. We'll be fine for decades, they said. Who knows where this "global warming" is really going, others said. And evacuate to where?

Solomone had listened respectfully to all points of view. He knew the majority of the council was in denial and that it would take time to bring them around. He responded that it was important for Viatupu to be among the first to take this step. Many other islands throughout Polynesia, Micronesia and Melanesia were facing similar problems.

"Tuvalu, as you know, is listed as number eight on the list of countries that will be most affected by rising ocean levels. Many other islands will need to evacuate. We need to be among the first while there are still places willing to take us."

He asked for and received permission to contact Global Relocation Services, a new NGO offering evacuation assistance to countries in the top 20 on the list of most affected.

"They will visit, evaluate our situation and make recommendations. If it comes to that, they will find and negotiate for a suitable place for us to go and handle logistics of the evacuation. But, initially, we will just talk," Solomone said.

A month later, the NGO's representative, a youngish woman from its headquarters in Los Angeles, arrived after an eight-hour trip on the almost-weekly boat from Funafuti, site of the country's only airport. Lisa Markus had been in transit for 36 hours and was exhausted. She stayed with the Lomus and slept initially for 12 hours. For the next few days she struggled valiantly with jet lag.

Solomone was her primary contact and spent hours answering questions and escorting her around the island. Initially he'd taken her to the very spot where he was now standing. As she surveyed the island, she had a strange look. Solomone wasn't particularly skilled at reading *haole* expressions, but it seemed to combine awe and sadness.

Without taking her eyes off the emerald waters of the island's central lagoon, she said: "This is unbearably lovely. What a tragedy that the people who contributed least to the causes of the warming are the ones who bear its greatest burdens."

She stayed two weeks and became a close friend of the Lomu family, adapting readily to the rhythms of island life. When the time came, she clearly wasn't ready to go.

Departing loaded with fragrant leis and Solomone's copy of Michener's *Hawaii*, which she said she had never read, Lisa promised to complete her report to the agency within two weeks. Her recommendation, she confided, would be for the NGO to grant priority assistance.

The report arrived by email three weeks later. The school had satellite internet connection. He printed it, provided copies to each council member and called a special meeting to discuss.

Lisa's recommendation for priority relocation had been approved. The agency offered to negotiate with New Zealand for emigration of up to 1,000 Viatupuans, virtually the entire population. It ranked the likelihood of success "high" because both Tuvalu and New Zealand were members of the British Commonwealth and there were ethnic and cultural links.

Discussion was contentious. Would relocation be voluntary? If so, who would want to go? Despite evidence to the contrary—steady out migration by the island's young people—some "grey hairs" couldn't believe the people would abandon their ancestral home. How would migrants make a living? And, a more practical question, what would happen to Motofuoa, the secondary school, and its 500 boarders from throughout Tuvalu?

"Would the government even permit us to leave?" asked Tamiela Umbari, apparent leader of the anti-evacuation clique.

Solomone listened until the issues had been raised. He had foreseen most, if not all, of the arguments and had answers ready. "Of course emigration will be voluntary. No one would be forced to leave who wants to stay. The island will support a smaller population for some time to come. It will, however, be more difficult for those who stay to migrate later when conditions dictate."

He went on to recommend that a meeting of all family

heads and single adults be held to obtain input about the proposal.

"But first," he said, "I ask permission to authorize the NGO to negotiate with New Zealand to see if arrangements actually can be made. There's no sense in talking further until we are certain the option exists and is satisfactory to us. In the meantime, I will contact the Departments of Interior and Education to discuss the possibility of mass emigration and what to do about the school."

The vote was not unanimously in favor, but Solomone received the authorization he sought.

As a final thought, he said: "I know how difficult it is to keep secrets in our small, tightly knit community. But it would be best if we kept this to ourselves until the appropriate time to talk to the people. We don't want to have to deal with rumors...."

He knew it was unlikely the proposal would stay under wraps. His greatest fear was that hostile counselors would spread disinformation among their constituents and begin lobbying against it. Can't be helped, he told himself. But I do hate politics.

———————

Shortly after, Solomone contacted Tomasi Malolu, head of the Tuvaluan Interior Ministry, and asked for a meeting. They were slightly acquainted. As a senior member of the island school's staff, he was more familiar with Lemeki Ganilau, the education minister. For his convenience, the two meetings were set for the same day. Lemeki invited him to stay with his family.

The crossing to Funafuti was rougher than usual. A strong low-pressure system was moving into the area. I don't care, Solomone thought, as long as it brings some rain.

Funafuti is the largest and most unusual of the

country's nine atolls. About one-square mile of land, parsed into 29 islets, surrounds the 100 square-mile *Te Namo* Lagoon. Most of Funafuti's 5,000 residents are clustered on the eastern side of the island near its airport. The strip was built in 1943 by U.S. Seabees to serve as a base for B-24s raiding Japanese-held islands including Tarawa. By 1945, the strip had been abandoned and was developed later as a commercial airport. It was the airport that supported Funafuti's position as Tuvalu's primary island.

The meetings went well. Malolu praised him for his foresight. He said a report was being prepared by ministry staff considering the eventual necessity for the evacuation of all Tuvalu's islands. But he was years away from going public.

"For all intents and purposes," he said with apparent sadness, "this would mean the end of our country as we know it. I wish you weren't considering unilateral action. It may raise the issue countrywide before the ministry is prepared to deal with it. But we are a democracy and in no position to bar our citizens from emigration if that's their desire, even *en masse*."

He asked to be kept informed and wondered if Solomone would consider consulting with the ministry's taskforce as it planned for the country's future.

He and Lemeki didn't need to go to his office to discuss the fate of the school. They retired to the *lanai* after dinner the first night and had a long talk. Lemeki said it was important that the school remain in operation. There simply was no money to build another to absorb its 500 students. In addition, as Solomone knew, the ministry had recently spent thousands of Tuvalan dollars to upgrade the school's solar-diesel power plant and its computer facilities.

The ministry, he said, would continue to support the school financially, providing jobs for faculty and staff that might stay. An effort would be made to provide suitable replacements for those who emigrated.

"I know it would be peculiar for students to greatly outnumber permanent residents for much of the year," he said thoughtfully. "Education would become Viatupu's sole industry, not that there are many others at present."

The two laughed at the prospect of dealing with 500 adolescents as the island's primary population.

Solomone realized he'd been standing for a long time. So he sat on the knoll and watched the soaring kites.

About 10 years earlier, a new headmaster for the school arrived with his wife and two boisterous young sons. They introduced the island's kids to kite flying. Viatupu's often strong and steady prevailing winds were perfect for kites. By the time the family left several years later, the kids were hooked. There was hardly a day in which kites weren't flying somewhere.

Dozens now flew off the beach over the heads of boarding émigrés. Children who were remaining, including some from the school, had organized the mass kite fly as a tribute to those who were leaving. And, flying high above them all was Joeli Maraiwai's enormous kite, the largest ever built on the island.

The story of its construction had become legend. Joeli had appropriated one of his mother's *muumuus* to provide the fabric. Mrs. Maraiwai was a woman of some substance, so he had plenty of fabric with which to work. The kite's split bamboo frame was eight-feet across. Though it was difficult to get airborne, when it took flight, no other kite could fly as high or majestically. And no other kite could match its beauty. The fabric was decorated with huge purple hibiscus.

Mrs. Maraiwai had taken Joeli's transgression in stride. Even though it had been her favorite *muumuu*, she came to enjoy seeing it aloft.

Solomone watched as the kites were joined, as often happened, by frigate birds diving on them, flying between them. They were not aggressive; they just seemed to be playing. Below the aerial display, the line was appreciably shorter. It appeared the loading process would finish close to sundown.

———————

Six weeks after Solomone's return from Funafuti, he'd received the results of the NGO's negotiations with New Zealand. They were amazingly generous. As a humanitarian gesture, the government had agreed to transport up to 1,000 Viatupuans with a moderate amount of personal goods to Wellington, the capital. There, free housing would be provided for up to one year. Job counseling, training and placement would be provided. School-age children would receive public education. Men ages 18-24, if medically fit, would be required to accept two years of service in the New Zealand military with salary and training opportunities. Those extending for two more years would be offered free university education.

He took this information to the council along with the blessings of the Interior and Education Ministries.

Solomone was happy to see the information diffuse much of the hostility. As predicted, the island had been buzzing for weeks about the potential for evacuation. In response, he had promised an island-wide meeting to discuss the matter just as soon as all the necessary information had been gathered.

The rumors actually had one positive effect. Islanders had begun to talk seriously about Viatupu's increasingly precarious situation and to make tentative decisions about who might go or stay and under what conditions.

———————

There was no building large enough to accommodate all meeting attendees, so the council arranged to conduct it out-of-doors. A speaker, amplifier and mic were borrowed from the school and lights were strung on poles in what served as Asau's central square. About 250 heads of household and single adults were invited to attend. Expecting that many others would also infiltrate the group, it was made clear that only invited attendees could speak. Viatupuans were known for their volubility. Without some restraint, the meeting could have stretched into the next day.

After solving the inevitable feedback "screech," Solomone ascended the small riser built for the occasion.

"We're here tonight to decide the fate of our island," he began simply. "This is probably the most important meeting ever held by the people of Viatupu. Thank you for coming. Once I've made my remarks, we'll open the meeting for questions and discussion.

"There is no one here who doesn't know that our island is in serious trouble. Rising sea waters have poisoned our wells. Catching rain is not a dependable source of fresh water. The rising waters are eroding our land. We are watching it slowly dissolve. The warming ocean is killing our coral. They can no longer offset the island's subsidence. Our reefs no longer protect our shores as they have for centuries.

"This is the truth. It is a sad truth we all must face and accept. It is a truth that requires action.

"For weeks I know everyone has been talking about what must be done. You all know that your council has been investigating evacuation of the island as one approach. Not everyone on the council agrees, and those who oppose will be given the opportunity to speak, but the majority recommends we take this unprecedented and almost unbearably sad course of action.

"It is the belief of a council majority that we must make this move as soon as possible. Before long, many other islands, those of Tuvalu and throughout the Pacific, will come to the same conclusion. We must find a place for our people while other nations are still willing to accept immigrants.

"And let me answer this question before it is asked. Relocation is voluntary. Those who wish to stay, and accept the fact that emigration will be much more difficult later, may stay. Our island will be able to support a substantially smaller population for some time to come."

Solomone stopped and looked out at his audience, faces and names he'd known all this life. They were listening somberly.

He then explained the process the council had taken to reach this conclusion: the visit of the NGO representative, her report and the agency's negotiations with New Zealand, the approval of the Tuvaluan government, the stipulation that the secondary school remain open.

He next outlined what New Zealand was offering. He was pleased to see a number of smiles when he completed the list. "If agreed," he continued, "relocation would take place six months to a year from now, once planning is completed and those who are going can wrap up their affairs here. What you must do now is decide who is going to relocate. I realize this is a big decision, but we must hear from all of you in the next two weeks. Please inform your councilman of your decision, whether it's stay or go.

"And, before I conclude, let me answer another question that's sure to be asked. As I said, relocation is voluntary. But, with advice, the council has determined that a remaining full-time population of no more than about 200 would be best. You must remember that Motofuoa will stay open at government request and with its continued support. That means island population would swell to about 700 for much of the year.

"I know what a difficult, even terrifying, decision this is—one my family faces just as yours do. It is almost impossible to think that generations of friends and families who have lived, laughed, suffered and worked together will, in many cases, be separated forever. But I'm sure those who stay will keep *Fiafia* alive as long as possible, hoping all Viatupuans will be able to return to celebrate.

"The NGO representative who visited said something that I thought was profound. In so many words, she said it's a tragedy that the people who have contributed the least to the warming of the Earth are the ones who suffer most. She's right, of course. But blame and bitterness will change nothing. We must act."

His fellow Viatupuans were unnaturally quiet. Solomone offered the podium to members of the council who wished to speak in opposition. To his surprise, there were no takers.

After a few easily answered questions from the audience and some brief discussion, the meeting adjourned. Solomone didn't know if that was a good or bad thing.

Solomone stood to stretch his legs and wondered if his wife and daughter were still among the crowd of well-wishers. Adi and Felise were in the throng not only to say *tōfā*, goodbye, to lifelong friends, but to see the Lomu boys off. Emori and Teatao had decided to join the exodus. Solomone, who couldn't abide long and tearful farewells, had said goodbye to his young adult sons the night before.

Solomone, Adi and Felise were staying. He'd accepted the position of temporary headmaster at the school. Felise would finish school this year and had just learned she'd earned a scholarship to her dad's alma mater. The boys, who would have probably gone off island soon anyway, welcomed the opportunities offered in New Zealand. They'd decided to enlist in the navy together for the mandatory two years. If it went well, they'd consider reenlisting in order to get free college.

The sun was settling into the sea. There were few émigrés left on the beach. Loading would be completed in the gathering twilight. The ships' high-powered spots tracked the amphibs as they approached.

The bonfire had been relighted. Over the sound of the surf, Solomone heard snatches of suitably somber songs as people gathered around the dancing flames.

Two weeks after the big meeting, the council convened and each member reported the number of his constituents who would relocate. The tally was 827, a pleasant surprise for Solomone. It was well within the hoped for population limits.

Many families were going as a unit. In some cases, elderly islanders were staying because they were concerned about making the necessary adjustments or because they simply wanted to die where they had always lived. In these cases, a family member had usually volunteered to stay to help care for them. Once they passed, families would help the caretaker join them. Most young unmarried islanders readily accepted relocation as an opportunity to broaden access to the opposite sex, get work and an education.

But, despite the apparent advantages of relocation, a palpable sadness pervaded the island's people.

Everyone knew the exodus marked the end of Viatupu as it had been known to its people since they arrived some 3,000 years earlier on large sailing outriggers from islands to the west. Of the 50,000 migrants out of Africa who had originally overspread the Earth, they were among the last progeny to settle permanently.

The 100,000-year-old migration from civilization's African cradle had finally been completed, only to start once again.

Viatupu—one of thousands of fly specks in the 70

million square-mile watery vastness the world calls Polynesia—would slowly sink under the unrelenting waves, its people dispersed to new lives in what all hoped would be safer lands.

Solomone stayed on the hill long after loading was completed. He watched the lights of the two naval vessels carrying his sons and 825 friends and relatives sink slowly beneath the horizon.

THE PERFECT STORM
BANGLADESH
OCTOBER, 2029

"We opened the Gates of Heaven with pouring water. And We caused the Earth to gush forth springs, so the water met according to the decree which has been ordained."
—The Qu'ran, Chapter 54, Versus 11-13

"Embark therein; the Name of God will be its course and its anchorage. Surely my Lord is oft forgiving, most merciful. So it sailed with them amidst waves like mountains."
—The Qu'ran, Chapter 11, Verse 41

*T*hey moved slowly, watching their footing. The waters of the Shahbazpur Channel had receded slightly, uncovering the ancient path the Ahmed brothers trod almost every day to the family paddies. The path was sodden, its compacted clay surface slippery. Barefooted, they skirted debris left by the flood waters. And, above all, they watched for snakes that would be using the path to slither to safety.

Sumon, the elder brother, walked in front with his walking stick at the ready. A vigorous man who, at 49, seemed to have escaped the vicissitudes of life in this Bangladeshi backwater, carried the stick only for defense. Ashik padded quietly behind, saying nothing. These days he rarely spoke. Since his Anika died in childbirth, Ashik had folded into himself like the petals of a water lily at dusk. He and his son, Rana, had moved into Sumon's household with his wife and three children. Ashik's grief had made dealing with everyday life difficult for him.

Ashik put his hand on Sumon's shoulder. They stopped and watched a black and yellow-banded krait moving sinuously across the path and into the undergrowth.

"I am thankful they are colorful. It is Allah's way of allowing us one more day. *Insha'Allah*," Sumon said, invoking the Arabic phrase he'd learned as a child. Krait bites, he knew, were not always fatal if properly treated. But medical attention was scarce in rural Manpura.

It was October, near the end of the monsoon and cyclone seasons in Bangladesh. This recent monsoon had not been remarkable. Weeks of relentless rain had swollen rivers throughout the country and the small island known as Manpura, far to the south near the Bay of Bengal, was surrounded by floodwaters collected from the Brahmaputra, Ganges, Jamuna, Padma and Meghna Rivers that flowed around the island.

Sumon knew little of the world beyond the island. The Ahmeds had lived for generations near its southern tip, close to the village of Rahmanpur. The farthest he'd traveled had been to Manpura Town in the north to get medical attention for Anjama when she was having difficulty with her second pregnancy.

What he knew of Bangladesh and the rest of the world he'd gleaned from his prized possession—a used solar-powered radio he'd saved for years to buy. Anjama had been against it. She had rattled off a long list of things they *really* needed.

"What good is knowing about a world you will *never* see, a world about which you can do nothing?"

"Ah!" Sumon had said, refusing to back down, "Surely, I do not believe I can do anything about the world. But I would like to know what it is doing to us. I fear there are things going on in the world that will bring us harm. We need to prepare as best we can." He had said these things, not really understanding why he had said them.

Anjama had looked at him with a strange expression. But nothing further was said.

Now it was a family tradition to listen to the radio each morning at breakfast before the children walked to school and the day's work began. After dinner they'd listen again. The radio picked up several stations in the capital, Dhaka. Some of what they heard made little sense, particularly the politics. But weather, agricultural programs and music had made the radio a good investment.

As the brothers rounded a bend in the path, they saw a boat grounded on a sandbar in the middle of the river. Here small islands divided the channel into many streams.

It was a traditional fishing boat, but not one they'd ever seen. It looked about 30-feet long, its paint-less wood planking dark gray with age. The prow was long, pointed and high. It had a flat, inward angled stern, also high. A cabin, whose roof was partially covered with remnants of blue plastic sheeting, sat toward the stern. The rudder appeared to be intact. If there were a propeller, it was underwater.

Sumon shouted, "Hallo!" Then again. But no one

appeared to be on board or nearby.

The brothers stared at each other.

"Let us take a look."

Ashik seemed reluctant. "Is it too deep here? What about the current?"

"Someone might be injured," Sumon persisted. "We will walk farther upstream. It will be easier to wade with the current. It is not that deep here," he assured him.

They walked 50 more yards and then slid a few feet down the bank into the water. They could feel the current. The bottom was mud. Good footing. They watched for floating debris as they angled toward the boat. After dodging a small tree trunk, a door and the carcass of what appeared to be a goat, they reached the stern and waded onto the submerged sandbar, standing about knee deep.

Sumon "halloed" again, then hauled himself up over the stern. As he climbed, he noticed there was no name. Once there might have been. But it had long faded into obscurity.

The cabin was large, but showed little sign of recent habitation. The storm had torn away its plastic protection from the elements, allowing rain to soak the interior. He found a panel of simple instruments for the motor and a starter button.

The two moved forward and opened two hatches covering the hold where he assumed the catch would be stored. There was about a foot of water, less than he'd expected. Further inspection showed that a frayed rope tied around the bow timberhead had parted, probably freeing the boat for its journey.

"I wonder how far it has come?" He looked at Ashik. "The boat seems sound. We could bail out the hold, get it off the bar and float it home."

Ashik looked at him as if he were crazy. "But it does not belong to us? Anyway, what would we do with a boat? We grow rice; we are not fishermen."

He was right, of course, thought Sumon. I know very

little about boats. But, *Masha' Allah*, God has willed it. For some reason He has given us a boat.

He said as much to Ashik. "Who are we to question the will of Allah?"

They found two large, rusty cans and began bailing. Sumon joked that sweat pouring from their bodies might overwhelm the bailing effort. But, after two hours, he could feel the boat start to bob slightly in the current. They jumped overboard, grabbed the rope attached to the prow and pulled. Without too much effort, it floated free. They quickly climbed aboard.

Sumon told Ashik to check the hold for leaks. He threw him a handful of rags from the cabin. "Stuff them in if you find any."

He rushed to the tiller, pointed the prow at midstream and the current slowly carried them toward home.

In that first short voyage, Sumon learned several important things about boats. First, a rudder is only effective if a boat is motoring or under sail. Try as he might to steer, the vessel simply went where the current dictated. The channel was widening, the current taking them farther from shore. How, he wondered, could he beach it without the ability to steer?

The second important lesson was always to check your equipment before shoving off. The two had missed the fact that there was no anchor on board. An anchor, Sumon thought, would at least have allowed me to stop the boat when needed.

Hoping against hope, Sumon hit the motor start button. Nothing. Not a sound. He was sure the battery was dead.

The only solution that came to mind was to tie a rope to the stern, wade or swim to shore and tie it off. But, was there rope?

"Ashik," he yelled, "we need a lot of rope. There's a storage bin in front of the cabin. Check there. I can't steer. We need to jump in, make it to shore and tie it off. Otherwise, we're going to lose the boat."

"Yes, maybe 100 feet," was the response.

Sumon tied the rope to a timberhead on the left rear of the stern and its end around his waist. He jumped in but couldn't touch bottom. Ashik followed and they began to swim the 100 yards to shore as quickly as they could. Soon the rope played out and Sumon found himself being dragged along by the boat—still no footing. To relieve the tension, he turned toward the boat and swam parallel and diagonally toward the shore fast as he could, using the current for additional speed.

Just as the rope again began to lose slack, he touched bottom and dug his feet into the welcomed mud. Ashik was close behind. He, too, grabbed the rope and planted his feet. They stopped the boat's forward motion, waded to shore and, with effort, tied it off on a large mangrove trunk.

Winded and soaked, the brothers sat on the muddy trail.

"Why are we doing this?" Ashik asked, once he'd caught his breath.

"I, too, wonder. But, my brother, something tells me it is the right thing to do."

The Ahmed compound was just around the next bend.

Sumon had been so focused on freeing the boat and floating it home he hadn't considered the next steps. Where would he keep it? He couldn't just tie it off in front of his compound without raising unwanted questions. He was not ashamed of what he'd done. This is not, he told himself, stealing. If the boat's true owners showed up, he'd gladly return it.

But, perhaps that was best. Take it home. Let people see it. Explain that he and Ashik had saved the boat from being washed out to sea. If its owners turn up to claim it, *Insha' Allah*.

So the brothers hefted the rope and staggered down the path, dragging the boat about a half mile to home. There they pulled the prow, hand over hand, onto the small beach they kept clear between the mangroves. Ashik ran off to find the sledge hammer and a stake to secure the boat.

Hearing the commotion, Anjama and the children, already home from school, gathered on the beach and regarded the boat as some sort of apparition. Everyone had questions. Sumon raised his hand to quiet the hubbub. He explained, turning the story into a tale of high adventure for the kids' benefit. Anjama, as always, looked suspicious.

"And if the owners don't come to claim it, then what? We are stuck with this old wreck?"

Sumon wasn't going to tell her about his plans to repair and make it seaworthy. He'd keep that argument for later. "Well, after a time, we could probably sell it to one of our fisher folk friends," he said with feigned enthusiasm.

Anjama, obviously, wasn't convinced, but decided not to pursue the discussion.

The next few days found Sumon and Ashik tending to the family paddies. The second crop of the year was nearly ready for harvest. The Ahmed's fields were among the highest in the area, about 10-feet above the average river level. The advantage was they were less prone to flood damage, either by a monsoon's fresh water rushing down from the north or salt water pushed up river by a cyclone blowing in from the Bay of Bengal.

Sumon knew rising sea levels were forcing salt water

ever farther inland throughout southern Bangladesh. To the west of Manpura, mangroves in the 8,000 square-mile Sundarbans National Park—the world's largest mangrove forest—were gradually were dying. The park was also a reserve for the few Bengal tigers still roaming free.

The disadvantage of their elevation was the need to pump water up from the river when irrigation was required. The ancient pumping system, constructed generations ago, required constant attention. In preparation for the coming dry season, Sumon had disassembled, cleaned and oiled the large hand pump. He also made new gaskets from discarded inner tubes. Gaskets for the pump hadn't been available for decades. The family was waiting for a government grant to buy a small diesel-powered unit, but never seemed to rise to the top of the waiting list.

As they walked home after a long day in the fields, Ashik asked Sumon what he really intended to do with the boat. They walked in silence for a moment while Sumon considered his answer.

"I intend to fix it up; make it seaworthy. I wish I could give you a good reason. But I cannot explain it. I am not a visionary man. But I believe the boat is important to our family. Will you trust and help me?"

"Brother," Ashik said, "I have never known you not to have good reasons for the things you do. So I am with you in this."

———————

Sumon had a cousin and childhood friend who operated an engine repair shop, catering primarily to area fishermen. Early one morning he rode the family bicycle into the village to visit Rasel.

After customary greetings, Sumon mentioned the rescued boat he'd hope to repair.

"I have heard of this, cousin," he said with a smile. "It

is much talked about among my customers."

"And what are they saying?"

"Well, for one thing, they hope you do not decide to become a fisherman. They fear for their livelihoods!"

They laughed.

"I cannot today, but tomorrow I will come in the morning to see what needs to be done."

As Sumon rode home he wondered how he would pay his cousin should it come to that. Perhaps we could help him harvest the small paddy he tends to supplement his income, he thought. Or exchange rice for work after the harvest.

True to his word, Rasel peddled his ramshackle rickshaw, tools and equipment bouncing in the back, into their yard just after breakfast. Sumon and Ashik were waiting. Anjama, he knew, was watching from the house. There would be a reckoning later.

"Well," Rasel said, slightly out of breath, "let us see this glorious hulk of yours."

He picked up his tool box and gave Ashik a grimy battery to carry. "I thought we might need juice if we are to get it started. And I brought some diesel if we need it."

Rasel waded alongside the boat, lifted his tool box up and clambered over the side. He reached down, took the battery from Ashik, and quickly moved to the cabin. The two brothers followed.

He removed the engine cover and, whistling out of tune, surveyed the compartment with a flashlight. "A Deutz 150-HP diesel, air cooled. Chinese. Common around here. Should not be hard to get parts if needed. Looks pretty clean and dry. That is good," he said, almost to himself.

He pushed the starter and got the same silence that had greeted Sumon. He crawled into the compartment, unhooked the battery and, with a grunt, heaved it up onto the deck. Sumon handed him the other battery.

"Hit the starter, Sumon. Let us see if it turns over."

Sumon did and it did. But the engine didn't catch.

Rasel probed the fuel tank and found a few inches. Probably moisture, he said, and asked Rashik to return to the rickshaw and bring the can of fuel. While waiting, he checked the oil level. With fresh fuel, the engine sputtered reluctantly into life, but not without Rasel's expert ministrations involving the choke and throttle.

Once it had warmed up and was running more-or-less smoothly, he shouted, "Is the prop free?" Sumon said it was, so Rasel carefully slipped the engine into gear— forward and then reverse. He revved it slowly, watching the tach. He listened carefully and shut it down.

As he wiped his greasy hands on a rag, Rasel delivered his diagnosis: "Probably just needs the plugs cleaned or replaced, fresh oil, filter and, of course, a battery."

"And will I have to sell the goats to be able to afford this?" Sumon asked nervously.

"No, cousin, but I might consider taking your first child."

Even Ashik laughed.

Rasel told them the labor would be minimal. In fact, the brothers could probably do it themselves. As for parts, assuming the plugs were okay, he said that oil, filter and used battery would be about 500 Taka.

"I'm afraid I would need cash. That good looking young goat I saw might bring that much. Or I'd be happy to wait for payment until you've marketed your surplus rice."

They walked up from the beach. Sumon said he'd think about it and let him know soon. As Rasel rattled off, Sumon began mentally to prepare for the imminent confrontation with Anjama.

By the time Sumon returned for dinner, he had marshaled all his arguments. He could see she wasn't happy, but nothing was said during dinner. In fact, she had prepared his favorite spicy dal—red lentils, onions, garlic, tomatoes, spices and cilantro—with freshly baked roti.

But, when they crawled into their bed, Anjama asked quietly why he hadn't asked her about repairing the boat. Sumon was caught off guard. He'd expected a tirade.

"I just wanted to learn how bad it was and whether we could afford to get it running before I spoke with you. I did not want you to worry without reason," he said.

"Can it be fixed? And at what cost?"

He related what Rasel had told him.

"Our best doe? Or 500 Taka in rice? That is the cost? And you would have us pay this?" she asked, voice rising slightly.

Sumon nodded, then realized she couldn't see him in the dark. "Yes."

"Sumon, I do not understand why you would waste what little we have in this way. You are not a fisherman. Nor do we have time or money to take pleasure cruises on the Shahbazpur. What is it you would do with this boat?"

Sumon sighed. "I do not know. All I know is that Allah gave us the boat for a reason, *Allahu Akbar*. If you do not trust in me, then trust in Him."

Realizing she had lost the argument, Anjama rolled over and said nothing. Soon he heard her breathing quietly. Sumon lay on his back and watched as moonlight filtering through the window traveled slowly along the wall. The moon was down before he slept.

The repairs proceeded in fits and starts. It was time to harvest the rice and the days of backbreaking labor left little time to devote to the boat. Still, Sumon tried to do something every day.

The first big project was—when the boat rode high on the tide—to slip palm logs beneath and place props to hold it upright when the tide receded. Sumon had begged a supply of pitch from friendly boat owners to caulk leaks. Almost to a man they had smiled and shook their heads as Sumon walked away carrying pots of the sticky substance. It would have to be heated before it would flow between cracks in the hull.

With the children's enthusiastic help, they cleaned trash out of the cabin and scrubbed it down. Sumon and Ashik tore the remnants of plastic from the roof and replaced them with a double layer of tarp, tacked down with strips of wood.

They also cleaned the hold and found, to their surprise, a bilge pump they hadn't noticed before. Sumon tore it apart, cleaned, oiled it and—as was his custom with their irrigation pump—fashioned new gaskets from an inner tube. The hatch covers didn't fit tightly, so he also outfitted them with rubber seals to help keep the hold dry. He did the same for the engine cover.

For an anchor, Sumon had the blacksmith tap the lid of a large oil can and weld an eye bolt. He filled the can with sand and the blacksmith welded the lid shut. It took the two brothers to carry the anchor to the boat, hung on a thick plank supported on their shoulders.

Meanwhile, Anjama, with a heavy heart, found a buyer for the goat. She did well and raised enough to pay for engine parts and diesel fuel. Sumon pulled the plugs and took them to Rasel for advice. He checked the gap and proclaimed them usable with cleaning. Sumon paid him for the oil, filter and used battery. He also paid for fuel and bought two beaten up jerry cans so Rasel could deliver it with the parts.

As Rasel had predicted, the brothers were able to make the repairs and, to their great satisfaction, the engine was soon running smoothly.

The end of the month was near. With November would come cooler, dry weather and the end of the monsoon and cyclone seasons until they began again in April. But Sumon had heard on the radio that, because of the warming Earth, the seasons were lengthening. He had noticed this even before it had been announced on the morning weather program to which the family listened.

Insha'Allah, he thought, there will be no more bad weather this year.

But, over the next several days, weather news on his radio was disquieting. One morning, he heard that a low-pressure system forming in the North Indian Ocean had the potential to create a post-season cyclone.

"We'll be watching to see how it develops," he promised.

The next day, they were told that unseasonably hot temperatures made it possible the monsoon season would continue into November. Sumon knew that heavy monsoon rains were caused by hot air rising above the land, sucking in cooler air from the ocean. In the same broadcast, a weather expert also explained that continuing heat in the region was causing snow and ice on the mountains of Nepal to melt faster than normal.

"This additional water," he warned, "will flow into the Brahmaputra, among others, and is likely to raise the level of our river system to some degree, perhaps beyond flood stage in some low-lying areas."

And, if that weren't enough, it appeared the low-pressure system had coalesced and been upgraded to a cyclonic storm with sustained winds of 55 miles an hour. Its direction was indefinite, but, if it continued to gain strength, the historic path for these storms would be north into the Bay of Bengal, with possible landfall on Bangladesh.

"I know radio listeners can't see the satellite picture I'm holding, but let me describe it to you. Imagine a length of white cotton fiber wrapped very tightly and flat. Imagine it is rotating counterclockwise with a bright blue eye in the center. That's how the storm appears. It has been named '*Sagar*,' the next name on list for Indian Ocean cyclones."

Sumon went to bed that night with a sense of foreboding. As the rains began pattering on the tin roof, he made a decision.

During the long and sleepless night, Sumon made a mental list of all that had to be done. He woke everyone before the usual time. Complaints from the children quickly quieted when they saw the look on his face.

"We have much to do," he said, "and very little time." He asked Anjama to prepare a quick but filling breakfast while he explained.

"We are facing very dangerous weather. I believe there is nothing to be done but to fill the boat with food, drinking water, our animals and more fuel so we can ride out the storm. We will not be safe on land," he said. The children looked at him, round eyed.

Sumon assigned tasks for everyone.

Ashik would take the bicycle to the village and fill the two cans with more fuel, using what money they had left. Considering the muddy road and pathway, he would probably have to push the bicycle home with the cans hanging on either side. If necessary, he would go back for more to ensure the tank was full.

He and the boys would put the chickens in the small coop. When the time came, they would load the coop and their two remaining goats in the hold. They would also fill all the plastic jugs they could with water from the well.

Meanwhile Anjama and the girls would pick the ripe and almost ripe vegetables and fruit in the garden, packing them in baskets. Anjama would also supervise packing necessary clothing and household items in boxes.

"Don't forget the brazier, charcoal and lanterns," he reminded her. "I will wrap as many bags of rice and beans in plastic as I can and store them in the hold," he said.

He stopped and looked at everyone. He saw fear and disbelief.

"We will come home after the storm," Sumi, his eldest daughter, stated with a hopeful look. "*Insha'Allah*," Sumon said. Her face fell.

The next three hours were a madhouse of activity with everyone coming and going. The increasingly heavy rain and wind made it difficult. Sumon checked the radio once more before sealing it in a plastic bag.

The news was worse. The cyclone had intensified. It was now Category Three with winds exceeding 111 miles-per-hour. The radio said it was heading for the Bangladeshi coast and, at its current speed, would arrive in less than two days. Landfall would probably coincide with a high tide, the worst of all possible situations.

Meanwhile, the monsoon had intensified and rivers throughout the country were rising rapidly. All that water, Sumon knew, was heading south and would rage around the island through channels on the west and east.

It was early afternoon when the goats were manhandled onboard and into the hold. Sumon had supervised the loading, trying to ensure weight was carefully distributed. He had placed the heavy sacks of rice and beans along the keel and tied them off.

The beach had already disappeared under the rising flood. The stake holding the boat to shore was underwater. With everyone and everything on board, he had Ashik wade out and untie the line. He backed the boat into the current, gunned the engine and turned upstream. His plan was to motor several hundred yards to the shelter of a small island at midstream, tie off the boat and shut down the engine to save fuel. This way, he reasoned, they could rise with the flood and be protected by the island's shadow from much of the debris hurtling downstream.

He had no idea what he would do when the cyclone roared ashore from the south.

The rain fell in sheets. Sumon often felt as if he were underwater. The straw hat he wore in the fields had quickly blown away. The rain cascaded over his face, blocking vision. He could have stepped into the cabin, but was afraid he might lose the tether to the island, requiring him to start the engine and maneuver the boat. In any case, the cabin didn't provide that much protection. It was open at both ends and the family, huddled together, tried in vain to stay dry. He suggested they get into the hold where it would be drier. Ashik was already there, working the pump.

Occasionally the heavy rain relented for a few moments. Sumon could see debris on either side of the island moving as fast as he could pedal the bicycle. Whole trees, animal carcasses, mangled structures paraded by. In the roiling waters it was hard to tell, but once he thought he saw a corpse. Another time, just as the rain began again in earnest, he swore he saw two people clinging to what might have been the wall of a shack floating like a raft on the swollen river.

Sumon suddenly had a strange vision. He saw a huge underwater city made of broken buildings, trees, boats and vehicles deposited on the ocean floor by the decades of flood waters. The city was inhabited by many thousands of ghosts floating aimlessly in and out of buildings and up and down crooked streets. Among them floated countless animal apparitions, livestock gathered in herds or flocks;

predators—including the last Bengal tiger—moving menacingly among them.

Sumon wiped the water from his eyes and with it, he hoped, the nightmare scene suggesting the fate of his people. *I must stay alert.*

Day was turning into night. The day had been so dark that, initially, it was difficult to tell the difference. But gradually, Sumon could no longer see the island only 25 yards ahead. The rising flood waters were slowly submerging the island. The time would soon come when the boat would no longer benefit from its shadow. He knew the current would scour away the soil, exposing tree roots. They would soon start to topple and menace the boat. His tether would be lost.

Insha'Allah, this won't happen until morning so I can see to take the boat to mid-channel and, with Ashik's help, avoid debris. He knew he would then have to use precious fuel to try to keep the boat in place. There would be no more shelter, and he couldn't let them be beaten south by the raging flood waters into the teeth of the coming cyclone.

Night descended—the blackest night Sumon had ever known. He was not a man prone to fear. But the all-enveloping darkness disoriented him. He had absolutely no point of reference. It was impossible to keep a lantern lit. Once in a while he would flip on the flashlight just for few seconds to provide some comforting light.

Barred vision, his other senses seemed heightened. He could hear the eerie keening of the wind in the now barren branches of the island's trees. He could feel the water rushing along the sides of the boat. The "thunk" of debris hitting the boat seemed magnified and sent shivers down his spine.

Sometime during the night, Ashik stumbled up from

the hold to report that the pump was keeping up with leaks. He gave Sumon water and a mango. He said the family was as dry and comfortable as could be expected and wondered if he could take over to give him some rest.

"Thanks, brother," Sumon shouted over the roar, "but I fear we may soon have to abandon our shelter behind the island when it is submerged. I need to be ready. It is best you continue on the pump. And please instruct Anjama and Sumi how to work it. They will need to replace you when we move into the channel. I will need you on the bow to help me avoid debris."

So Sumon sat, tiller in hand, waiting for whichever came first—loss of their umbilical to the island or daylight.

To occupy his mind, he thought of what he would do when the cyclone struck. It will probably be tomorrow, he thought. Sumon remembered that cyclone winds wrap counterclockwise around the eye. He had never owned a watch, but he knew what counterclockwise meant. That means the winds would be screaming in from the east. How damaging the winds and storm surge would be depended on where the center of the storm hit.

In any case, he believed the boat would best be placed as far from the gulf as possible and along the west side of the island. Manpura would help block some of the storm's fury. The east side would take the brunt of it. Staying as far north as possible would lessen the impact of the inevitable storm surge.

Over the years he had experienced the many storms that had hit the region. He hoped he understood the best thing to do, in this case with a boat. He knew, at some point, he would have to point it south into the coming maelstrom to survive its winds and the storm surge.

He prayed the fuel would last.

Sometime during the long night, the rain lessened to a

steady drizzle. The wind, which had been from the south, providing cooler air to fuel the monsoon, was shifting to the east, announcing the imminent arrival of "*Sagar.*"

In the grayness of dawn, Sumon could see that the island was completely underwater. The rope to the anchoring tree was submerged. Trees were toppling, being carried swiftly downstream, some coming close to the boat. He shouted for Ashik. They had to be ready to cut and run.

Before Ashik made it to the bow, Sumon felt the boat slipping backward. The top of the tree to which it was tied was slowly falling toward them into the water.

"Ashik, cut the line," he shouted. He hacked at it, wielding the machete left there for that purpose. Meanwhile, Sumon started the engine and, once the line was cut, backed away from island that had served them so well.

For the rest of the day, the brothers did the best they could to dodge debris flung by the raging flood waters. Sumon took cues from Ashik positioned on the bow. They couldn't miss them all. But the boat's long and narrow prow helped push debris aside. Sumi came up from the hold to announce that water was rising despite their efforts. She wondered if she could watch for debris so the pump could benefit from Ashik's strength. Sumon agreed and Ashik instructed her on what to do. Soon he was steering following her directions.

Sumon worked the throttle carefully. He picked a tree still standing on the edge of the river as a marker and tried to use only enough power to keep them abreast. But the current was so fast he was afraid he was using too much fuel.

Now he worried about when he should turn and head south to face the monster bent on their destruction. Late in the afternoon, that decision was made for him.

Wind screaming in his ear, rain blowing sideways, smacking the right side of his face, Sumon suddenly felt the stern dip slightly. He knew it was time.

He shouted to Sumi: "Go below. Tell everyone to hang on and Ashik to keep pumping."

Sumon tied himself to davits in the cockpit and, when Sumi was safely below, applied full power and wheeled the boat around. The maneuver was dangerous. He feared the full force of the flood might capsize the boat when broadside. He also prayed it wouldn't be hit by a massive tree or wreckage while turning.

The boat did tip when hit by the flood. But it quickly righted as he completed the turn.

Now he was speeding south along with the current, debris matching his speed to left and right. He looked ahead and his heart almost stopped. Before him was a wall of gray-green water towering at least 20 feet above the channel. The top was curling. White froth blew in sheets from the crest, powered by winds of unimaginable fury.

Instinct told him to apply full power and hit the wave head on. If not, all was surely lost.

It was only seconds, but it seemed like an eternity. At first the sharp bow cleaved the water, sending it rushing down the sides of the boat until it climbed over the gunnels and rushed toward Sumon like a raging water buffalo. The boat rose higher and higher, climbing the mountain of water. Then it seemed to slip backwards. The stern was underwater. Sumon was submerged, saved only by the ropes. The engine screamed. Sumon hung onto the tiller, trying to keep the boat pointing straight. As the curl crashed over the boat, it was entirely underwater.

Then the boat crested the wave and slid down its backside, shedding water as it went. Sumon watched with horror as the prow plowed farther and farther underwater back to the second hatch cover before it leveled and, like a cork, popped back to the surface.

"*Al-hamdu-lillah*, thanks be to Allah," Sumon shouted.

But the ordeal wasn't over. Smaller following waves had to be crested. And Sumon had to motor carefully as close as possible to what was left of Manpura's western shore to help block the furious winds that buffeted the sodden craft.

Ashik climbed out of the hold.

"Everyone is okay," he shouted over the wailing wind. "Some cuts and bruises. I think Rana may have a broken arm. Sprained, at least. Everything went flying. We have over a foot of water, but I think the pump can hold it."

Sumon asked him to check the fuel level before going back to pump.

"Looks like less than half a tank."

Early the next afternoon, the storm had dissipated as it pushed in over the land. Sumon brought out the radio to learn whatever he could. Anjama and the girls brought the brazier up and heated water for tea and their first hot meal in three days.

To conserve fuel, the brothers wrestled the anchor overboard. The boat rocked, not too gently, close to the southern tip of Manpura. Sumon, exhausted almost beyond salvation, called the family together.

"We have survived the storm, *Al-hamdu-lillah*," he said. He surveyed the cuts, bruises and Rana's right arm in a sling. "But we are far from safe yet. What I am going to say will not make you happy. But it is what we must do."

He took a sip of tea.

"We cannot go home because there is no home. You heard the radio. All of southern Bangladesh is destroyed.

"Yes, our land is still there. But it has been ruined by salt water. Even if we could rebuild, we couldn't support ourselves. Even if we could rebuild, there will be more and more storms like this one to destroy us again and again.

"The government is setting up refugee camps, but they won't be ready for weeks. And how could we get there? We don't have enough fuel.

"The only answer is to resettle in the hills of Chittagong. We will be safe there. We can sell the boat and use the money to buy a place away from the ocean where we can live peacefully. We have food and our animals to get us started. Chittagong is only about half a day east and I think we have enough fuel."

He stopped. Anjama wept silently, but there were no arguments.

"The boat is taking water, so we must push on. I don't want to travel at night but we have no choice. Everyone eat, drink and rest."

With the anchor back aboard, Ashik took the tiller. It would have been safer to hug the coast, but, to have enough fuel, Sumon told him to take a southeast heading around the tip of neighboring Hatiya Island and then east across bay. He lay down in a corner of the cabin and slept. Anjama covered him with a thin blanket that, miraculously, had stayed almost dry.

The sky was lightening to the east when Ashik shook Sumon's shoulder. Anjama was at the tiller. "There is something you must see, brother," he said, pointing toward the dawn. On the horizon were smudges—the hills of Chittagong.

"We have several inches of fuel left. I think we'll make it," Ashik said.

Sumon gradually got to his feet. Everything hurt. He walked to the bow and looked down at the prow as it neatly split the water. The ocean was amazingly flat with only the slightest of swells.

Ahead and on the right he thought he saw something in the water. He was about to warn Anjama to steer left, when the object resolved into a large tree truck with what appeared to be two people clinging to it.

"Stop the engine and steer right," he shouted.

Sumon jumped into the water and swam the short distance to the tree trunk. It was light enough to see it was a woman and what appeared to be a young boy. They were tied to the tree. As he got closer, it was clear they were dead.

He reached the boy first. His head was above water. His eyes were closed; face peaceful. One arm, possibly broken, was in the water waving in the current as if to greet him. The woman was face down, her long hair floating like a black halo around her head. He pulled out his knife, cut the rope and turned her over. Her frozen expression was also peaceful, accepting. Her eyes were open; he closed them.

There was nothing he could do but cut their bonds and let them sink to a watery grave. He tied them at the waist so they would remain together on their journey. He let them go, watching as they sank slowly into the dark waters. Her hair floated above her head, undulating gently in current. The boy's arm continued to wave as he sank out of sight.

As Sumon swam back to the boat, he again saw his vision of the undersea city of the dead.

The hills of Chittagong were now sharply etched on the horizon as the sun prepared to rise behind them. Sumon was sitting at the bow. The pink disk of the sun peeked above the hills. It shot a streak of light across the gently rolling, silver-gray waters. The rosy light seemed to quiver and pulsate as it skipped over tops of the swells.

Sumon thought he should pray to give thanks for their deliverance. But he was too agitated. Not agitated, he thought. Angry. As he watched the sun slowly rising, the anger built. He looked directly into the sun, hoping it would burn away the things he had seen. He had never known such anger.

He said: "Lord, are we not already among your poorest, most humble, most downtrodden people. Are our sins so iniquitous as to cause you to destroy us in this way? To wash men, women and children off the face of the Earth? To banish whole generations of your people to watery graves? Why, Lord? Why?"

Sumon bowed his head. The sun's afterimage glowed behind his closed eyes. He listened.

There was no answer.

FRANCESCA AND PAULO
VENICE
APRIL, 2032

"To build a city where it is impossible to build a city is madness in itself, but to build there one of the most elegant and grandest of cities is the madness of genius."
—Alexander Herzen, writer and philosopher

"The experts are right, he thought. Venice is sinking. The whole city is slowly dying. One day the tourists will travel here by boat to peer down into the waters, and they will see pillars and columns and marble far, far beneath them, slime and mud uncovering for brief moments a lost underworld of stone...."
—Daphne du Maurier, author and playwright

"Is it worthwhile to observe that there are no Venetian blinds in Venice?"
—William Dean Howells, author and playwright

*F*rancesca stood at the top of the dark, narrow staircase. Clear, bare bulbs barely illuminated the passage, casting dancing phantasms on its rough, stone walls—shadows of volunteers who, like herself, were passing carefully waterproofed boxes from the second floor of the *Museo Marciano* to be carried through the flooded first floor to barges bobbing gently at the south end of the Grand Canal near *Piazza San Marco*.

Paulo, her boyfriend, was one step down, accepting packages from her—another link in the long chain of young and old helping to remove the museum's massive collection of historical art, small sculptures, glass, gold and silver religious and profane objects, ancient books and manuscripts. Larger pieces—paintings, sculptures, tapestries and those frescos that could be removed—had been carefully crated and transported earlier to the *Santa Lucia* rail yard at the other end of the canal, a long reverse "S" that bisects the city.

She knew Paulo was upset with her. He was careful not to show it because he understood. But she knew. Francesca couldn't help but hold each package a little longer than necessary as it came to her. She simply *had* to scan the manifest to learn what treasures were passing through her hands.

Born and raised in Venice, Francesca was intimately familiar with its museums, palaces, churches and what they contained. She had recently completed her Second, a Master's Degree, in art history at Venice's *Università Ca' Foscari*. It saddened her beyond words to see the magnificent museum's walls denuded, its display cases and archives emptied. And it wasn't the first, nor would it be the last, as the much of the city's cultural heritage, dating to its founding 1,200 years earlier, was gradually transported to a newly constructed facility in Rome to save it from the rising waters of the Adriatic and its penetrating damp.

The last box traveled down the human chain around 10:30 p.m. Francesca, Paulo and a couple of friends, physically drained by the 12-hour ordeal, decided to get something to eat. They walked a short distance across *Piazza San Marco* to *Caffè Florian*, a place they wouldn't normally go because it was usually inundated with tourists and prices were correspondingly high. But the hour was late.

Actually, they had to wade. The four wore *stivali di gommas*, rubber boots, to protect their shoes. They were ususally just referred to as *gommas*. The plaza, one of the lowest spots in the city, was covered with about eight-inches of water in what was known as an *acqua alta*, a high water incident. *Acqua altas* used to be infrequent, resulting from an unusual combination of high tide and wind. Now, because of the rising sea level and continued subsidence of the city, many areas flooded on a regular basis.

Francesca looked at her *gommas*. They were black and unadorned, although they had become available in colors, abstract patterns and with graphics to cater to Italians' sense of style.

Florian had the unique distinction of being the oldest continuously operating cafe in the world. Founded in 1720, its elegant surroundings had attracted the likes of Dickens, Vivaldi, Proust, Byron and Goethe. Some of its early appeal, no doubt, had to do with the fact that it was then the only coffee house in town allowing women patrons.

An obviously tired waiter escorted them to a small table in the back of the main room. The warm and aromatic atmosphere helped raise their spirits a bit as did the bottle of red table wine. But, overall, it was a somber meal.

"Tell me," Paulo said, "wasn't there a project some years ago to try to enclose the *Laguna Venetia* to keep the rising waters out of the city?" Paulo lived and worked in Rome and was visiting Francesca for a few days.

Giovanni snorted. "Some project! That crook Berlusconi promoted a system of 78 huge floatable gates to be fixed on the seabed across the three entrances to the lagoon. When tides were predicted to rise about four feet, the pontoons were to be filled with air, float to the surface and block incoming water."

Marco seemed amused by his partner's tirade.

"As an experiment, four gates were installed at a cost of five billion euros across the smallest of the three inlets. The government termed it a success and vowed to continue the project. But charges of gross corruption, poor engineering and adverse environmental impact held the project up in court for years. As the economy continued to worsen, the project eventually sank from sight." Giovanni smiled at his metaphor.

Paulo professed not to understand the validity of the concept. "Isn't the problem caused by a combination of high tides *and* rising sea levels? How could a temporary structure designed to control tides deal with the rising waters *added* to tides? And, if it *were* designed to be a permanent form of sea wall, wouldn't it have needed locks?"

Giovanni looked at Francesca. "You've found yourself a smart one," he said, teasingly.

"*Esattamente*," he said. "Initial planning for the project did not factor in rising sea levels. Many *idioti* early in the century did not accept implications of the warming."

"So," Paulo said, "the city, essentially, is helpless."

"There are plans *floating* around to build an actual seawall with a lock on the Lido Channel to wall off the lagoon. But the problem is that the many miles of sandbar between the three channel openings are, themselves, barely above water. For the plan to work, they would have to be covered with millions of tons of stone. No one knows where the money would come from," Giovanni said.

There was a pause in the conversation as panini arrived. It was just as well, Francesca thought. The topic had cast a pall over the gathering. Later, coffee came with a "we're-about-to-close" look from the waiter.

Outside they said, "*buona notte.*" Holding hands, Giovanna and Marco sloshed like kids to the *Riva degli Schiavoni* and headed east along the lagoon past *San Marco* and the *Doge's Palace*. The three-quarters moon overhead turned the wakes of their *gommas* into irridescent waves. At canal *Rio de la Pieta* they'd catch a *vaporetto*, a water bus, north to their apartment near *Scuola de San Georgio degli Schiavoni*, an art museum where they worked as curators.

"Carapacio's 'St. George and the Dragon' brought us together," Marco liked to joke.

Francesca and Paulo sloshed the other way past *Teatro la Fenice*, where her parents had given them tickets for the following evening's *homage* to Vivaldi, a Venice native. They caught a *vaporetto* at the Grand Canal that took them across to canal *Rio Nuovo*. Her apartment was near her alma mater where she worked as a research assistant in the *dipartimento di arte*.

As they moved away from *Plaza San Marco*, the narrow streets began to dry. Moonlight turned water in small depressions in the cobblestones into diamonds. They laughed because Paulo's borrowed *gommas* were too big and flopped as he walked.

They were tired, so lovemaking in her small bed was delightfully slow, sweet, languid—very unlike the frenzied exuberance of the previous night following Paulo's arrival. He was soon asleep, lying on his back, softly snoring. Francesca, who had always slept very little, turned on her side to study his features. Moonlight bathing the room gave his face the appearance of an alabaster sculpture.

A nice face, she thought. A noble nose. Full mouth. Long lashes. A profusion of thick black hair with a slight curl. Not exactly handsome in the classic sense, but nice. I don't think I'd want him too handsome, she ruminated. Handsome men can be so vain, egotistical—used to getting their way with women without having to work very hard.

I wonder how long this will last, she thought, as she carefully rolled onto her back. Her track record had not been very good. From the way men looked at her, she knew she was attractive. But her relationships were usually short-lived. Her mother, who was hoping for grandchildren from her only child, was starting to despair.

"Your problem," she'd said after each breakup, "is that you think too much. Men don't like smart women. They make them feel inadequate." She was beginning to think she was right. Carlo, her last boyfriend, had said as much in breaking off the relationship.

"You're always asking questions," he said. "They're often rhetorical, but you go on to answer them anyway, usually at length. Many times I feel I can't hold up my end of a conversation. I don't think you mean to, but you frequently make me feel *molto stupido.*"

I've always been a motor mouth, she thought. Her parents told her it started early. At nine months, during services at St. Mark's, she uttered her first words. Pointing at a stained glass window, sun streaming through its colorful panes, she said, "pretty light."

She looked again at the sleeping Paulo. Men, she thought. Such fragile creatures. Despite all the bluff, bluster and *braggadocio*, they can be such children.

But, with Paulo, she had vowed to mend her ways. Since their backgrounds were so different, it might be easier this time. Paulo was a *Romani*, born and raised in Rome. He was trained in computer science. That's the reason they met.

Francesca had traveled to Rome's *Archivio di Arte Italiana in Pericolo* to conduct research for her master's thesis—the same facility to which Venetian art, and endangered art from many coastal cities, was being sent for safe-keeping and restoration. The computer in the research cubicle she had been assigned was malfunctioning and Paulo was the technician sent to help.

After restoring the system and giving her a few operational pointers, he asked if she had plans for lunch. She did not and he offered to return to pick her up.

As they left the huge, warehouse-like building, Francesca remarked how odd it seemed that some of the world's most beautiful *oggetti d'arte* were housed in such a plain structure. It rose several stories above the grimy industrial street—concrete block, no windows or skylights, only one entrance and loading docks in the back.

Paulo, obviously, had never considered the irony.

"Most of the money was spent on the inside," he said. "Actually, this is the most hi-tech and expensive facility of its kind anywhere in the world. It's not just a warehouse with elaborate climate-controlled vaults. We also have a state-of-the art restoration department that does amazing things to restore and preserve paintings, frescoes and tapestries. We can use high-resolution printing to create two-dimensional reproductions so real it takes an expert to tell the difference. We have a lab in which 3D modeling is used to manufacture perfect replicas of sculptures and other dimensional objects, right down to coloration. Modeling is also used to recreate substrates for paintings—brush strokes and textures—onto which the reproductions are aligned and printed.

"Then, too, we make images of all the works in our care available to researchers like you. If you were studying dimensional objects, many are available as holos.

"Incidentally," he said, "did you know that Italy has about 6,000 miles of coastline with hundreds of cities at risk, many with art that will need to be protected? Venice, as the worst case, is among the first. But, in the coming years, we will be receiving much more. That's why the building is so large."

"What happens to the reproductions?"

Paulo explained that many museums and other venues—those still able to do so—can display them in place of the originals. "Of course, it's made clear to patrons. But many still come to see the works in their original settings. There are also plans to mount traveling exhibits of reproductions, allowing people to see the works who might otherwise never have the chance."

"Do originals ever go back to their respective museums?"

"Placing art works here is completely voluntary. Any organization that requests the return of objects is accommodated. But, of course, if the situation requiring them to put the art in our hands in the first place hadn't been resolved, it would be foolish to ask for their return."

They stopped at a Ducati motorcycle in the parking lot.

"I hope you don't mind," Paulo said, handing her a helmet. "Like so many, I can't afford a car. Not only is there the high cost, but bribes for one of the limited number of permits to drive in *Roma* are outrageous."

As she put on the helmet, Francesca decided not to tell him that she had never ridden on a motorcycle. With a flutter in her stomach, she threw her leg over the back seat. She was glad she had worn pants.

The bike's electric motor made a quiet, whirring sound. "I wish I'd been old enough to get a *real* motorcycle before they were banned here. I loved the rumble of the Harley Davidson. I've always wondered why they are called 'hogs.'"

At lunch that day Paulo asked what brought her to the *Archivio*.

"The thesis for my Second." She explained that she was remotely related through her mother to the Bellini family of Renaissance-era painters. Rather than launch into a detailed explication about the Bellinis, she asked if Paulo knew very much about Italian Renaissance Art. She wanted to be sure she didn't talk down to him, remembering her mother's admonitions.

"My first real exposure to art has come through my work. So I know very little from the academic point of view. Let's just say, as one often hears, I know what I like when I see it," he said with a self-deprecating grin.

"The Bellinis, primarily Giovanni and his brother Gentile, are among the best known Venetian painters of the 16th Century. Giovanni, in particular, is said to have revolutionized the Venetian painting school, moving it toward a more sensuous and colorful style with deep, rich tints and detailed shading. His work is thought to have had tremendous influence on Titian, his best known student, who art historians claim went on to eclipse his master's best work."

Basta, thought Francesca. Let's not bore him.

"In my paper," she said, "I'm working to identify Bellini's specific influences. It's my belief that Titian's work was more derivative of Bellini's and, therefore, less revolutionary than has been thought."

She explained that the *Archivio* has several examples of each painter's work that she is reviewing digitally in side-by-side comparison, with magnification and by overlay.

"These cleaned and restored pieces are showing minute details not seen since they were painted almost 500 years ago. Gradually, I'm finding good support for my hypothesis." She had barely touched the *anti-pasti* when *rissoto* arrived.

To refocus the conversation, she asked about his background. Paulo said he grew up in the southeastern part of the city not far from *Cinecittá*, cinema city, a large studio considered the hub of the Italian film industry. He'd studied computer science at *Instituto Tecnico Industriale Statale Hertz* near his home.

"I really wanted to work in movies. But the job picture

was so grim that I settled for IT. *Archivio* was my first job. While I like it, I still want to make it in the film business. 'Film,' of course, is a misnomer since everything has been digital for more than 50 years. So my computer skills may still give me a chance."

Still unable to sleep, she slipped out of bed and padded softly across the small apartment to a table under its only window. If Paulo had been awake he would have enjoyed seeing Francesca's slender body silhouetted against the window as it moved within the folds of her diaphanous nightgown. She watched the moon, now fat and golden, as it sank toward the horizon across the lagoon, throwing a tawny highway of light across the still waters.

This is why I took the place, she reminded herself. Though little better than a garret, it had the best view she could afford. Some mornings she could sit with her coffee and watch the rising sun paint her city's marble spires, towers, domes, tile roofs, saints, sinners and gargoyles in pink and rosy hues.

Back in bed, before sleep finally came, she mapped the route for the day's sightseeing. She had served in the role before, showing the city to visiting friends and relatives. They could tour until about 1 p.m. to hit some highlights. Then it was time for lunch with her parents. She wondered if her mother would vary the cuisine this time. Over the years, she seemed to have created a standard menu for the first meeting with a boyfriend.

As they breakfasted quickly on coffee and pastries, Francesca checked her tab. It appeared most of the itinerary she had planned was dry. Where there was some flooding, they would take advantage of a system of wooden walkways that was getting more and more extensive as waters rose.

On the way north they passed her university and place of work. She would have liked to stop, but there really wasn't much of interest inside, particularly not her tiny cubicle. Playing tour guide, she informed him that the school was founded in 1868. The Venetian Gothic building was a palace purchased and restored by Doge Francesco Foscari in 1452 because it was strategically positioned in the center of the city on a major bend of the Grand Canal.

They meandered down tiny alleyways and across several small canals. It was sunny and pleasantly warm for April. At one point they stopped to watch workmen on a small barge doing something to the side of a building.

"They're injecting a plastic compound into the wall along its length," she explained. "You see this being done everywhere. The rising waters are rotting the bricks. It seems to help, but so many buildings in the city require this treatment. Lately buildings have been collapsing all or in part at the rate of about one every month or two."

"But what about below the waterline," Paulo asked.

She told him that they were probably treating the whole wall right down to the foundation. It is also possible, although infinitely more expensive, to restore walls with new waterproof bricks.

"How much do you know about the construction of Venice?" she asked.

"I've heard some things over the years, but not very much."

Francesca thought he might be interested in an abbreviated version. "In one sentence, here is the problem: Venice was built on a salt marsh, at sea level, in a sinking area, and, unfortunately, the sea level is rising."

The city, she explained, consists of 118 small islands interspersed with a network of 160 canals. It's built on millions of sunken wood pilings that do not rot in the airless environment below water. Most foundations resting on the pylons are marble and also very resistant to degradation. It's the brick and stone comprising building walls that are deteriorating when submerged or exposed to the salt water.

"Despite their age, the pilings are doing their jobs, but the lagoon is slowly subsiding—an estimated three-inches per century for the last 1,200 years. Subsidence worsened to nine inches last century as the city pumped increasing amounts of fresh water from aquifers beneath it. Once that was stopped, subsidence returned to the previous rate.

"Then there are our famous tides. The North Adriatic is quite narrow and subject to unusual tides that can quickly rise four or more feet. Historically, it's these tides, teamed with continued subsidence, that have done most of the damage.

"But, in recent decades, warming-induced sea level increase is the real culprit. As you said last night, the gate solution for high tides did not consider rising water levels. And you were right. At the time, engineers factored in an eight-inch increase, choosing to go with what was then the best-case scenario. Today, the oceans have risen almost three feet and the increase is accelerating."

This dissertation was not something she had planned. But she thought it would help him understand some of the things he would see.

They continued wandering crookedly northward toward the center of Venice, the San Polo District. She wanted to show him where, as a young girl, she first encountered the works of Bellini and Titian in the *Basilica del Frari*. The church, dating to the 13th Century, houses some of the most magnificent art in the city. They entered the relatively simple tan-gray brick building through its massive iron-bound door.

The basilica was long and narrow, its windowed-clerestory roof warmly lighting the interior. In the nave above the massive flower-bedecked altar was Titian's

"*Assunta,*" commissioned in 1518. In hushed voice, Francesca told him there are art historians who call this the most beautiful painting in the world. They also viewed his "*Madonna di Ca 'Pesaro,*" painted from 1519-1526.

She led him to the sacristy to see the triptych by Giovanni Bellini—madonna with child and four saints. It was this monumental creation, completed in 1488, that launched her on her comparative analysis of the work of her distant relative and his more famous student. She noticed that its massive carved, inlaid wooden frame was badly in need of restoration. Its gilt was tarnished to a dull bronze, some inlays were loose or missing, victims of the pervading dampness.

On their way to another landmark, the *Ponte di Rialto,* Francesca took him to the *Campo San Polo,* the city's second largest square and virtual center of the city. She slipped again into tour-guide mode.

"The space was originally devoted to grazing and farming," she said. "It was paved in the 1490s and used for the secular and the profane—bull fighting, masked balls and mass sermons. It's also remembered as the place where Lorenzino de' Medici was assassinated around 1550. Today it's a popular location for annual *Carnevale* events, open air concerts and screenings during the Venice Film Festival."

Paulo was a little difficult to read at times. She thought he was enjoying seeing the sights, but he was a bit more inscrutable than usual. She would have been just as happy quietly walking hand-in-hand enjoying the early spring sun, but felt a host's obligation to point out some of the highlights of her beloved city.

As they headed for the Grand Canal, walking along canal *Rio San Polo,* he stopped and pointed to a barge with some odd looking equipment and divers in the water.

"Ah," she said, "another sign of the times." She explained that Venice was not sinking at a consistent rate across the city. The result was that many large buildings were sinking unevenly, causing one end of the building slowly to sink lower than the other.

"In some cases, the effect is quite profound. Not only can you feel as if you're walking slightly up or down hill in its halls, the irregular subsidence causes serious structural strain.

"See over there." She pointed across the canal. "That building has steel rods running inside along its entirety. See the large plates midway up the wall that anchor the rods? The rods literally hold the building together."

Nodding at the barge, she explained that a newer hi-tech solution—used for large buildings thought to be of significant historic or cultural value—had divers cut a number of submerged pilings at each end and in the center of the structure. They then inserted powerful permanent hydraulic jacks controlled by a GPS system to level the building gradually, maintain the level and counter the subsidence. Obviously it's a big commitment. Not only is it expensive, but, once a building is level, divers must also shim up other major pilings to distribute the weight.

Paulo looked at her. "How do you know all these things?"

"When you meet my father at lunch, you'll understand. He's a retired public works official and I've been hearing all about the city's woes since I was born."

Approaching the Grand Canal, they had to sprint to catch a *vaporetto* to take them to the Rialto Bridge. The distance wasn't great and, if they had all day, she would have rented a gondola. But, with lunch looming at 1 p.m., they'd have to hurry along.

As the water-bus wove between traffic on the canal, she pointed out the empty gondolas docked along *Riva del Via* on the left bank, and knots of gondoliers, many in their old-fashioned costumes—beribboned straw hats, white nautical shirts and black pants—sitting on the stone parapet smoking.

"The day was when there were literally thousands of

gondolas in the city. Today the number is about 300. Declining tourism means declining demand. But, more significantly, the rising waters have made it impossible for gondolas to pass under many of the 438 bridges.

"The four bridges on the Grand Canal are high enough at present but may have had to be raised, not for gondolas, but for taller water craft. How or when to raise the iconic white-marble clad Rialto, a magnificent single-arch stone bridge completed about 1590, is the subject of fiery debate and many rejected plans."

They exited the *vaporetto* on the right bank at the foot of the bridge and climbed stairs to the covered inclined ramp leading to the central portico. As they walked across the bridge, bells in church towers around the city began to chime. Based on variations in their sonorous clanging, Francesca could identify each basilica. It was noon.

They walked down one row of shops on the bridge to the left bank and then returned to the right bank along shops on the other side. Since the 1400s, she told Paulo, shops had lined both sides of the bridge. The rent had helped pay for maintenance of the early wooden structure. The shops remained after construction of the new stone bridge.

"Not a good place to shop," Francesca sniffed. "Much of the merchandise is cheap reproductions of Venetian and Murano glass, fake designer purses, clothing and the like."

Back across the bridge, the two strolled through the Rialto market, from which the bridge got its name. From time immemorial this was the site of the city's largest market. It was crowded this day, vibrating with the sound of hawkers and shoppers haggling over prices, arguing about freshness. They passed a bakery tent and were tempted by the smell of fresh bread and pastries. The morning's outing had kindled their appetites.

"I'd take you to visit the nearby home of who is arguably the most famous Venetian," Francesca said, obviously testing, "but we won't have time."

"Ah, that would be Enrico Bataglia, forward for *Azzurri*, the national soccer team," Paulo said with a completely straight face.

"Right. Actually, we dated for a time while I was in secondary school."

They both laughed.

"It's not really worth visiting Marco Polo's home," she said. "The building on the site is not original. But it would have been nice to go a bit farther north to visit the Ghetto District." She told him it's the area of city in which Jews were compelled to live starting early in the 16th Century. In Venetian Italian, "*ghèto*" is the word from which the English "ghetto" is derived.

"So, leaving out Bataglia and Polo, who's the next most famous Venice native?"

"Sorry, I'm running out of soccer players."

"Actually, it's an unfair question. This resident was a fiction created by Shakespeare. Shylock, 'The Merchant of Venice,' who sought but never received his pound of flesh as collateral for a bad debt."

I can tell he's getting bored with this. Mother would never approve.

They walked east along canal *Rio del Apostoli*. To save time, they hopped a launch that dropped them near her parent's place on *Ramo Dona*. The third floor of the faded pink three-story Venetian Gothic had been the Barzini home for generations.

Francesca explained it had been built by a wealthy merchant about 1680 in the style of the times—the first floor was a warehouse, the second was opulent living quarters and the third was for servants. Much later it was remodeled into two apartments above with retail space below. Though smaller, the family had purchased the third floor for the partial view of the Lagoon. Also typical of the times, the servant's quarters had its own staircase leading to the second floor and street to minimize contact between servant and master.

"Any words of warning or encouragement before we go up?" Paulo asked.

"Don't worry. My parents have never met a boyfriend of mine they didn't like." She grinned.

They were met at the door by Bianca and Aberto with the usual flurry of awkward welcomes. Settled in the living room, her mother offered *bellinis*, named in honor of their family's remote ancestor. The drink—champagne-like *Prosecco* mixed with white peach juice—was introduced at Venice's infamous Harry's Bar and said to have been enjoyed by Hemingway.

Drinks served, the two women repaired to the kitchen to put out lunch. The men found a common interest in *futbol* and discussed the merits, or lack thereof, of the current national team.

As she surveyed the kitchen, Francesca thought her mother must really be getting desperate. Not only was the menu different than the usual "new boyfriend" lunch, it was extravagant. Now I know why she looks tired. She's probably spent the last two days in the kitchen.

She had made many traditional Venetian dishes. For *antipasto*, in addition to *formaggi*, *salumi* and *crustini*, there was *Sarde in Saor*, marinated sardines with onions with pine nuts and raisins in a sweet and sour sauce. The *primo* course was *Risi i Bisi*, a unique combination of a soup and thick risotto made with fresh peas, rice and cooked with chunks of *pancetta*, thick Italian bacon. *Secondo* was *baccala' mantecata*, Venice's most notable dish—softened, dried, salted Baltic cod prepared in olive oil, garlic, parsley and creamed. And, her mother said, in case he doesn't like fish, there was *grigliata mista*, mixed grilled meats served with *polenta*.

It went on and on—a fresh garden *insalata*, *formaggi e frutta* and *tiramisu* for *dolce*. Several cities in Italy vied for recognition as the originator of *tiramisu*, but Venice was the frontrunner.

Francesca wished, for her mother's sake, that food was the answer.

———————

Paulo, who was trim and maintained his weight by not overeating, took the meal in stride. He tried everything, was effusive in his compliments and successfully navigated the usual questions the new boyfriend had to endure at the Barzini table. She liked the way he handled the polite but pointed interrogation. She had noticed that, no matter what the situation, Paulo seemed comfortable in his own skin.

After lunch, the two men carried snifters of *grappa* to the small balcony overlooking the east lagoon a block away. They quietly contemplated the watermelon and azure sky, colored by the late afternoon sun. Shadows of buildings along the waterfront were long and spilled onto the choppy lagoon.

Aberto pointed to *Isola San Michelle*, an almost square island only few thousand feet from shore. It was the site, he said, of a large Greek Orthodox cemetery. And beyond it, the storied Murano, source for 900 years of famed Murano glass.

"We have one piece of old Murano," he said. "It's an heirloom passed down for several centuries. You may have seen it in the living room. The white vase? It's an example of *lattimo*, milk glass, developed as an alternative to porcelain that was then far more expensive. It will undoubtedly be the most valuable item in Francesca's dowry." He looked meaningfully at Paulo and then broke into a big whiskered grin.

They drank in silence for a minute.

"Venice has been called many things over the centuries," Aberto said. 'City of Light,' 'City of Water,' 'City of Bridges,' 'City of Canals,' 'The Floating City,' 'City of Masks,' '*Serenissima*'—the serene republic. I call it the city that should never have been. He paused, probably for effect.

"Our founders made a mistake. A grand mistake, no doubt. But to build a city here was pure folly. Of course, what did they know in the 8th Century about matters of hydrology and subsidence? How could they have predicted that someday the Adriatic would rise to swallow their creation? All they wanted was a citadel, surrounded by water, safe from Germanic tribes raping the mainland after the fall of Rome.

"Today there are two schools of thought among Venetians. One is *pessimistico*, or, as some prefer to call themselves, *realistico*. This school believes the demise of Venice is inevitable. They compare the city to a sugar cube, crumbling and dissolving in *caffè*. Others are *ottimista*. They believe that Venetia has survived for 1,200 years by creatively adapting to whatever conditions have arisen. They believe the impact of the warming will be less than now anticipated, or, if not, new technologies will save us.

"After almost 40 years of helping the battle to save the city, sadly, I must confess that I'm a *pessimistico.*"

"But I've heard of plans to build a seawall to enclose the lagoon," Paulo responded.

"No one takes it seriously. You've been on and around the canals. Tell me. What color are they? And how do they smell?"

Paulo thought. "The color is a kind of murky gray-green. Smell? Well, not exactly fragrant."

Aberto explained that Venice has no central sewage system. With the exception of a number of buildings, primarily public that have retrofitted septic tanks, all the sewage goes into the canals. "The only thing that saves us is the cleansing effect of daily tides running into and out of the lagoon. They flush out the canals, including the industrial and agricultural pollution seeping into the lagoon from the mainland. Closing it off with a seawall would create the world's biggest cesspool."

"But surely there's something that can be done."

Paulo stared momentarily at the distant lagoon.

"Well, there is something. Probably a long shot that, if it happens, may well be too late for *Serenissima*. Officials of the Union for the Mediterranean based in Barcelona, the largest city on the sea, have developed plans to turn the Mediterranean into a lake.

"I know it may sound impossible, but all that has to be done is run a seawall with locks across the narrow Strait of Gibraltar at one end and close off the Suez Canal with a wall and locks at the Port Said entrance to the sea. That would turn the Mediterranean—including the Adriatic and Black Seas—into a massive salt-water lake, safe from the rising Atlantic to the west and Indian Ocean-fed Red Sea on the east."

But Aberto explained that complications were many from financial, engineering and political standpoints.

The UFM completed the plans in 2031. The price tag is a heart-stopping 40 billion Euros. From an engineering point of view, the plans are feasible. The most complex and expensive part of the project would be dealing with the nearly 1,000-foot depth of the Strait along the wall's 8.9 mile run between the "Pillars of Hercules."

The deal was sweetened by including a four-lane toll road and rail line atop the wall. Connecting Africa and Europe across the Strait had always been a dream.

But the stumbling block for the proposal has been political. All 22 countries bordering the sea's 29,000 miles of coast and the Island of Cyprus have to agree to a proposed shared-funding scheme based on the length of their coastlines. The holdout has been Slovenia whose coast on the Adriatic is a mere 27 miles, stretching from Italy to Croatia. Its bill for the project was proportionately small. But the country pled poverty, lack of benefit and has refused to sign on.

"It's rumored that Slovenia is now on board. But I wonder if the country has actually agreed to pay or its wealthier neighbors, whose seaside cities are really beginning to suffer, passed the hat.

"Could the project be completed in time to save Venice? Who can say?

"Centuries ago," he continued, "Venice was the richest city in Europe, a mercantile powerhouse sitting at the end of the Silk Route to Asia. Today it relies primarily on the ever shrinking tourist Euro.

"The day was when Venice, with a population of fewer than 100,000, hosted one million tourists a year. Today the population is 60,000 and tourism is down by half. Tourists find a little decay to be charming, romantic," he said. "But Venice is starting to resemble a city in the Third World. Then, too, through no fault of yours, our cultural heritage that's not nailed down is being carted off for safekeeping. Before long, Venice will be a sad city of crumbling buildings, bereft of the artistic glories that have attracted visitors over the ages."

Paulo kissed Bianca on both cheeks and shook Aberto's hand, thanking them for a wonderful afternoon. Aberto gave them the tickets for the theatre and her mother rushed back to the kitchen, returning with two sandwiches wrapped in paper.

"For the train tomorrow, Paulo," she said. "We know how terrible the food is."

Francesca stuffed them in her purse. As they headed for the door, Bianca gave them an umbrella, saying rain was possible later.

A feathery mist began to form halos around street lamps

as they approached *Teatro La Fenice*. Francesca explained that the theater had burned twice, resulting in its unusual name, The Phoenix. First built in 1792, it is one of the most famous theatres in Europe.

They were escorted to their seats in a box near the middle of the third of five gilt-encrusted levels. The plush burgundy seats were a bit threadbare; the gilt more the color of bronze than gold.

For Venetians, it was "oldies but goodies" night featuring hometown-boy Antonio Vivaldi. Though he had reputedly written 50 operas, none had been terribly successful, not of the caliber of those by Verdi, Rossini or Puccini. But the program contained one of his better-known arias from "Griselda." Featured that evening would be the four violin concertos known as "*La Quattro Stagioni*." Another violin concerto and flute concerto would round out the performance.

A chamber orchestra drawn from the Venice Symphony took the stage. In a few minutes, Francesca closed her eyes for the first movement, "*La Primavera*," of the "Four Seasons." It was her favorite concerto of the four and she had done this since she was a child. The music spoke to her of new leaves shivering in the breeze, soft spring rains streaking windows, water sluicing down gutters, trilling golden finches and bright spring flowers bursting through winter grey.

The two were up early the next morning to catch Paulo's train. He threw his things into a duffel and they walked in a light rain, huddled under one umbrella, to catch a *vaporetto* to the *Stazione di Venezia Santa Lucia* at the northern end of the Grand Canal. Much of the trip was made in the uncomfortable silence of goodbyes.

As they approached the station, Francesca noticed a line of covered baggage carts being wheeled down the platform to a waiting train. They were stacked with boxes and wooden crates stenciled *Museo Ca'Rezzonico*. More cultural refugees heading for Rome, she thought, probably on the same train with Paulo.

She pointed and Paulo nodded. They sat in the station to stay dry until his train was called.

"I'm really sorry about your city," he said. "I can see how much you love it."

She was touched by his concern.

Suddenly. "Can you come to Rome to meet my family? It won't be as splendid an affair. Mom cooks for the whole family on Sundays, so you would have to contend with my siblings, nieces, nephews, grandma and a stray aunt and uncle or two."

I thought you'd never ask, she thought. "I'd love to."

"Oh, and don't worry," Paulo smiled. "My folks have never met a girlfriend of mine they didn't like."

She poked him in the ribs.

SMILEY'S PEOPLE
YUNNAN PROVINCE, CHINA
OCTOBER, 2036

"The fact that you can only do a little is no excuse for doing nothing."
—John le Carré, *A Most Wanted Man*

Zhang Ahlim watched in the cracked and grimy mirror with some amusement as she smeared greasy black paint on her face. The contrast between her pale, white skin and the black blotches was striking. She had been told not to cover her full face—the skin needed to breathe. That left the question of pattern. Do I use stripes or irregularly shaped blobs? Rather than look like a zebra, she chose blobs.

A single bare bulb swung overhead, casting moving shadows that made her look even more sinister. Paint job completed, she stood back and almost disappeared into the gloom of the small, dilapidated toilet. She rolled the black turtle neck up to cover her white neck. Under the turtle neck, her body was encased in warm, tight-fitting black silk underwear. Over everything was a two-piece suit made of a thick but relatively lightweight black canvas-like fabric with more zippered pockets and pouches than she could imagine needing.

She completed the outfit with a tight fitting hood that covered all but her face. She'd had to pull her hair back and bind it in a compact bun.

She sat carefully on a rickety bench and laced up heavy high-topped boots. As a girl accustomed to sandals and flip-flops, she wondered how comfortable she was going to be over the next 24-hours in this formidable footwear.

Fully attired, she stepped into the office of what had been a manufacturing plant south of Kunming, capital of the Southwestern Chinese province of Yunnan. The plant had been abandoned for years and was in such a deteriorated state that it was condemned as unsafe, making it the perfect location for clandestine operations. Seven others in her cell were already dressed for the action to come. Some paced, one sat with a leg nervously tapping an erratic rhythm on the stained concrete floor. Others lounged on cracked plastic chairs in feigned or actual calm.

At precisely 10 p.m. the cell leader made his appearance. He quickly closed the door and shed his night-vision goggles. The only light in the building was provided by several dim bulbs in the interior office. Otherwise, the plant was pitch black and almost impossible to navigate.

"Good evening," Smiley said quietly—without smiling.

Ahlim first met Smiley about a month earlier after she arrived in Kunming. She had been recruited in her home city of Chengdu, 800 miles north, just after completing a degree in elementary education at Sichuan Normal University. "Recruited" probably wasn't the right word. She had volunteered. The process was difficult and risky.

Obviously, the organization didn't put up recruiting posters or conduct public rallies. But, through cautious persistence, she was able to get hooked up through the friend of a friend of a friend. After extensive vetting, she was accepted.

The organization had no name, but its eco-activism throughout China was well known. The media, badly in need of a label, had come to call it "The Shadow."

Her burly initial contact, code name "Bear," had tried to make clear the distinction between eco-terrorism and activism. Eco-terrorists, he said, were indiscriminant. They kill people. "We target only offending infrastructure. We are never armed."

He was to be her only contact. She would become a sleeper to be awakened if or when there was an assignment. That, he said, could be weeks, months, a year or never.

"We have become very high profile and the authorities are working diligently to shut us down. So we are quite decentralized. Individual cells operate almost independently. Each cell has only one contact with the central organization. Cell members know only as much as they absolutely need to know about each other and details of a particular operation. Cells are formed for a single operation and then dissolved. Secrecy and security are of utmost importance," he warned. "We use no electronic communication."

Her only task initially was to read daily the online classifieds in a somewhat obscure local news net and look for an ad offering a red 26-inch mountain bike. If the ad ran two days in a row, she was to meet with her handler at their initial meeting place at 11 p.m. the following day.

His last question: "What would you like to use as your code name?" Code name? She thought for an instant. The name came quickly.

"Mouse," she said. Her handler raised an eyebrow, but didn't ask the obvious question.

"Mouse, it is."

———————

Mouse.

Her younger brother had stuck her with the nickname. At around age 4, when he learned she had been born in The Year of the Rat, he decided that she was too cute to be a rat. So he named her Mouse. At first, like any good 12-year-old, she was annoyed. But she adored her brother and let him have his way.

Chanming was the center of the Zhang family universe. China's One-Child Planning Policy allowed several exceptions. Rural families could have a second child if the first is female or a disabled male. The commonly accepted explanation for "son preference" is that sons in rural families are more helpful in farm work. Sons are also preferred because they provide the primary financial support for parents in their retirement.

Arguably, the Zhangs, as residents of suburban Chengdu, were not rural. But, because the family operated a small truck farm, the authorities allowed them a second child.

Ahlim remembered there was great joy when her parents returned from the hospital with the infant boy. She was eight and felt some twinges of jealously. But, from the beginning, he smiled a lot and liked it when he wrapped a little hand around her finger. Soon she was in his thrall.

Unfortunately, the family's happiness was short-lived. As Chanming grew, it became evident he suffered from asthma. The condition was made more severe by poor air quality in the region. The Zhangs lived several miles downwind of a massive coal-burning power plant that spewed noxious fumes. The plant, one of 800 throughout China, was supposed to be using desulphurization equipment and scrubbers for CO_2 and other pollutants. But it was common knowledge that the equipment was either faulty or simply turned off to increase the plant's efficiency.

The Zhangs sat helpless as Chanming suffered. Their small savings were eaten up by visits to specialists. They tried Eastern and Western medical treatments. An air purifier ran around the clock. They kept him indoors as much as possible, wearing a filtering mask. They taped the windows—even in the heat of summer.

Still his condition worsened. He was small, pale and usually too sick to go to school. Probably the best advice they received was to move to a cleaner environment. But it was advice they couldn't take. The truck farm was all they had; it would be impossible to start over. And, though Chanming might have been sent to live with relatives elsewhere, her parents couldn't bear the thought of parting with him.

So, Ahlim watched him struggle. She cried at night because he was so brave, smiling and rarely complaining. Her anger at the power plant smoldered and burned to the point that she would dream of blowing it up single-handedly.

She took responsibility for Chanming's education. When she returned from school each day, they would spend a few hours working on reading, writing and math. She would often read to him of legends, superheroes, history or about strange, faraway countries.

On days when the air was relatively breathable, Chanming was allowed to play in the yard. His favorite activity was watching several varieties of caterpillars lazily crawling on their many feet. Some were quite exotic—colorful with stripes or feathery spines. So, in return, she nicknamed him "Caterpillar." He loved it.

Father, though, was careful to hide the fact that he sprayed insecticide on the vegetables and fruit to kill the pests. When he couldn't afford it, he would wander the garden when Chanming was asleep, crushing his little friends between thumb and forefinger.

At night she would take turns with her parents watching him sleep, waiting for his inevitable respiratory distress. One night, when he was almost seven, she awakened to labored and raspy breathing. She put on his oxygen mask, but he still couldn't catch his breath. His skin was turning a pale blue; his forehead was terribly hot.

They sped to the hospital, Chanming cradled in his mother's arms. Ahlim, in the back of the truck, hung on as her father skidded madly around corners.

He had contracted pneumonia and died early that morning, a tiny doll in a big hospital bed. He lapsed into a coma before the end. So he went quietly, peacefully. His rosy parchment-thin skin gradually whitened as the fever radiated from his inert body.

When Bear had asked why she wanted to volunteer, she didn't tell him the story of her brother. She knew most of the group's activities targeted emitters of greenhouse gases. Her personal vendetta would be against the air polluters who killed her brother. So she told him what he wanted to hear: that the effects of the warming could only be halted by curbing CO_2 emissions; that rising temperatures were making it difficult for her family to make a living with their truck farm.

After several weeks, the ad for the red bike ran. She met Bear as arranged and was given an assignment. She was to join a cell in Kunming. On arrival she would rent a post office box and run a personal in a local news net that was to read: "New girl in town looking for fun." She would run the ad daily until there was a response with instructions from someone named "Smiley."

Bear told her she could not tell her parents, friends or anyone where or why she was going. Ahlim expected as much and had a story prepared. She would tell people that she'd been offered an elementary teaching post in some relatively distant city. She could still keep in touch since net communications were not location specific, unless someone with the necessary skills really wanted to know.

Ahlim was embarrassed by the sendoff her parents and friends gave her. Lying didn't come easily, but she knew it was necessary. She talked in vague terms of her school, her duties and exuded as much enthusiasm as she could muster.

Her best friend stayed on after the guests left, offering to help clean up. Ahlim had come to realize that she'd have to break her promise of silence, at least in part. What would happen, she wondered, if I were to be captured or die on a mission? She knew there were risks involved. Her parents would probably never know what happened to her or why.

Before Leang left, she took her into the garden to talk. "I have lied about where I'm going," she said quietly, pausing to let the statement sink in. "I belong to an eco-activist organization and am joining a cell in a city whose name I can't divulge. When Chanming died, I promised I would find a way to revenge his death."

Leang looked incredulous.

"There are dangers involved. And I'm worried that, should something go wrong, my parents would never know what happened to me. If you agree to help, I will contact you at least once a week. If you don't hear from me for two weeks, assume the worst and please tell them what I've told you. Otherwise, tell no one. Will you help?"

Her request was met initially with shocked silence. "Don't do this," Leang said. "How can you help Chanming by getting yourself killed or arrested? He's gone. Nothing can bring him back. Aren't there less dangerous ways to protest?"

Ahlim told her she had considered all the alternatives

but believed only direct and dramatic action could make a difference. She was committed.

Leang looked at her for a moment; then nodded. "I will help and I will pray for you."

The train ride took all of a day. She arrived late at night at the city's Northern Railway Depot.

Ahlim knew little of Kunming except its reputation as the "City of Eternal Spring." Situated in the south of China at an elevation of 6,000 feet, Kunming boasted the best climate in that vast country. It was also, she knew, called the "Flower Basket of China." Its temperate, year-around growing season made it an agricultural mecca. Kunming's gigantic daily flower market was a major tourist attraction.

As she stepped off the train and was swept along with the tide of passengers and baggage carts, Ahlim noticed that the air seemed light and fresh in stark contrast to the chemical-tanged miasma she had breathed in Chengdu.

She took a taxi to the inexpensive hostel she had booked. She would share a room with three others, but it was all she could afford. It was after midnight when she arrived, reluctant to wake her roommates. But they seemed to take it in stride. One showed her the bathroom they shared.

All three rose early to get ready for work. One asked if Ahlim needed a job. She said she did. The girl believed work was to be had at their factory and offered to check. Ahlim smiled in appreciation. She would have to work to support herself and keep up appearances.

"What does the factory produce?"

The girl laughed. "Artificial Christmas trees for export to the West."

Every day after work Ahlim checked her post office box. Some days it contained lewd or repulsive invitations "for fun." But nothing from Smiley. After a week she began to wonder if there actually *were* a Smiley. When the note finally arrived, it simply contained a day, time and location with the admonition to memorize and destroy the note. He also requested that she wear a red ribbon in her hair.

Great, she thought. I don't have a red ribbon to tie up a ponytail. I don't even like red.

Two days hence, a Sunday, she was to wait at 11 a.m. for Smiley at the Donhua Noodle and Rice Shop across from the paddleboat lagoon in Green Lake Park. She got directions and bus routes online and found it was across town, requiring a bus transfer.

———————————

Sunday morning, their only day off, her roommates invited her to join them for lunch and a shopping excursion. Ahlim declined, saying she wasn't feeling well and would probably rest and read.

After they'd left, gaily chattering about shopping and the hope they'd meet some boys, Ahlim caught a bus. The trip, with one transfer, took less time than expected. She arrived early and located the noodle shop. The day was sunny and pleasant so she decided to walk in the park.

The paddleboats had plastic shells in animal shapes— lions, giraffes, swans, hippos, elephants. They were faded and cracked, but hordes of kids and harried parents didn't seem to mind. They paddled without much skill around the lake with frequent collisions that sent boaters into paroxysms of laughter, but, fortunately, not to the bottom of its murky green waters.

Walking on she saw two black limos park in front of a large, colorful and elaborately tiled pagoda with reflecting pool. They disgorged a wedding party intent on photos.

The bride was beautiful, raven hair piled atop her head in an intricate coiffure. The dress was full-length white silk decorated with seed pearls, the train of diaphanous lace. The photographer herded the party as best he could into various poses using the pool and ancient building as a backdrop.

And here I am, thought Ahlim. Twenty-two years old, never had a serious boyfriend and unlikely to find one while working in the obscurity of this shadow organization. "New girl in town looking for fun!" Right! At least I've not signed a life-time contract. There's nothing stopping me from returning to a normal life once I feel I've had my revenge.

She had almost circled the park when, on the other side of the lake, she came upon a knot of serious kite flyers. Their gaily-colored kites frolicked about a thousand feet above the park, lines attached to large reels held in two hands. The reels had knobs for reeling in or playing out line and braking mechanisms to hold the kites at altitude. The kiters were old men who bantered back and forth, deriding their compatriots' kites and their skill in flying them. Ahlim couldn't tell if there were a competition of some sort going on.

To avoid being late, she hurried on to the noodle shop and ordered Kunming's most famous dish, "crossing-the-bridge" noodles. When she picked up her order she asked the old cook about the strange name.

"The most popular story is that centuries ago the wife of a scholar studying for his imperial exams in the seclusion of a small island brought him food every day. But she found that, by the time she got there, the soup would be cold and noodles soggy. So she began to load an earthen pot with boiling broth and a layer of oil on top to keep the broth warm. The noodles and other ingredients were kept in separate containers and mixed when she arrived. It worked, but we don't know if he passed his exams," the cook laughed.

Ahlim had almost finished her soup when a young man, tall and thin, entered. He casually surveyed the shop, made eye contact and walked to her table. He smiled. It was the first and last time she'd see him make the effort.

Quietly, as he extended his hand, "We are old friends, so greet me warmly." She stood and they hugged awkwardly. "It's so good to see you." She played her part.

He sat down and he asked how she liked the soup. "They make it well here."

She praised the soup and asked if he believed the story of its naming.

He shrugged. "Who can say? It's as good a story as any, I suspect." They continued to make light, animated conversation. But his eyes continually roamed the room.

"Now," he said in a low voice, "we'll leave the shop as friends and, once outside, go our separate ways. He took a piece of paper from his shirt pocket. He stared for a moment at the paddleboat pond. Then his long fingers quickly and deftly folded the paper into an origami swan and placed it before her. She smiled in wonder and surprise.

"For you." He paid for her soup and, with another "friendly" hug at the door, they walked casually in separate directions. After a few feet, he turned and waved.

As she waited for the second bus, Ahlim unfolded the swan. The message told her to report in two days at 7 p.m. to a specified classroom at Yunnan University.

Ahlim assumed she should dress like a student for the meeting. Since she'd graduated only recently, that wouldn't be a problem. The classroom was in an unprepossessing building near the east gate of campus facing a busy commercial thoroughfare. It was on the first floor near a rear entrance. She walked by casually, saw a few people sitting at desks, entered and sat down near the door.

Gradually, others filtered in and dispersed around the classroom. Most looked ahead; others scanned the room, sizing up their compatriots. Soon there were eight of them. Six were males who appeared to be in their 20s.

A little after the hour, Smiley walked in, opened a bulging briefcase and pulled out a stack of slim textbooks. He walked to the blackboard and began writing in English. Ahlim spoke little English, but she recognized some words or phrases about food.

"This is an introductory class in English," he said, as he passed out the textbooks. "Turn to page 38. Should someone come in, follow my lead. We will repeat and discuss the terms and phrases on the board. If I feel we have been compromised, you will follow me to the back entrance and disburse quickly and separately. If the meeting is blown, check your post office boxes for the reschedule.

Smiley scanned the room, inviting questions. None came.

"I'll save you the need to wonder about my code name. I took it from the main character in a series of Western spy novels. I learned much of my spy craft from George Smiley. And I have relied on General Sun Tzu's ancient text, *The Art of War*, for help in developing strategies and tactics."

Surely, Ahlim thought, these can't be his only qualifications. I wonder if spy craft includes folding secret messages into origami swans?

"Understand this clearly. We are at war with those who are ruining the planet. Our mission is to strike the very heart of China's CO_2 emitters and show the world that there are Chinese who oppose what this country is doing. I needn't remind you that our country continues to be the world's greatest source of greenhouse gases."

Smiley's delivery was quiet, matter of fact and strangely uninspiring. If meant to rally the troops, it failed to feed the passions of those in the room. But, while his intonation was flat, his deep-set eyes burned with the intensity of a zealot. This, thought Ahlim, is a complex and dangerous man.

"Our cell is small of necessity. We have secrets to keep. The government is increasing its efforts to hunt us down. But, as General Tzu wrote: 'Great results can be achieved with small forces.'"

Smiley said that, for the sake of security, details about the mission would not be divulged until the cell goes to ground a few days before the action is to take place.

"Two of you have been selected for special training over the next few weeks. You know who you are. Preparation for the roles performed by the rest will take place when we've gone to ground. There is no need to meet again until that time. Check your boxes daily for instructions."

"Questions? If not, class dismissed." Smiley picked up the text books.

October stretched into November. No word from Smiley. In Chengdu, Ahlim would begin wearing heavy sweaters or padded jackets about now. But, while the temperatures in Kunming had cooled slightly, the air remained spring-like.

As the eldest of her roommates, she, uncomfortably, had assumed the role of mother figure. The girls were still in their teens and came from the same rural community a half-day's drive from Kunming. They were good, hard-working girls who sent most of their earnings home. But they were giddy, very naïve, and dealing with their first experience in the big city. At times they were overwhelmed by urban life and its complexities. And each week Ahlim had to help at least one recover from a broken heart.

When it comes to matters of romance, Ahlim thought, I'm like the blind leading the blind.

As the Christmas season neared, the factory began

shipping thousands of lighted plastic "spruce" trees a week to Wal-Mart for distribution in North America. Ahlim was responsible for testing lights on one of the three tree sections as it came down the assembly line. Mind numbing work. And for what, she wondered? What does a fake tree have to do with the supposed birth of the Christian's Christ?

Her roommates couldn't understand why she didn't get a teaching job. They knew she had an elementary education degree. Ahlim explained that she was looking, but that good teaching jobs were hard to find.

I wish I *could* get a teaching job, she lamented. The inactivity was making her restless; making her question her decision to devote her life, even if only a part of it, to the "cause." But, when commitment flagged, images of Caterpillar's lifeless body would come, unbidden, to remind her why she was making the sacrifice.

During the second week of the month, the long-awaited message came: *"Be at the Donbu Bus Terminal next Monday before 6 p.m. Mingle with the crowd in the main waiting room. If I am there, follow me discretely to a waiting mini-bus. Bring only one small bag with a change of clothes and necessary personal items. Everything else will be provided. You will not be returning to Kunming, so make arrangements for other belongings. If you don't see me at the terminal, the mission has been postponed. In that case, check daily for further instructions."*

The bus ride to their "base," as Smiley called it, would take about two hours. Her sense of direction was not particularly acute, but she believed they were heading south or southeast.

Before leaving, she told her roommates that her mother was ill and she had to go home for a while. On Monday morning she quit her job using the same excuse. At the hostel she packed a small gym bag she'd purchased for the trip. Her other belongings went into her one suitcase. The only thing she could think to do was store it in a locker at the bus station. Smiley said they wouldn't be coming back, but she thought it might be possible to retrieve it someday.

Smiley sat next to the driver. There were more than enough seats for other members of the cell. Several large black duffel bags were stored in the back. She sat next to a window and watched the city get dingier and darker. At some point, residential and commercial turned to industrial.

Her seat mate was the other woman in the cell. They hadn't been introduced so they exchanged code names. "Martini," she said. "My favorite drink." Ahlim told her "Mouse" was a nickname. They shared a chocolate bar Ahlim had purchased at the terminal. She could sense that Martini would like to talk, but both knew they were not to get personal. So they rode in companionable silence.

Just after dark, the bus pulled up to the gate of what appeared to be an abandoned factory. The driver turned off his headlights. Smiley opened a box at his feet and pulled out night-vision goggles, one for each of them.

"May as well start getting used to these," he said. "Operation is simple. Put it on, tighten the straps, activate with the switch on the right side and focus as necessary by rotating the lenses."

The driver opened the gate and drove in without lights. Ahlim was amazed. Though a strange shade of green, the dilapidated building looked almost as bright as if it were being seen in daylight. He parked in a shed. Smiley and a couple of the men hefted the bags and he led them into the building. Inside was a shambles—a jumble of twisted equipment, pipes and crates. Their feet crunched on glass fallen from broken skylights.

Home for the next few days would be an interior space, formerly an office. Smiley apologized for the accommodations. "It's not exactly the Hilton and there is no room service. We have bottled water and military-style rations. There will be no calling out for pizza."

He pointed to the single toilet, foam mats and sleeping bags scattered throughout the room. Roughly in the center, an area had been cleared for folding chairs and a table. It looked like a classroom.

"Pick a mat and settle in. We'll put out what will serve as dinner in a few minutes. Then, at 2100 hours, we'll tell you why we're here and what we plan to accomplish."

So now we're starting with the military jargon, Ahlim thought. I assume that's 9 p.m.

Smiley started without preamble: "Our mission is to cause as much damage as possible to the coal-fired power plant near Kaiyuan City about 150 miles southeast of our location. The plant, with two 300-megawatt units, went on line in 2006 and serves the Kunming power grid. Like all China's power facilities, Kaiyuan is corporately owned.

Using a small digital projector, he threw an image of the plant on a sheet tacked to the wall.

"When constructed, the plant was equipped with Amine scrubbing technology for help in CO_2 removal. But its low efficiency and high operating cost led plant operators to shut the scrubbers down. And the government looked the other way. Since then, more effective and efficient scrubbing methods have been developed, but, because of the high cost of retrofit, they have not been installed.

"So the plant is dirty—not just emitting huge quantities of CO_2—but other air pollutants as well." Smiley paused and scanned the room. He was surprised to see Ahlim smiling.

"I'm sure you wonder how a small group of volunteer activists is going to cause significant damage to a power plant. This sounds more like a military operation, but only two of you have prior military training. So the plan I've developed is relatively simple and yet has a high probability of success. Over the next two days, necessary training will be provided."

Smiley turned and manhandled a large case onto the table. He opened the latches and pulled out several components.

"This is a rocket-propelled grenade launcher—the Type 69 Chinese knockoff of the famous Russian RPG-7 developed in the 1960s. Old technology, yes. But still highly effective. We have acquired two of these and four grenades."

He picked up a tube with a hand grip and trigger. He then attached what looked like a sight. "This is the basic launcher. It's about three-feet long and, with night-vision sight, weighs 22 pounds."

He put the launcher down and picked up a smaller case.

"This is the business end of the launcher, the grenade. It comes in two pieces and is too unstable to be assembled until it's ready to be used. We have two called bunker busters that are engineered to penetrate very thick walls. So, they can only deliver a relatively small explosive charge. The other two are high-explosive grenades that carry a real punch. Each weighs about eight pounds. We'll practice until you can deliver the second warhead in less than 15 seconds."

He explained that the cell will be divided into two four-person teams. Each team will tackle one of the two generating units.

"'Elvis' and 'Spider Man,' who have had military service, will serve as gunners. They have already received necessary training. Each will carry the basic launcher into the field. 'Buddha' and 'Red' will assist the gunners and carry the sights. 'Martini,' 'Mouse,' 'Brain' and 'Tattoo,' will each carry one of the grenades.

"I know this sounds complex. But, to avoid detection, you will each move to the initial rendezvous separately to minimize the risk of discovery. We have built redundancy into the plan so that, should some of you be neutralized, enough components may still make it to assemble at least one of the RPGs. Once you're all together—assuming everyone makes it—the teams will move to their launch positions."

Tattoo tentatively raised his hand. He was aptly named. Both arms were festooned with vivid figures of dragons intertwined with other mythical beasts. "Why not just have the gunners carry the assembled RPGs? Do we need all the additional personnel?"

"As indicated, the assembled RPG weighs about 22 pounds. It's awkward to carry over long distances. The sight is also quite delicate and needs to be handled separately. In addition, the grenades must be assembled at the launch site. The unit cannot be carried loaded. There are too many components and too much assembly required for single gunners.

"As you know we have already seriously damaged several power plants in other parts of the country. So the power industry has gone screaming to the government, demanding help in protecting facilities. Fortunately, our beloved bureaucrats work slowly, so little has been done to date except to provide some military units to increase security.

"We have a well-placed source inside the plant who tells us that two companies of reservists, about 160 troops, have begun patrolling the area, installing roadblocks and are soon to begin building watch towers and additional fencing.

"The good news is that the security efforts are quite traditional and directed outward. No one expects a small force to penetrate the plant in a more creative way. As Sun Tzu said: 'Attack him where he is unprepared; appear where you are not expected.'

"That's the reason we have assembled here. You've no doubt heard the sounds of the rail yard next to the plant.

Coal trains destined for Kaiyuan stop here to pick up new engines and crew. In two nights, we will stow away on a train in the coal cars, each to one car to help reduce the chance of detection. At the end of a 4-5 hour ride we will be *inside* the plant perimeter. Our source assures us incoming trains are not being checked."

He projected a satellite view of the plant.

"From the train you will each move separately over about 250 yards of open terrain to the cover of this building near the base of the first smokestack where the two teams will assemble and then each move to the optimum sites for launch. RPG's are used primarily as anti-tank weapons and the Type 69 has a 96 percent hit rate at 100 yards for a moving target. But our targets are the bases of the plant's smokestacks. So accuracy should be much better."

He used a laser pointer to draw attention to key features on the satellite image and the launch sites near the bases of the two 200-foot smokestacks.

"Why the smokestacks?" He projected a schematic of the plant.

"Penetrate the base of the smokestack with the bunker buster and then the high-explosive warhead and you blow up the furnace. The exploding furnace may, in turn, rupture the high-pressure steam boilers that drive the turbine generators, causing even more damage. In addition, there's a good chance the smokestacks will collapse, destroying a lot of what's left of the structures. Coal dust in the air may also ignite adding a fireball to the round out the destruction."

Ahlim felt a rush. Smiley was recounting her childhood dream; the retribution she so badly wanted to inflict on the power plant that killed her brother.

"The plan for extraction is relatively simple," he continued. "In the confusion following the attack, all will return to the rail yard. I will be waiting in a track maintenance vehicle on the first spur. Its rotating beacon will be easy to spot with night vision. We will exit the yard, and, about five miles down line, switch to a delivery van. You will each be given a change of clothes, bus tickets to differing destinations and some money to help get you started."

Ahlim had never been more uncomfortable in her life. The chunks of bituminous coal dug into her no matter where or in what position she lay. She finally huddled in a front corner of the car where the coal level was lower, squatting against the bulkhead. At least here she was less exposed to the cold wind as the train hurtled through the black night, swaying back and forth, wheels clattering rhythmically. Occasionally she had to stand to relieve cramps in her legs.

She had been told to keep the night-vision goggles off as much as possible to save the batteries. So, for most of the seemingly endless ride, she could see nothing but the lights of an occasional village as the train barreled through. The tea provided in a thermos was now cold. She was too nervous to eat, but mechanically chewed biscuits to help rid her mouth of the foul taste of sulfur emanating from the coal.

Well, she thought, nobody said eco-activism was going to be glamorous.

She spent much of the time in her head reviewing the steps for assembling and arming the grenade. She also repeatedly reviewed the mission plans and her specific role. Occasionally she allowed her mind to wander, thinking of Caterpillar, her family, friends and the small life she had led in that dusty village near Chengdu.

She must have dozed. Sensing the train was slowing, she woke and switched on her goggles. They were entering the yard. In the distance to the left loomed the power plant, its stacks pouring green smoke almost straight up into the calm night air.

She gently swung the backpack on her shoulders and switched on her radio. There was a hissing sound in the ear buds.

The train came to a jarring halt as momentum slammed coupler against coupler down the line. She was almost knocked off her feet as she scrambled over the loose coal to reach the ladder. Once there, she waited authorization to get off. In about a minute, Smiley quietly said "go."

As Ahlim clambered down the ladder, she lost her footing before she realized how stiff her legs were. Once down, she quickly crossed an adjoining track and sprinted toward the first smokestack. As promised, the 250 yards to the rendezvous *was* open ground. She felt very exposed. As she ran, she tightened the straps on the backpack to minimize jostling of the warhead.

Her car had been one of those nearer the plant, so she was second to arrive in the cover of a maintenance shed. She leaned against the wall to catch her breath. Quickly, out of the green gloom, other running figures appeared. Soon all eight were assembled.

"Team One in place," Elvis said. Spider Man radioed the same for Team Two.

"Go," said Smiley's disembodied voice. "And good luck."

Team One had drawn the short straw and moved out to attack the second generating unit about 200 yards to the west. Team Two had only to move to a nearby position to achieve the desired firing range of 100 yards for the other stack. Ahlim, assigned to Team One, ducked and ran with the others toward the distant position.

As they ran, Spider Man announced that Team Two was ready. "Hold," Smiley responded.

Ahlim's team reached the cover of a large garage and immediately began the assembly process. Elvis would only have to step to the left of the building to make his shots. She unpacked the grenade and carefully placed the powder charge in the rear section that would shoot the missile from the launcher. Then, fingers flying, she attached the section to the sustainer rocket motor that would hurl the warhead to the target at about 1,000 feet-per-second.

She finished first, handed the bunker buster to Red, and, following the plan, turned and ran toward the distant rotating beacon that marked the escape vehicle. The back blast of the launcher was about 60 feet, so Ahlim and Tattoo had to be well clear before firing.

"Team One ready," Elvis announced.

"Teams fire!"

By then Ahlim was approaching the middle of the open ground. Out of the corner of her eye, she saw a bright plume of fire, the back blast of Team One's bunker buster. She heard a loud "whump" as the missile hit home.

Suddenly night turned into day. She was nearly blinded, even though the goggles compensated almost instantly. She froze. She could see her shadow.

"Flare!" Smiley said, without his characteristic calm. "Take the shots and get out of there."

Ahlim didn't know if she should continue to run or hit the ground. Before she could decide, something like a huge fist punched her in the stomach, knocking her on her butt. She couldn't understand why, suddenly, she was sitting down. She tried to stand, but her legs wouldn't cooperate. She couldn't feel them. She reached down to check her stomach and looked at her hand. It was covered with a warm, black liquid.

The realization came. I've been shot. *I've been shot!*

Then the ground trembled and she saw fire from the furnaces shooting up and out of both smokestacks as they began to collapse. There were more tremors as boilers exploded and coal dust ignited. The sound and pressure wave hit Ahlim an instant later, knocking her on her back.

She was very cold. Her blood was soaking the ground

beneath her. She watched a universe of embers floating high above like a huge field of fireflies on a summer night. As embers burned out, their ashes floated down, covering her body with a thin blanket of warm snowflakes.

For you, Caterpillar, she thought. *For you.*

She watched as the fireflies dimmed and, suddenly, all winked out.

DEEPEST AND DARKEST
SOUTH SUDAN, AFRICA
FEBRUARY, 2039

*"Amid the diverse social and political causes, the Darfur conflict
began as an ecological crisis, arising at least in part,
from climate change."*
—Ban Ki-moon, UN secretary-general

*"Rising temperatures are likely to cause drought and increase natural
hazards.... These may cause increased strife over dwindling resources
in the areas directly affected, but also migration and, in turn, conflict
with host communities. A common theme of these scenarios is that
climate change will lead to local scarcities, which will increase the
risk of conflict."*
—Environmental Impacts Risk and Opportunities
Assessment, Ministry of Environment, South Sudan

*"I once spoke to someone who had survived the genocide in Rwanda,
and she (said) that there was now nobody left on the face of the earth,
either friend or relative, who knew who she was."*
—Christopher Hitchens, author

Dr. Jean-Philippe Bertrand—J.P. to family and friends— stepped from the plane into the bright and broiling Juba afternoon. The cracked and patched tarmac was soft and sticky. Carry-on in hand, he moved quickly to the terminal's baggage claim to retrieve his large medical case. He'd hated to check it, but the plane was small and he'd had no choice.

Lines at immigration were short. The few passengers disgorged from his nearly empty flight made only two lines. His agent, a young woman, suffered from a pronounced case of amblyopia, "lazy eye." It was disconcerting when she looked from his passport to his face and back several times.

"Reason for visit?" she asked in British-tinged English. J.P. showed her his *Médecins Sans Frontières* identification.

"I'm here to visit our regional headquarters for meetings," he lied. As a precautionary measure, MSF had warned him not to divulge his actual destination.

While she checked the computer, J.P. took a closer look at her. Dinka, he thought, based on her slightly elongated head, apparent height and facial scars. Of course, Dinka would have been a good guess in any case since it was the largest tribe in South Sudan and, after decades of civil war, very much in control. Jobs such as hers would probably only go to Dinkas.

She stamped his passport and visa.

"Next."

Two armed soldiers lounged by the door to the lobby, machine guns slung insolently over their shoulders. One looked him up and down and, moving in slow motion, pushed the button to open the steel door. As J.P. stepped into the waiting room he was assaulted by the noise, heat and smells of the seedy African airport. Outlaw taxi drivers accosted him, some aggressively pulling at his bags. And the body odor. That would take getting used to again.

Vendors clamored for his attention. Particularly poignant were the kids trying to sell him bottled water.

One girl dressed in rags—a single bottle in her hand— looked more desperate than others. He pressed a dollar in her hand and took the bottle. He would not drink it, of course. Though it had a well-known label, it almost certainly had been refilled with who knows what.

He pushed his way through the crowd to the taxi stand. First in line was a mottled green rattletrap. The driver gave him a big betel nut-stained smile, probably in appreciation of his effort to take an official taxi.

"Juba Bridge Hotel," J.P. said.

It was not the best of the few decent hotels in town. But it had sentimental appeal. He and Marie had spent their short honeymoon there 30 years ago. It sat adjacent to the Juba Bridge, the only White Nile crossing in all of South Sudan. Then it had been a tranquil and serene hideaway in the hubbub that was Juba.

They'd met in Sudan shortly before the country split into Sudan and South Sudan in 2011. MSF had posted them to its clinic in Yei, a town near the borders with Uganda and the Central Africa Republic, Sudan's two major trading partners. She was assigned to be his nurse and soon became his bed partner. Their clientele consisted primarily of refugees escaping the genocide in Sudan's Darfur Province to the north.

Later they wondered why they'd married. It seemed almost on a whim. Perhaps it was because, now in their early '30s, neither had had a long-term relationship. Perhaps it was their rootlessness. Each had been on the road with MSF for several years, ministering to the impoverished, the starved, and the torn, battered, catatonic, crazed victims of genocide. Or, perhaps, it was the need to have someone to cling to when the black waves of helplessness, frustration and depression rolled over them.

After Sudan they'd returned to France to start a family and try to live a normal life. But the relationship was never quite the same. Normal life—married life—soon seemed humdrum, colorless. Boredom led J.P. back to MSF to take short-term assignments, leaving Marie home to raise their two sons. Each had affairs. But they'd gotten through it. They stayed together, initially for their sons; later for themselves. With retirement came travel plans and a modest summer place in Arles overlooking the Rhone.

Then she died. A mercifully short encounter with cancer. The nest was empty. He had nothing but time on his hands. So he returned to MSF, asking for a posting to South Sudan.

Despite his age, J.P. was welcomed back. The warming had dramatically increased the need for the organization's services, but funding and volunteers had dropped significantly. Famine-related disease was increasing exponentially. Ethnic cleansing and outright genocide were being actively employed against minority populations around the world—whether religious or ethnic—to make more of the limited food and water available to a country's majority. Minorities were also being forcibly removed from their homes and lands to make room for a country's elite, displaced by the ocean's implacable inundation of coastlines.

Why South Sudan? Why not? Was there any other place more or less deserving of his efforts? But, deep down, he knew the real reason. It was nostalgia, as illogical as it might seem. Nothing good happened to him in Sudan. Nothing but Marie. Perhaps that was reason enough.

Not surprisingly, the taxi's air conditioning wasn't functioning. J.P. mopped his forehead with a handkerchief. Betel Juice caught his eye in the rearview mirror and shrugged apologetically.

Exiting the airport, they were confronted by a large billboard and the smiling face of a much younger President Samuel Jiir wearing his signature black cowboy hat. J.P.

guessed no one had ever dared mention to Jiir that black hats were associated with bad guys in American cowboy movies.

Jiir, who billed himself the "Father of South Sudan," welcomed visitors and invited them to enjoy the wonders of the world's newest country. After decades of violence, Muslim northern Sudan allowed its essentially Christian and Animist southern half limited autonomy in 2005, with the promise of a plebiscite on full independence within six years. When the time came, the vote was just shy of 99 percent in favor.

J.P. was intrigued that Jiir was trying to erase from memory the fact that John Garang was the country's true father. He led the Sudan People's Liberation Army from its inception in 1983 to the peace agreement leading to partition in 2005. But, shortly following the end of hostilities, Garang was killed in a helicopter crash under suspicious circumstances. Jiir, then his deputy, was suspected of his assassination, but never formally charged.

Less than two years after separation, the new country descended into civil war, pitting Jiir's majority Dinka against the only slightly smaller Nuer Tribe. The bloody conflict lasted for years until Jiir's forces finally subdued the Nuer White Army—named for the white chalk with which they painted their faces—and either jailed or executed its leadership.

It was rumored Jiir had the support of the Chinese government as it sought to protect its control of South Sudan's oil. With Africa's fourth largest reserves, the country exported 70 percent of its crude to China. Oil revenues accounted for about 90 percent of its income. To facilitate shipment, the Chinese had bankrolled a pipeline through Uganda to a port in Tanzania on the Indian Ocean. The Nuer, on the other hand, had vowed to nationalize the country's oil, cutting out the Chinese.

Once Jiir had consolidated power, he ruled as the stereotypical African strongman for 28 years without materially improving the country's economy, health and well-being of its people—with the possible exception of his Dinkas.

In an ironic twist, Jiir today was tacitly supporting the Nuer in its genocide of the Murle Tribe in Jonglei State in the country's northeast corner. The two tribes had fought for as long as anyone could remember over grazing land for cattle, the cornerstone of their economic and social lives. Jiir's strategy was to placate the Nuer to help diffuse any further dissention. The Murle was a relatively small tribe, one he believed could be easily written off.

J.P.'s eventual destination was the MSF clinic in the town of Pibor in Jonglei State, near the center of the fighting. Jiir's government was not happy that MSF would locate there to provide medical assistance, primarily to Murle combatants, women and children being hunted by Nuer forces. But world opinion would side with MSF; Jiir was reluctant to take any more public relations hits.

It was a dangerous posting, but J.P. wanted back in the game.

———————

The taxi turned south and wheezed its way down the oddly named Havana Avenue. At Mboro Avenue they turned southeast, heading for the White Nile—so named because of the light-colored clay sediment it picks up on its long journey north from Rwanda. The river's two branches meet in the Sudanese capital, Khartoum, where the increased depth of the merged river changes its color to blue.

Scant numbers of vehicles and pedestrians were on the streets, most of the population fleeing burning mid-day temperatures. Decades of increasingly high temperatures and drought had turned the once green city dusty, drab and dun-colored.

Just before the bridge, the driver made a hard left into

the hotel entrance. J.P. could see that a valiant—and almost successful—effort had been made to maintain the lush landscape he remembered. Under the bougainvillea-shaded portico, he gave the driver U.S. dollars for the fare. South Sudan's hyper-inflated pound was virtually useless for cash transactions.

Once in his room, he luxuriated in the air conditioning. The old wall unit was cacophonous in its efforts to cool the small room. He stripped and showered. There was no hot water. But that wasn't a problem. The cold water spraying from the shower was almost bath-water warm.

He was more tired than hungry, so he sprawled on the bed in the darkened room, lighted only by a slash of hot light streaming through a crack in curtains that didn't quite meet. Eyes closed, he tried to remember the room in which he and Marie had spent their three-day honeymoon. It was on an upper floor on the river side and had a small balcony.

Actually, the two were more excited about having three days off than the honeymoon itself; they'd been intimate for months. While there was plenty of sex, they exalted in clean sheets, showers, room service and the escape from 12-hour shifts and the misery they confronted each of those hours.

He remembered them sitting on the balcony in the cool of early evening, gin and tonics in hand, watching dhows with colorful, patched lateen sails moving silently up and down river. They were starkly etched by the setting sun. The scene looked like a print from a 19th Century travel memoir.

As he drifted off, his last thoughts were of his flight over the Sahara that morning, sunrise throwing marching rows of enormous dunes into high relief. And marching they were. Drought and prevailing northwest winds were inexorably expanding the desert, robbing viable land from Mali, Niger, Chad, Sudan and Eritrea.

J.P. dreamed not of Marie as he thought he might.

Instead he witnessed a sea of sand submerging everything in its path. He ran but was overtaken and quickly buried.

He awakened in a hot, stifling room. Sometime during the night, the air conditioner had gasped its last....

"*Merde*," J.P. muttered as he stood in the bathroom, splashing water on his face and toweling off the sweat.

The meeting at MSF headquarters was next morning. It was a relatively short ride on Mboro Avenue past the stone facades of the University of Juba. The office was located across from the large John Garang Memorial Park and Tomb and within sight of the South Sudan Parliament building. J.P. was intrigued that Jiir had let Garang's Memorial stand, although it was clear that maintenance of the grassless and trash-filled park was not a priority.

Regional Director Dr. Hamish MacDonald loomed large in his small, cluttered office. He rose and extended a hammy hand that engulfed J.P.'s. "Welcome to South Sudan. Or, should I say welcome back," Hamish said with a Scottish brogue so thick J.P. could barely make it out.

"Thanks," he said. "You're not from around here, are you?" Hamish broke into a big grin. "How could you tell?" They sat.

"Looks like you were posted here about 30 years ago. Much has changed but much is the same." Mercifully, he was making an effort to lighten the accent.

"Frankly, I'm not sure how viable Pibor will be in the short term. Hostilities have been increasing and the UN is considering withdrawing the small contingent of African Peacekeepers posted in the state."

J.P. knew that UN peacekeeping operations worldwide were severely hampered by rapidly diminishing financial support from member nations. Many had simply stopped paying dues to divert funds to help meet warming-created internal needs. Many countries had also declined to volunteer troops, opting to keep them at home to deal with their own internal conflicts.

"The situation out there is grim and Jür has made no effort to intervene. I know he wants us out but is afraid of world opinion. But, should the peacekeepers go, he may not stop the Nuer from moving against us, claiming it was the UN's fault for withdrawing.

"Bottom line is—do you want to go? The guy you're to replace is burned out, but might be willing to stay on until things clarify. I'll abandon the mission immediately if he recommends it."

Hell, J.P. thought, I've come this far. "I'll go and make sure we're ready to pull out quickly if necessary."

Hamish looked at him with a thoughtful expression. "Okay, but don't take any chances. I haven't lost anyone yet and don't want to start now. We'll load the truck with supplies today and assign a driver. You'll head out in the morning."

The unmarked white-panel truck was crammed with medical supplies. Hamish, sweating profusely, head covered with a floppy straw hat, handed J.P. the manifest—plasma, intravenous fluids, antibiotics, pain killers, anti-diarrheals, syringes, surgical dressings. There was also a large supply of fresh water and military-style rations.

Hamish introduced his driver. "Charles has been driving with us for years and has made this run a number of times. You're in good hands." Charles, who was small, wiry with a silver-fringed bald pate, smiled shyly.

"Considering the situation, I've requested that a couple of UN vehicles meet you at the Jonglei border. The truck is a tempting target for either of the factions."

He wished him "*bon chance*"—a Scotsman's version of *bon chance*—as he stepped up to the passenger seat.

"Radio us when you hit the border and again when you arrive at the clinic."

They passed his hotel as they drove onto the bridge spanning the sluggish, somewhat diminished Nile, now more brown than white. As the truck turned north on the Nile Highway, J.P. noticed the sky was bleached white by the intense heat.

The highway took them between the river and Bandinglio National Park. Charles informed him that the 4,000 square-mile park hosts the world's second-largest animal migration, primarily various species of antelope.

"Serengeti's first, of course," he said. "And Tanzania has made the most of it for tourism. Here the government chose to spend our money on oil, so Bandinglio has never been adequately developed and is the least-visited major national park in the world."

Ironic, J.P. thought. Now South Sudan's oil reserves are dwindling and prices continue to drop with diminishing demand. But a push to build tourism infrastructure to diversify the economy, even if money were available, would be doomed because of the warming and continuous bloody ethnic violence.

The truck's cab was warm. Charles said he had to keep the air conditioning on low to avoid ice buildup on the coils. He also thought better gas mileage would help them make it to Pibor on one tank.

"Not good to stop unless you have to."

So J.P. nodded off. He hadn't slept well the night before. The air conditioner had been fixed, but he was wound pretty tightly. Instead he'd begun reading a book by Antoine Saint-Exupery he'd thrown into his bag as he left the apartment. He remembered with pleasure reading *Le Petite Prince* to his boys when they were young. He also remembered trying to help them understand its key messages: *"Et maintenant, voici mon secret, un secret très simple; c'est seulement avec le coeur que l'on peut voir à juste titre, ce qui est essentiel est invisible pour les yeux."*

"And now here is my secret, a very simple secret; it is only with the heart that one can see rightly, what is essential is invisible to the eye."

"Vous êtes responsable pour toujours de ce que tu as apprivoisé. Vous êtes responsable de votre rose."

"You are responsible, forever, for what you have tamed. You are responsible for your rose."

The book was *Night Flight,* recounting Exupery's experiences as an airmail pilot in Argentina in the early '30s. He'd found the book soothing, elegiac.

He awoke with a start, lifting his chin off his chest. Charles had stopped. Ahead were several vehicles lined up at what appeared to be a checkpoint. He didn't look at all concerned as he took the manifest from a side pocket.

"Doctor," he said, "you might like to take out your passport and MSF identification. This is probably a routine weapons check. The government makes a show of trying to keep weapons out of Jonglei, but everyone knows the arms dealers bribe officials to turn a blind eye. In any case, the Murle can't afford to buy weapons. The dealers are primarily supplying the Nuer from Malakal in the north."

Charles was right. After a cursory look at the manifest and J.P.'s identification, they were waived through. In a few miles, Charles drove off the road into a dirt parking area.

"This is where we are to meet our UN escorts," he said, looking at his watch. "We're a few minutes early. Would you like to get out and stretch while I radio Juba?"

J.P. needed to visit a bush, so he stepped into the dusty early afternoon heat. When he climbed back in the cab, Charles handed him the radio phone, looking concerned.

"J.P.," said Hamish, "I have unsettling news. I just heard from the UN. Escort vehicles won't be coming. There's been a flare up north of Bor and they've had to deploy all their resources to that sector. This shouldn't affect you since you'll be heading east from Bor. You're more than halfway to Pibor—about 120 miles remain—so I think you'll be okay. Over."

J.P. was unfamiliar with the phone. Charles pointed to the send button. "Okay, we'll proceed. Ah, over."

"Good, I'll expect to hear from you in about three hours. Out."

Bor, Jonglei's adobe-colored capital city, spread below them in a small, hazy depression as Charles wrestled the truck east on a rutted dirt road—a bypass, he said, that would get them more quickly to the main highway to Pibor.

Along the road, a small group of young boys, ebony skin glistening with sweat, played a dispirited game of soccer. Puffs of dust accompanied their footwork as they kicked the scuffed, partially inflated ball up and down the dirt field. The goals were made of rusted pipe that probably had never seen netting.

It was cattle country. As they turned onto the graveled main road, J.P. saw boys tending herds of thin, dusty white, very long-horned cattle.

"Abigar," Charles said. "The breed most common in Sudan. Families count their wealth in cattle. So they're used for milk; rarely killed for meat."

He said these were Murle. Farther north, on the ever-shifting border with the Nuer, cattle rustling and murders happened almost daily. And the Nuer, with superior numbers and arms, were moving steadily south.

"The people have long memories. Over the decades, thousands have been killed, many more injured and tens of thousands made homeless. Countless children have been kidnapped. And many thousands of cattle have been stolen. Both sides have committed atrocities. And, as the warming continues to shrink grazing land, the conflict has intensified."

J.P. couldn't help but wonder where all this was heading. Even if the Nuer eliminate their rivals, they still face the impact of an even greater enemy—the warming. How many generations will be able to retain their traditional way of life in the face of the south-bound march of the Sahara and the desertification that will make obsolete the term "Sub-Saharan?"

Charles pointed to a cooler behind his seat. "Hungry?"

J.P. retrieved the cooler and found flat bread he remembered as *kissra,* some local soft white cheese, two Styrofoam containers of savory-smelling stew and bottled water."

Charles asked for bread and cheese so he could continue driving. J.P. tucked into the stew. Even after all the years, it tasted familiar—lamb, onions, peanut butter. As he ate he noticed they'd entered a marshy area known as the Kenamuke Swamp that extended as far he could see. It was part of Boma National Park, coming up on his right.

"Boma is another undeveloped resource," Charles said, brushing crumbs off this shirt. "The annual migration here is only slightly smaller than that of Bandinglio, but more diverse. Pibor is another 40 miles or so."

Nearing their destination, they were confronted with another roadblock consisting of two mangy pickups parked across the road, each with a 50mm machine gun mounted in its bed. A contingent of scruffy Murle milled around, looking suspiciously at the approaching truck.

"No problem," Charles said. "They'll welcome us."

He rolled down his window and spoke to a guard in some dialect J.P. didn't recognize. After a minute of what appeared to be amicable conversation, the guard smiled, nodded to J.P., and turned to order a truck to back up.

As they drove through, about six Murle piled into one truck and it pulled out in hot pursuit, tires spitting gravel.

"Don't worry," Charles laughed. "We're being provided with an escort to the clinic. I just hope they're around if you actually need them."

Their raucous arrival brought spectators out of a large Quonset hut and olive-drab military tents strung in a row behind it. The pickup circled the compound at high speed, kicking up a dust cloud and then fishtailed onto the road, heading back to the checkpoint. Most gawked, but one figure in white came forward looking haggard but pleased.

"I'm Robert Davies, clinic director. You must be my replacement."

"J.P. Bertrand at your service." Davies invited him in for refreshments, to meet the staff and tour the facilities. He nodded at Charles.

"Please drive around back and I'll get you help unloading."

As they walked toward the pewter-colored, rust-stained building, Davies told him it had long ago been a regional police headquarters.

"We gutted it and installed a walk-in clinic, dispensary, surgical theatre and 20 beds. Staff members staying on-site live in the tents out back. Most are occupied by ambulatory patients and families waiting for relatives to be released."

Once inside, Davies presented the clinic's other doctor, Omar Ondimba, a Gabonese who had received his training in that former French colony in West-Central Africa.

"*Bonjour et bienvenue*," he said, clearly enjoying the opportunity to speak French.

"*Mon plaisir. Je suis impatient de travailler avec vous*," J.P. responded.

Davies turned to a portly, red-cheeked young woman.

"Meet our head nurse and only RN, Margaret O'Rourke—Maggie."

"Welcome to Hades," she said brightly with an Irish lilt. In turn she presented her assistant, Athieng Ayun, a tall, gaunt woman of indeterminate age who looked impassively at J.P. and nodded.

Davies's overview of the clinic and its operation was thorough, but he was clearly more than ready to abandon ship. The three-month tour had, he said, done him in. "The staff is competent and hard working. But there are too few of them.

"My advice to you, good doctor, is not to be a hero. The Nuer occasionally raid in the area and, if the UN pulls out, the clinic will be a tempting target. At the first hint of trouble, get out with Omar and Maggie. Athieng and the others are local and should be okay. I have an old station wagon hidden close by in the bush. It's fully fueled and stocked with basic medical supplies, food and water. If it turns ugly, radio Hamish and head for Bor. He may be able to convince the UN to meet you en route with an escort."

With that, he took an ignition key from around his neck. "I'd keep this with you at all times...."

It took J.P. two or three days to get back into the rhythm of clinic life. At his age, the 12-hour shifts seemed like an eternity. The patient load was heavy and not always related to the genocide. Many patients suffered from the usual maladies stemming from poverty, hunger, unsanitary conditions. There certainly was variety. He and Omar could go from treating rickets to gunshot wounds in a matter of minutes.

The day after he arrived, a van tore into the parking lot and disgorged seven Murle men with bullet wounds ranging from superficial to mortal. The two of them worked side-by-side for hours in the small surgical theatre, repairing what could be repaired and closing the eyelids of those they weren't able to save.

He very quickly came to respect Omar, Maggie and the taciturn Athieng.

Toward evening the fourth day, J.P. was taking a break in front of the clinic when he saw figures in the haze, some distance down the road. As they came closer, they resolved into a boy with a girl riding on his shoulders and a small boy holding his hand. As he watched, the boy stumbled and fell. The older boy put the girl down, sat and cradled the fallen boy's head in his lap.

J.P. jogged toward the children. He could see they were in bad shape. The three were rail-thin with slightly protruding bellies. They had infected insect bites and he could smell the stench of diarrhea, probably the result of dysentery.

The boy looked up at him, eyes vacant. J.P. sprinted back to the clinic shouting for orderlies to bring a stretcher.

Once in the clinic, he ordered a saline drip, ampicillin and antibiotic cream for the bites. The three were undernourished, dehydrated, had high temperatures and were lethargic. Later that evening, once their conditions had stabilized, he asked Athieng to speak with the boy. She sat by his bed, quietly questioning him.

"They are Nuer," she said. "A Murle party raided their farm to steal cattle and killed their parents. They saw their father beheaded and mother raped and shot. The children were kidnapped. The next night the men became very drunk and they escaped. He thinks they have been walking for three days, drinking water from roadside ditches. He said neither his brother nor sister have spoken since they were abducted."

She told the story in a monotone, without affect.

J.P. asked their names and ages. "The older boy is *Kaaria*. He believes he's 10. The girl, *Sabiha*, is three. *Abasi* is six."

———————

In a few days the Nuer children had recovered sufficiently to be moved to J.P.'s tent. There was some discussion about what to do with them. Murle families in the area would not take in more mouths to feed, certainly not Nuer children. The nearest UNRWA refugee camp was north of Bor, but not secure. Orphaned children languished. The best they could hope for was to be shipped to one of the few overcrowded state-run orphanages for what could only be called warehousing.

J.P. found himself becoming fond of them. *Kaaria*, obviously intelligent, quickly picked up English words and phrases. To avoid confusing him, J.P and Omar did not speak French in his presence. The boy, *Abasi*, had begun speaking again, but suffered from nightmares. His screams woke not only J.P. but inhabitants of neighboring tents. To get him back to sleep, *Kaaria* would cuddle with him in his cot and softly croon a Nuer lullaby, probably one sung by his mother. The girl remained catatonic. She would eat when presented with food but slept almost around the clock.

———————

J.P. and Hamish spoke almost daily. The situation continued to deteriorate.

Hamish called early one morning. Two UN Peacekeepers had been killed the day before in a skirmish with Nuer raiders, pushing the UN to decide to remove its forces from Jonglei, effective in one week.

"I don't think you have any recourse but to start packing and be ready to move out," Hamish said. "I want you and the other foreign staff out of there before the UN withdraws."

J.P. called the staff together and told them of the decision. No one seemed too surprised. Others had heard of the peacekeepers' deaths and suspected the withdrawal was coming. He asked people to continue to do their jobs as best they could until the clinic shut its doors five days hence.

"We need to stop in-take of patients needing hospitalization, so, effective today, we'll close the hospital wing and try to get the remaining patients ambulatory before the deadline. In four days, we'll start loading the equipment and supplies to be taken to Juba for distribution to other MSF clinics."

He thanked the staff for its dedicated, hard work.

But the Nuer didn't wait for the UN to withdraw.

Three nights later, when J.P. was checking on "the kids," as they had become known around the clinic, two explosions in rapid succession almost blew his tent off its wooden floor. Instinctively, he threw himself down, crawled to the cots and pulled the kids to the floor with him. The canvas walls of the tent glowed bright yellow and orange as the conflagration consumed the clinic. Automatic weapon's fire sprayed around the compound. There were screams, shouts, cries. Shadows of running figures flickered on the tent walls.

J.P. stood to open the back flap of the tent so they could escape into the chaos. As he did, bullets tore through the tent. He was hit in the upper left leg and fell. It felt as if he'd been stabbed with a hot poker. He rolled over to assess the damage. The kids sat mutely, their eyes wide and glowing like coals. There wasn't much blood. Probably no major arterial involvement. Though it hurt like hell, it appeared the femur had been missed. It certainly was more than a flesh wound. He couldn't tell in the dark of the tent, but the bullet may have passed through.

Grimacing, he pushed the kids along the floor and out the back of the tent. He crawled with difficulty, dragging his leg. He gestured to *Kaaria* to stay low as he crawled ahead of them.

He had checked on the car enough times so, in the burning night, he was able to get his bearings. Behind him, the screams had stopped as raiders finished off the dying. It took only a few minutes—though it seemed like an eternity—to get to the hidden vehicle.

He was surprised to see Maggie sitting on the ground, leaning against the driver's door. She seemed dazed. Some of the hair on the right side of her head was gone. She didn't appear badly burned, but parts of her shirt were smoldering.

"Omar?" J.P croaked. "Dead," she said.

"Okay, let's try to get out of here." He unlocked the car, opened the rear door for the kids. Maggie moved unsteadily to the other side. "I'm hit in the left leg, but I think I can drive. I'm just not sure how soon we should go. This was probably a hit and run, but they still may be in the area. What if we encounter them on the road to Bor?"

He decided to take the chance, started the car and rolled slowly, lights out, toward the gravel highway. The remaining flames were bright enough to light his way. He looked left at the burning compound. No sign of raiders. So he pulled onto the road. To his chagrin, the muffler was bad; the car was loud.

He asked Maggie to call Hamish, pointing to the radio phone.

J.P. looked at his leg. There was a good deal of blood soaking his shorts. But bleeding wasn't excessive. He was in a great deal of pain and wondered if he were going to go into shock. If that happened, he'd have to lie down in the rear of the station wagon and let Maggie drive. For now, he thought he was okay. He gestured to *Kaaria*, pantomiming taking a drink. The boy looked behind the rear seat and passed around a couple of bottles of water.

Hamish must have been sleeping with the phone. Maggie passed it to him. "We've been hit, badly. The clinic's destroyed. Omar and many others are dead. Maggie and I plus three orphans are on the road to Bor in Davies' station wagon. I don't know if the raiders are still in the area."

"Let me get the UN on the line and see if they can provide an escort. Heading to Pibor, did you see the road into Boma National Park? Drive down that road and look for cover. If I can get help, they'll meet you on that road. Anyone injured?"

"I was hit in the leg, but doing okay. Maggie lost some hair and has what appear to be third degree facial burns. The kids are okay. When we get to Boma, we'll break out the medical supplies."

The next couple of hours were a blur. There wasn't much cover on the Boma access road. He backed into a clump of acacias so they could watch the road in both directions. The night was like pitch; cloud cover, no moon. In the weak dome light, they went through the medical kit, pulled out sulfa and dressings for his leg, morphine for the pain and burn ointment for Maggie.

No one was hungry, but J.P. thought they should try to eat. Maggie hydrated a couple of packaged dinners. They shared one; *Kaaria* fed himself and the little ones from the other.

The radio beeped. Hamish reported that the UN promised to send an escort from Bor to arrive in about an hour. He said they'd call when they hit the Boma Road. Just in case, he gave J.P. a frequency to use to contact the escort if necessary.

"The UN Mission Hospital here has been notified and will be ready for you. How are you doing?" J.P. told him they were okay and thanked him for his help.

The morphine helped. He hadn't injected much; just enough to dull the pain. Blood leaked through the dressing, but it had staunched most of the flow.

The little ones slept, the girl with her head in *Kaaria's* lap; *Abasi* leaning on his shoulder. J.P. couldn't be certain in the inky blackness, but he thought the boy was awake. Maggie cried softly, the night's horrors finally taking their toll.

J.P. closed his eyes. The adrenaline high was gone. He was beyond tired. If it weren't for the pain—though now somewhat muted—he thought he might sleep forever.

What am I doing here he asked Marie, seeing her face where the windshield should be? I think I came back to find us as we were then. I was a fool. Nothing remains of us here. There's just death and tragedy—the disintegration, unraveling of this sad cobbled-together country.

The beeping phone interrupted his reverie. The voice at the other end—a Lieutenant Deng—asked him to turn on his parking lights so they could find him. J.P. did and in a few minutes he saw headlights. To be certain they saw him, he flicked his high beams several times.

One of the men offered to drive the station wagon and helped J.P. hobble to the machine gun-topped Humvee where he could lie down. He allowed himself to sleep, waking three hours later as he was helped onto a stretcher at the hospital.

He was released two days later, walking with a cane. Hamish picked him up and drove to the small apartment he had rented for him, Maggie and the kids. She opened the door, face partially bandaged.

"Ain't I a beauty? Actually, it's not as bad as it looks."

Kaaria walked into the room, dressed in new shorts, sandals and t-shirt. J.P. gave him thumbs up. The two others joined him shyly, also in new outfits.

Maggie said they'd already eaten, but she had some lunch ready for the two of them. They sat and talked.

"Including Omar, 17 dead, most in the ward," Hamish said. "By the time of the raid, many of the local staff had gone home. So it could have been worse. Two RPGs. Omar was doing rounds and died instantly."

They sat quietly for a moment.

"Any thoughts about what to do with the kids?"

J.P. had thought a great deal about exactly that as he lay in the hospital. His decision scared him and he knew it would be viewed as crazy by almost everyone.

"I want to try to take them home with me. They have nobody. I have nobody. A match made in heaven," he joked.

Hamish put down his soup spoon and looked quizzically at him.

"I can see you're serious. I'm sure you've considered what you'd be getting yourself into. And you must also be aware of the roadblocks. I'm just a simple Scottish country doctor, but I don't think France is going to be easily persuaded to open its arms to embrace three South Sudanese orphans. Then there's the problem at this end of getting permission for them to leave. Unfortunately, what's good for the kids will be the last consideration."

"I know," J.P. said. "But I need to try."

Three days later, J.P. sat uncomfortably across from French Ambassador François Dumond in his over decorated and stuffy embassy office on Kololo Road.

Dumond, a small, fussy-looking man, glanced at J.P.'s request sitting on his leather-rimmed blotter. Drumming his fingers, he looked up and smiled a thin-lipped smile. "Dr. Bertrand, I trust you are recovering well. You've had quite an ordeal."

J.P. thanked him for his concern.

"As for your request," he looked down, "to return to France with three Nuer children—well, you must appreciate the complications. Even if you are successful convincing the South Sudanese to grant you guardianship, it is uncertain France will allow their immigration. As you know, the warming has—as with many other countries— required us to reduce quotas. In Africa, preference is given to former French colonies...."

"Yes, I am aware of the complications," J.P. interrupted. "But the local government tells me I cannot obtain guardianship unless I can prove the children will be allowed to return with me to France. So, the process must start here."

Dumond rocked forward in his high-backed chair, putting his elbows on the desk.

"May I ask why it is you wish to take these children to France? I'm sure you have become fond of them, nursing them back to health and sharing, as you have, this terrible incident. No child should have to suffer what they have suffered. But, with all its challenges, this is their country and culture. And, as orphans, there are facilities to care for them."

"Are you familiar with these—*facilities*? They are little better than warehouses. They are unsafe, unsanitary. The conditions are deplorable. It is unlikely they would receive the psychiatric counseling they need. And there's no guarantee the children would be kept together."

Dumond sighed, glancing at the clock on the wall behind J.P. He obviously wanted to bring the meeting to a conclusion.

"Doctor, I'm aware that conditions could be better. But there are literally thousands of children in the same situation. Do you really think that taking these three to

France would make any real difference?"

J.P. was stunned, struck speechless. Anger rose in him like a tide. As he struggled to control himself and frame a suitable response, the words of their fellow countryman, Saint-Exupery, came to mind: "You are responsible, forever, for what you have tamed."

The pompous ass would never understand. So J.P. stood, hobbled two steps to the desk. Maintaining eye contact, he leaned over and rested both fists on the desk. His knuckles were white.

Dumond looked alarmed and pushed his chair back from the desk.

"And what, *monsieur,* is wrong with reducing that number by three?"

The ambassador broke eye contact.

"*D'accord, d'accord,*" resignation in his voice. "We will forward the request, recommending that it be approved, pending your receipt of guardianship. An undersecretary will contact you to complete the necessary paperwork."

It took three months to work through the system and gather all the authorizations. J.P. spent many of his days moving slowly from office to office, trying to push the process along. Persistence eventually paid.

Meanwhile Maggie went to work for the UN Mission Hospital and got her own place. She had healed nicely, although the hair that grew back was a slightly lighter shade of red. She talked about returning to County Cork for an extended visit.

The kids were rebounding as kids often do. *Sabiha* was talking. *Abasi's* nightmares had subsided. *Kaaria* continued to pick up English at a rapid rate. Because of his obvious facility with language, J.P began speaking with him in French as well. The three children were a tight unit, bound not only by blood but what they'd experienced. Sometimes

J.P. felt he was more an observer than participant in their little lives.

When the time came, Hamish and Maggie drove them to the airport. They said their goodbyes outside security. Maggie teared up and vowed to stay in touch.

Hamish shook J.P.'s hand. "*Bon chance, mon ami,*" said in his best Scottish-French accent.

At the gate, *Kaaria* herded the little ones into line. As they neared the door, he looked up solemnly.

"I never come back."

"*Oui,*" J.P. said. "*Moi Aussi.*"

TALE OF TWO CITIES
MIAMI AND NEW ORLEANS
SEPTEMBER, 2045

"The big lesson I learned from Hurricane Katrina is that we have to be thinking about the unthinkable because sometimes the unthinkable happens."
—Mike Leavitt, EPA administrator, 2003-2005

"In Chaos Theory, the 'butterfly effect' describes the dependency on initial conditions in which a small change at one place in a non-linear system can result in large differences in a later state. The name of the effect is derived from the theoretical example of a hurricane's formation being contingent on whether a distant butterfly had flapped its wings several weeks earlier."
—Attributed to Edward Lorenz, mathematician and meteorologist

"The first rule of hurricane coverage is that every broadcast must begin with palm trees bending in the wind."
—Carl Hiaasen, author

Atlanta, GA
September 5, 2045, 7:45 a.m.

Bryan James's vehicle slowed with the traffic as it approached the interchange on I-75. His mind was elsewhere, wondering how the tropical disturbance he'd noted the day before forming in the Atlantic's "hurricane alley" had developed overnight. When able, he moved from the automatic lane and manually turned onto Interstate Parkway. In a few minutes he pulled into his parking space in front of The Weather Channel.

He smiled a greeting at the receptionist as he walked in the front door. Swiping his ID, he entered the inner sanctum and grabbed a cup of coffee on the way to his office. "Director, Hurricane and Severe Weather Team," read the plaque on the door.

As he hit the AC-strip to activate his computers and monitors, Bryan reflected that it had been a pretty quiet hurricane season. Only Barbara, a Cat 2, had come ashore so far—in the Carolinas. With winds at about 100 mph and storm surge averaging six feet, damage was not heavy. There'd been a couple other larger storms, but they were near misses. Of course, the season was only about half over.

Globally, on the other hand, the year thus far had produced a record crop of deadly typhoons and cyclones.

Putting on his computer glasses, Bryan checked the latest NOAA satellite image. There it was, still looking pretty innocuous. He ran the time-lapse for the past six hours. It had grown. And counter-clockwise rotation was evident. He pulled up the current Doppler radar data. Rotational winds around 60 mph. Still a tropical disturbance. It wouldn't deserve to be called a hurricane until sustained winds clocked more than 74 mph. Directional speed was about 10 mph on the relatively common northwesterly course.

And how warm is the water? On another computer, he

accessed readings from Argo free-floating weather stations in the area. Ouch. The water's really warm—averaging 88°F at the surface. He knew that the higher the water temperature, the more energy that was available to fuel the storm's intensity.

We're going to have to watch this one.

Atlanta, GA
September 6, 2045, 3:30 p.m.

The 7th Grade science class was particularly attentive. He'd spoken to junior high school classes before and realized that teaching at this level was the last thing on Earth he would want to do. The kids could be cute, but also completely uncontrollable.

He started off with his nickname to get that out of the way. "My name is Chad Wigglesworth," he said. "My friends call me 'Wiggles.'"

Actually, his friends knew better than to call him that, to his face anyway. When he'd joined The Weather Channel fresh out of his meteorology graduate program at Penn State, management suggested he consider a slightly less comical on-air name—something like "Chad Worth." Chad vetoed the idea. Though he'd suffered with his last name his entire life, he'd come to feel it was distinctive, memorable.

For the next 40-minutes or so, Chad talked about hurricanes, supported by holographic imagery. There were some good questions and he left the school feeling better than usual about these celebrity appearances management "encouraged."

The school was on the other side of town, so he arrived just a few minutes before his shift. He was on 6-midnight with co-anchor Brenda Smith. Brenda, with a smarmy southern accent and a taste for provocative outfits, was a commanding presence. More than once management had asked her to tone down the attire. But not too strenuously. Her ratings were high.

The two were quite a contrast. Chad dressed conservatively and projected a somewhat scholarly air. Around the station, their shift was known as the "Brenda and Wiggles Show."

The rundown for the evening included some special attention for a recently named Cat 1. Hurricane Herbert, nice alliteration Chad thought, was picking up steam in the Atlantic and heading vaguely, as they often did early on, toward Florida. Bryan had appended a note:

"This one's developing very rapidly. Water temp is high. 'Bertha' says this could be the real deal."

Bertha was the internal moniker for TWC's proprietary hurricane forecasting software. No one on staff knew where or how the nickname originated. Some World War II buff had recounted that the allies called any really large German gun, "Big Bertha." It was a stretch, but the software had given TWC a *big* advantage in its battle with weather-forecasting competitors.

Once every hour that evening, the two provided updates on Herbert. Before midnight, the storm was verging on Cat 2 with winds over 90 mph. Its direction? Straight as an arrow twanged at Florida's midsection.

Seattle, WA
September 7, 2045, 6:05 a.m.

Charlie Santore woke to the sound of thunder and fumbled for his tab. Everybody thought his "ring" was cute. But the blonde sharing his bed rolled over and pulled the pillow over her head.

"*What?*"

"Good morning to you, too." It was Bryan. "Sure hope

I'm interrupting something."

"Screw you. What do you need?"

"My, my. What a way to talk to your boss. But, since you asked so nicely, I need you in Miami by this afternoon. We've got a big one that looks intent on finishing up what Louise started three years ago.

"Herbert. I heard."

"Call when you get there. Download all the current data and check Herbie's progress on your way." With a click, he was gone.

Charlie sat on the edge of the bed trying to remember her name. "Sara," "Susan," "Sandy?" He'd picked her up in the hotel bar the night before. He was attending the brag-and-booze fest in San Diego officially known as the Investigators of Meteorological Phenomena (IMP) Annual Conference.

Storm chasers had recently been honored with membership in the American Meteorological Association and allowed to establish their own forum. The group's first task was to concoct a respectable sounding name. "IMP" was the calculated tongue-in-cheek result. Most thought calling themselves IMPs accurately depicted the approach to life and work of these meteorological misfits. Actually, the AMA soon rued the day it embraced them. The "forum" was so disruptive at its annual meetings, that leadership politely suggested they conduct their own.

Santore, widely known as the "weather warrior," was a ring leader. While he, like most of his compatriots, could talk isobars and isotherms, Coriolis Effect and the adiabatic process with the best of the traditional weather geeks, he much preferred the adrenaline-pumping action available in the field.

What's-her-name rolled over, sat up and demurely pulled the sheet up to cover her chest. She was tousled, fetching. "Where are you off to? Come on back in here." She patted the bed and dropped the sheet.

"Wish I could, sweetie. But duty calls. Got to get to

Miami for an appointment with a hurricane." He stood.

"Wow," she said. "You're ripped for your age. How old *are* you, anyway?"

Charlie turned around to give her a full frontal view and struck a weight lifter's pose.

"Trade secret, my dear," he said. "Only my mother knows for sure. Room's yours until checkout time. Just don't trash the place. I need a shower."

Later, as he toweled off, he reflected on how wacky the world had become—a world in which storm chasers were celebrities with groupies.

Santore wouldn't have had it any other way.

Atlanta, GA
September 7, 2045, 9:10 a.m.

Bryan sat for a moment after he hung up. Santore. What a piece of work. But viewers loved him, so Bryan played along.

Herbert was now a Cat 3; its winds had ramped up to 120 mph. It was barreling toward the mainland at about 20 mph, as fast as most hurricanes move. Its course? Still unvarying—west by northwest, almost equidistant between Bermuda and the Bahamas. It now measured well over 300 miles in diameter—just about as big as they come—and was located 1,500 miles from the Florida coast. At that speed, barring a course change, the outer wind field would hit in about 75 hours.

Introspection wasn't his thing. He had a scientist's healthy distrust of gut, of intuition. Still, it had happened in the past. Once in a while he just *knew* big trouble was brewing.

So far Bertha hadn't seen data suggesting an imminent course change. But it was early. Chaos Theory suggests that some unknown, perhaps unknowable, variable could throw the monster onto a different track or stall it out. But Bryan's gut told him otherwise. And his gut was batting about .750.

Okay, enough with the metaphysics. He walked down the hall to corner Ted Abernathy, head of programming. "Is he in?"

His support person shook her head. "No, he's in a meeting. Can I help?"

"Please mention that I stopped by and need to see him."

As he sat down back in his office, the phone rang. It was his counterpart at the National Hurricane Center, now located in Atlanta. After Louise pounded Miami three years ago, the National Weather Service decided to move the NHC to a less volatile location.

Despite the increasing frequency and severity of hurricanes, the center had been allowed to fall behind in the forecasting technology race. Funding cuts throughout the Federal government had made it difficult for many agencies to do their jobs. Since weather coverage had become a major money-maker for the commercial nets, the government seemed perfectly happy to let them take the lead in forecasting severe weather. So the NHC had become like a poor relative, frequently coming to the several major weather nets for help and advice.

"Hi Bryan," Adele Morris said. "Can I ask for your take on Herbert?" Without referencing his gut, Bryan told her it looked bad.

"We have no reason to expect a course shift. That would mean landfall in about 75 hours. I know you guys are supposed to wait 48 hours before a forecast landfall to issue a warning, but I'd do it sooner if I were you. I'm talking with programming today about gearing up for a full-court press."

"Thanks. I'll see if I can sell it to management. Do you mind if I check back occasionally to compare data?"

"Of course not. Let's keep in touch." He knew how she

hated to come begging.

Ted stuck his head in. "Herbert?" he asked while on his way to Bryan's only chair without piles of paper.

"Yeah, 75 hours to the Florida coast assuming same speed and course. If Herbie continues to grow and hits anywhere near the Miami metro, it's curtains. I want to expand to five-minute's coverage per hour. I'd like to put the Miami bureau on full alert and staff it up. Santore's on the way. I also suggest we get out the Louise footage and put together a special on what a hit from Herbert could mean. Oh, and I've got the money. It's been a light season to date and my budget's in good shape."

"Okay," Ted said. "Let's gear up...."

Miami, FL
September 7, 2045, 4:30 p.m.

Charlie closed his tab and looked out his business-class window at the soggy landscape below—The Everglades, an ecological disaster if ever there was one.

The plane was approaching Miami from the west, cutting across the tip of the peninsula and the 50-mile wide, slow and shallow "river of grass" that moved fresh water from Lake Okeechobee in the north to Florida Bay and the Gulf of Mexico. Agricultural and industrial development plus residential water diversion last century had reduced the Everglades to about 4,000 square miles, half its original size. The result? Extinction of hundreds of unique species.

Now, with the sea level up more than three feet, salt water was forcing its way ever higher, slowly killing off remaining fauna and flora relying on fresh water.

He thought about Herbert barreling in from the Atlantic. A direct or nearly direct hit from a storm this powerful would do more than pound metro Miami. It would flatten the 'glades and deliver significant destruction to areas on the gulf.

Just since morning, winds had reached an estimated 135 mph, moving it into Cat 4. It was still more than 1,000 miles out. The hope was that it would veer north and moderate over cooler water. Charlie had also seen megastorms peak early and lose steam before landfall.

The plane flew south of Miami International over Little Havana, Biscayne Bay and hooked north over the shuttered art deco hotels of South Beach then west. On approach, he saw that—since his last visit—dikes surrounding the airport had grown taller.

It was a quick and depressing taxi ride west on the Dolphin Expressway, then south a few miles past the airport to Florida International University where TWC had co-located its Miami studio with the National Hurricane Center some years ago. TWC stayed on after the NHC moved. The space was centrally-located, inexpensive and the university—facing precipitously declining enrollment—was happy to have the rent.

From the taxi window, Charlie could see that Miami hadn't rebounded from its encounter with Louise in '42. Many residents—particularly those among the tens of thousands living on Miami's sea level canals and lakes— had given up and relocated. At least those who could. With plunging property values, many found themselves underwater literally and financially.

Tourism was down and corporate headquarters were relocating. Unemployment was among the highest of major metropolitan areas. Population decline started in earnest about two decades earlier directly correlated with the increasingly severe weather and ocean level increases. Early in the century, Miami-Dade County was the nation's seventh largest metroplex with a population exceeding five million. It was 40 percent smaller today and shrinking rapidly.

Many former residents, he knew, had moved to

relocation centers—most outside of Florida—since the state was barely above sea level and the Atlantic and gulf were never far away. Most would be living in FEMAs, as the bare-bones trailers had come to be known. He wished he'd been smart enough to buy stock in the couple of companies with sweetheart government contracts to provide the "temporary" housing. They'd built many millions of units since early in the century.

Suitcase in hand, Charlie breezed into TWC's studios. "Heeeee's back," he announced. "Let's get to work!"

Atlanta, GA
September 7, 2045, 11:55 p.m.

Wigglesworth (MCU): Brenda and I are going to close the segment tonight with our final update on Herbert. The storm is nearing Category 5 status. Rotational winds are currently clocking at 150 miles an hour—five short of a Category 5. Herbert is about 900 miles out. At its current directional speed of 15 mph, about 60 hours from Florida landfall. Brenda.

Cut to satellite loop

Smith (VO): The National Hurricane Center has taken the unprecedented step of issuing a hurricane warning— that's a warning, not a watch—for Florida's entire Atlantic coast from Key West to Jacksonville. The Center normally issues warnings 48 hours out from a forecast landfall, so this is early. As Herbert's course clarifies, the NHC says it will make adjustments to the warning, narrowing it as appropriate.

Smith (CU): Everyone in the affected area is strongly advised to check with local media for evacuation planning information. Chad, Herbert could be a doozy.

Wigglesworth (CU): *Doozy?* That's not a commonly used meteorologic term, but pretty well sums it up. Perhaps hurricane-weary Floridians don't need a reminder, but Category 5 storms pack winds in excess of 155 mph, often throw up storm surges exceeding 20 feet and have been known to dump up to two feet of rain in a very short time frame.

Smith (CU): Stay tuned to The Weather Channel for continuing coverage.

Cut to commercial

Miami, FL
September 9, 11 a.m.

It was time.

Forecasters all agreed. There was a 90-percent probability that Herbie—as it was being called by the media—would hit Southern Florida within 24 hours. The NHC had refined its warning to include the coast from Melbourne south to Key West. Best estimates had the storm's eye making landfall near Boca Raton—just north of the Miami metro area—surrounded with winds of 160 mph pushing storm surges in some areas of up to 20 feet.

Charlie and the crew packed a van. He had negotiated for a location with a real estate company representing the defunct Best Western Atlantic Beach Resort in South Beach. What a mission impossible, he thought, trying to sell beach property where there no longer is a beach.

The hotel was faux Art Deco, designed to mimic the real deal in the once trendy area. The realtor agreed to open a sixth floor beachfront suite and have the plywood removed from the windows. Charlie paid $1,000 for two days and signed an agreement to repair any damage resulting from removal of window coverings.

He liked the location because it provided relatively easy in and out. The hotel was at the end of the Julia Tuttle Causeway. It became the airport expressway, giving him easy access to both the airport and TWC's bureau. The suite also had a balcony perfectly suited to what he had in mind.

As the van drove under I-95, Miami's major north-south artery, Charlie wasn't surprised to see that the expressway was a virtual parking lot. For evacuations, Miami Dade closed all south I-95 lanes to accommodate northbound vehicles. But six lanes apparently weren't enough.

Atlanta, GA and Miami, FL
September 10, 2045, 6 p.m.

Smith (MS): Good evening. Brenda Smith and Chad Wigglesworth here with a Weather Channel special edition. The long-awaited and feared arrival of Hurricane Herbert along the Florida Atlantic Coast is happening as we speak.

Cut to Miami for live video

Wigglesworth (VO): Herbert arrived a little later than expected. The storm's forward movement slowed to about 10 miles per hour earlier in the day. But it now packs winds close 180 miles per hour, only 10 miles per hours less than the record holder—Camille in 1969.

Substantial storm surges are expected in various locations. But surge forecasts at any one point on the coastline are difficult to make very far in advance. They require accurate forecasting of the hurricane's track, intensity and wind structure, as well as knowledge of the characteristics of the ocean floor and coastline.

What you're seeing is a live image of Miami's South Beach shot from a closed hotel property. Storm chaser extraordinaire Charlie Santore is ready to do battle with Herbert. Charlie, I suppose—in winds like this—being bald is an advantage.

Camera pans to Santore on hotel balcony

Santore (CU): True, Chad. Eliminates the need for hair gel. As you can see, winds are picking up as Herbert's front wall nears shore. We're clocking winds from the northeast at about 80 miles per hour. The rain is starting in earnest and visibility is declining. I hope we'll be able to show you a storm surge if one comes ashore at this location. But, if we can't see it, we'll certainly know if it hits. A wall of water that high will probably shake this eight-story hotel to its very foundation. Back to you.

Smith (CU): Charlie will be back shortly with more live coverage. Everyone stay with us.

Cut to commercial

Atlanta, GA and Miami, FL
September 10, 2045, 9:15 p.m.

Smith (CU): We're back with our coverage of Herbert's landfall.

Cut to time-lapse satellite image

Smith (VO): As predicted, the eye came ashore centered on an area from between Boca Raton and Boynton Beach. That's a scant 60 miles north of the Miami metro. Winds of close to 180 miles per hour are flailing the area. Rain is falling at the rate of about one-foot-per hour depending on the location. Surges have inundated various areas up and down the coast causing heavy damage. It's been impossible to determine their height because of nightfall and almost zero visibility in the thick, driving rain.

Camera Two cut to Wigglesworth CU

Wigglesworth: The Florida State Police reports that many motorists fleeing the storm are stranded in high water on stretches along I-95. Some communities are trying to help get people to shelter in schools or hotels. For a view that's up close and personal, we go live to Miami and Charlie Santore. Charlie, what's that you're wearing?

Cut to Miami live

Santore (MS): I'm sure I look like some kind of alien insectoid. It's actually military headgear that includes filtration, night vision and internal wireless microphone. I hope you're hearing me okay. I'm standing in the shelter of a corner of the balcony. Alf Nelson, my trusty cameraman, is shooting me from just inside the suite through the balcony's sliding glass doors. The doors seem to be holding, although the wind-driven rain is causing some leakage. My plan is to step into the storm to report what it feels like to be toe-to-toe with a Category 5 hurricane. That's why the headgear. Without the filtration, I doubt I would be able to breathe in the thick, driving rain. And night vision may allow me to see some of what's going on out there. I'm wearing a harness clipped to the railing in the strong likelihood I will be unable to stand up. Now, boys and girls, *do not try this at home*. Only a trained professional should be allowed to make a fool of himself like this. Here goes....

Wow! It feels like I've been hit by a truck. Even with a tether I don't feel very secure. I'm able to breathe, but just barely. The filters are designed to handle gas. The water is tending to clog the canisters. And, even with night vision, the water sheeting off the lenses is making it difficult to make out much detail. Here's a note to the military—try mini-windshield wipers. I do know there were palm trees out there earlier. No sign of them now. The boulevard running between the hotel and what was a berm is submerged. And the rain is really cold—probably around 40°F. I know that may not make sense, but you have to understand that the rain is pouring down from about 35,000 feet where the air temps are below freezing. Maybe having some hair wouldn't be a bad idea.

Smith (VO): Charlie, can you hear me through that roar? Was there evidence earlier of a storm surge in the area?

Santore (VO): Yes, I can hear. And yes, we felt rather than saw a surge perhaps an hour ago. We have no way of knowing its height, but this concrete and stucco building did shake. Well, kids, I think I've been out here long enough. My teeth are starting to chatter. Back to you.

Wigglesworth (CU): Charlie Santore reporting live from Miami Beach. Charlie, that's got to be a first. A classic confrontation between a man and nature—fought to a draw. Unfortunately, overall, Herbert is delivering a knock-out punch to the entire region. Stay tuned for continuing coverage.

Cut to commercial

Atlanta, GA
September 11, 2045, 8 a.m.

Bryan reviewed storm data that had streamed in overnight. One interesting thing stood out. Instead of slowing down or stalling over land, uncharacteristically, Herbert had actually picked up speed and was moving northwesterly at about 20 mph.

Good news and bad news, he thought. The storm will drop less rain on a given area as it moves more quickly across the peninsula. The bad news is that it shows little sign of weakening. It was now a Cat 4 with winds around 140 mph. Wind speed had dropped somewhat and the rain was lessening as it rolled along. But it was still a large and very dangerous storm. The eye had crossed Lake Okeechobee. Directly in its path was Ft. Myers and the gulf.

Alarm bells went off as Bryan's gut kicked in. When was the last time a hurricane crossed the Florida mainland and entered the gulf as a major storm? Andrew in 1992 came to mind. He pulled up the data. It had flattened the Bahamas as a Cat 5 with peak winds of 175 mph. It then rolled over the very southern tip of Florida, decimating the Keys. From there it blew into the gulf as a Cat 4 and hooked northwest to make landfall on the Louisiana coast three days later as a low-end Cat 3.

Katrina in 2005 had also crossed Florida's tip, but as a Cat 1. Within two days, warm gulf waters had fueled its growth to Cat 5. It made landfall two days later twice along the Mississippi and Louisiana coasts as a Cat 3 and then a Cat 4. Betsy in 1965 also grazed the Keys as a Cat 3, then hooked northwest to hit Louisiana as a Cat 2.

He compared Andrew and the other storms with Herbert. There were major differences. Andrew and most of the others just grazed Florida's tip and then moved immediately into the gulf, benefiting from a continued supply of warm water. But Andrew, though equally powerful, was substantially smaller—only 180 miles across. Herbert is almost twice as large and will straddle the peninsula, continuing to pick up heat from the Atlantic on the east while getting nourishment from the warm gulf waters on the west.

Bryan mused. I don't think we've heard the last of Hurricane Herbert.

Miami, FL
September 13, 2045, 8 a.m.

The crew spent an uncomfortable night in the powerless suite; they'd run out of diesel for the small generator. Their only solace was the generous supply of Jim Beam Charlie had thought to provide. At daybreak, he and the crew started packing. TWC had dispatched a large, rented Zodiac—gotten from who knows where—to get the team away from the coast. The van in which they had come was in water up to its windows.

They moved the water-proof cases to the second floor, sliding them down the stairs. Charlie abandoned the generator. The lobby was flooded; its front windows blown in by the storm surge. Soon the boat was tied off as close as possible to the hotel, bobbing over its front stairs.

They floated the cases out and the four clambered aboard.

Before they got far from the hotel, Charlie spotted a small dog struggling to keep its head above water. He pointed and the boat made a slow pass. He grabbed the dog and pulled it onboard. It looked like a Jack Russell Terrier, its bristly coat punked out, its heart pounding madly. The dog was shaking violently. The pilot threw a towel and Charlie wrapped him in it.

"Well, tough guy, if any dog were going to survive a

dunking like that, it would probably be a Jack Russell."

They carefully motored westward, skimming over flooded streets to the Biscayne Waterway and then across the Intracoastal, paralleling the Julia Tuttle Causeway. On the other side, a chopper, blades slowing circling, was waiting on one of the causeway's empty ramps. They motored as close as they could, wrestled the cases up the wet embankment and climbed onboard. Charlie carried "Tough Guy" still wrapped in his towel.

Once airborne, the copilot handed Charlie a headset. He mouthed, "It's for you" over the whump of the blades.

"Charlie, it's Bryan. You guys okay?" He didn't wait for a response. "Great job. Listen are you and the crew up for a trip to New Orleans? Herbert's gotten real hinky and is rebuilding big time over the gulf. It could get nasty along the Mississippi and Louisiana coasts. No pressure to accept. You guys deserve a rest. In either case, you're heading for Orlando for a flight out...."

Shit, he thought, I'm tired. I may be getting too old for this. Still, the chance to do a "two-fer" was very appealing—probably a first. "Let me talk to the guys and I'll get back."

With headsets on all around, Charlie presented the possibility. While no one looked overjoyed, all agreed. He wasn't surprised. He'd picked his crew because, with him, they shared the adrenaline-junkie gene.

The copilot passed around sandwiches and water. Charlie took the ham out of one and fed it to an appreciative Tough Guy. He cupped his hands and had one of the crew pour water for him.

For the rest of the flight, Charlie gazed at the watery world below.

I don't know what people expected, he thought. A peninsula with an average elevation of only three feet surrounded by an ever-more hostile ocean and gulf whose warming waters were about three feet above the historic mean. I wonder if Disney has an underwater theme park in the planning stages.

Atlanta, GA
September 13, 2045, 6 p.m.

Wigglesworth (CU): Good evening, everyone. Brenda Smith and Chad Wigglesworth with you from The Weather Channel. As we've been reporting for the last 36 hours, bad-boy Hurricane Herbert has blown across the Florida mainland, leaving unprecedented flooding and destruction. The death toll is rising with over 150 related deaths reported to this moment.

It exited the peninsula in the Ft. Myers area as a Category 3 and immediately regained strength, drawing energy from warm gulf waters. It's now on a northwesterly course, aiming—at the moment anyway—at the Mississippi and Louisiana coasts as a Category 4 with winds in excess of 130 miles-per-hour.

Camera Two cut to CU of Smith

Smith: We're only now starting to get some sense for the destruction and loss of life on the Atlantic coast and around Ft. Myers. Herbert did something no other hurricane on record has done. It failed to weaken substantially as it crossed the peninsula. It hit Ft. Myers with a nasty blow from behind. Because of Herbert's speed and the fact that its actions were unanticipated, the area had little warning. The west side of the state is more accustomed to dealing with hurricanes blowing in from the gulf.

Camera One cut to Wigglesworth CU

Wigglesworth: To be clear, other Atlantic hurricanes have moved into the gulf across Florida. But they just grazed the tip of the peninsula. Most Atlantic storms that hit farther north on the mainland weaken and dissipate.

Camera Two cut to Smith CU

Smith: If Herbert maintains its present course and speed, landfall is predicted in 24 hours in approximately the same area devastated by Katrina almost exactly 40 years ago. Katrina, as you may remember, almost wiped the Gulf Coast from Gulfport to Mobile off the map and then put large areas of New Orleans under 10 feet of water when several levees broke. Eighty percent of the city was flooded. To this day, it's ranked as the most destructive hurricane in U.S. history with 2,000 deaths and property damage estimated at $80 billion.

Camera One cut to Wigglesworth CU

Wigglesworth: It's a frightening thought, but Herbert—as it continues its rampage into the gulf—could easily knock Katrina out of top spot in that grisly list of worst-ever storms. Stay tuned for continued coverage....

Cut to commercial

New Orleans, LA
September 14, 2045, 8 p.m.

The drive from Louis Armstrong International to Hotel St. Marie in the French Quarter was relatively quick. Most traffic was heading the other direction, out of town in the face of the impending storm. New Orleans had fared well since Katrina. Because it was probably the most endangered of major American cities—at an average of six feet below sea level—a great deal of thought and money had gone into efforts to waterproof it.

But Herbert seemed malevolent—a force of nature intent on inflicting as much mayhem as possible in its short, violent life. With higher sea levels, The Big Easy wasn't overly confident about surviving this one.

The Marie was a small European-style hotel festooned with New Orleans' signature wrought-iron balconies. It had become Charlie's favorite over the years. He'd spent lots of time in the city. The hotel was located in the center of the French Quarter, just off Bourbon and a few blocks from the iconic Jackson Square. The Quarter was about 10-feet above sea level, making it a relatively safe location for reporting on a hurricane.

Charlie had no sooner dropped his bag on the bed and put Tough Guy's carrier on the floor, when his phone rang. "It's Bryan. Sorry to have sent you and the crew to New Orleans. Looks now like Herbie will not be a major threat. A pretty intense high-pressure system is forming centered over Missouri-Arkansas. It's slowed the storm and pushed it on a westerly course. Bertha thinks it'll peter out before hitting the Texas coast, maybe coming in at Cat 1 or a tropical storm. Looks like that butterfly somewhere flapped its wings.

"Tell you what. Since you're there, why don't you and the guys take some time to wind down? You've earned it."

"Thanks. Appreciate it. I'll tell the crew and check back in a few days."

Charlie let the dog out of his carrier. He seemed agitated. "Need to water a bush? Hang on, let me tell the boys the good news and we'll go for a walk."

Charlie put on the dog's collar and attached his leash. They were black leather and studded. The humor was lost on Tough Guy. His little chest actually seemed to swell with pride. You could almost hear him thinking: "Yeah, that's *what* I'm talkin' about!" Charlie had picked them up—along with the carrier—at a pet boutique in the Orlando airport. The clerk was kind enough to punch another hole in the collar so it wouldn't slip off his skinny neck.

They walked to nearby Bourbon. The joints were open—jazz, Cajun and blues floating through the sticky night air. They turned south on St. Peter and headed for Jackson Square, passing Pat O'Brien's—home of the famous New Orleans Hurricane Cocktail.

Filtering onto the street was the refrain from Randy Newman's tune, "Louisiana:"

> *"Louisiana, Louisiana—*
> *They're trying to wash us away.*
> *They're trying to wash us away...."*

Charlie wasn't particularly hungry, but he did hanker for the chicory-laced coffee and powdered-sugar beignets at Café Du Monde on the square.

The place was next to empty. A waiter, who looked as if he'd been there since it was founded in 1862, shuffled to the table, his apron coated with a day's worth of powder.

He looked at Charlie and the dog. "Do he bite?" His speech was Creole flavored.

"Tough Guy? Naw, he just looks ornery. How 'bout some coffee black and a couple of beignets?"

When he returned, Charlie asked if he could sit with them "for a spell" and have some coffee.

"Not s'posed to fratinize wid customers," he said. "But since ain't almost nobody here, might for a minute. Good to get off my dogs."

Looking at Tough Guy: "Meant no disrespect. As for coffee, t'anks, but had all I can take for one day. All's that keeps me going."

"Charlie." He extended his hand.

"I know. That guy from The Weather Channel. I'm Ezekiel, Zeke. You here for Herbie?"

"Well, I was. But Herbie's wimped out. He's losing steam and heading for the Texas coast."

Zeke looked pleased. "Den looks like we gonna live to fight 'nuther day."

Charlie pulled a hunk off a beignet and gave it to Tough Guy. The dog sniffed, coating his nose with powdered sugar. The two laughed when he gave a mighty sneeze. Then he attacked the beignet with gusto.

ESCAPE FROM L.A.
LOS ANGELES, CA
SEPTEMBER, 2047

"Cuervo Jones to Snake Plissken: "You might have survived
Cleveland. You might have escaped from New York. But this is
L.A.,vato. And you're about to find out that this fucking place can
kill anybody."
—"Escape from LA," a film (1996)

$\mathcal{A}$cademic conferences are notorious for being done on the cheap. Travel budgets for faculty are usually paltry. It's always been a *Catch 22*, Jeff Grant thought. Faculties are supposed to go forth and participate in the intellectual life surrounding their disciplines, but with limited support.

So organizers had booked this conference at the Hilton Long Beach. It hadn't aged well. The lobby had recently been refurbished; the rooms had not. The carpet in his room had stains. The drapes were partly unhung and dragged on the floor. The "art" bolted on the walls consisted of cheap prints that had faded in sunlight to a pinkish-blue.

According to his conference packet, presenters had been assigned times in the presentation hall to check their visual support and practice if they desired. His slot followed what was billed as an informal reception for presenters and participants in a private room off the hotel's restaurant.

He signed in at a table outside the restaurant and clipped on his badge. It was the typical "friendly" name tag—big "Jeffrey," small "Grant" followed by "PhD." His title and school followed. The badge sported a red ribbon proclaiming "Presenter."

Jeff wasn't much of a mingler, so he headed first for the bar where he had to settle for Johnnie Red. There was no food on the airplane, so next stop was the hors d'oeuvres table. He wasn't a fussy eater, but he passed on the shrimp—giant tigers. They looked firm and fresh, but he was almost certain they had been farm raised in China or Indonesia. He knew the chemical soup in which they were grown and wanted no part of it.

Drink in one hand, plastic plate in the other, he walked to an unoccupied round table and scanned the room. Unfortunately, the only person who looked interesting was heading for the door. She had two guys in thrall, happily joining her escape from tedium. A leggy brunette.

He saw a few fellow faculty he knew from previous conferences. He waved but chose not to join them. He wasn't in the mood for academic small talk. He checked his watch and was happy to see it was almost time for his practice session. He gulped his drink and headed for the conference venue.

The room had seating for about 100. He handed his tablet to the waiting hotel technician and asked him to project the holos he'd had prepared for the talk. Speaker Services at his school, Oklahoma State, had been happy to take what was left of his modest support budget to build the images.

The holos looked good. At least the hotel had a decent projector. Jeff's field was Earth Science—seismology, in particular. The paper reported his findings clearly linking the practice of hydrologic fracking for oil to serious seismic instability in heavily "fracked" areas. Fracking was finally banned in the '20s, but the damage had been done.

Jeff's presentation was next to last on the second day of the conference. By the time his turn came, the audience had thinned. He'd seen a number of attendees wheeling suitcases into the lobby after lunch, one of the downsides of presenting the last afternoon of a conference.

But, as he approached the stage, he saw that, potentially, the most important conference attendee was sitting third-row center. He caught the brunette's eye; she crossed her legs demurely and smiled.

Later that evening, Jeff had just finished some unremarkable bar food and was working on his second drink when, in the mirror, he noticed the brunette walking his way. He looked up again as she stood next to his stool.

"You looked so lost in thought, I almost don't want to intrude."

"Nope," he replied. "This is currently a no-thinking zone. I'll ask you to sit down, but only if you promise there'll be no thinking."

"I can handle that. I can be just as thoughtless as the next person. Name's Alex." She extended her hand. In what was a promising role reversal, she held Jeff's hand longer than necessary.

He looked at her name tag. "Alexis Matthews." He

squinted, "Department of Environmental Policy, UC-Berkeley." As she sat he asked, "What's a policy wonk doing at a gathering like this? Ah, before you answer, I'm forgetting my manners. What are you drinking?"

She asked for whatever Jeff was having. He waved two fingers at the bartender.

"We like to keep track of what's being discussed in the field and look for policy implications. So, tell me about Jeff."

For the next few minutes they exchanged abbreviated and carefully censored life stories.

When Jeff was through, she said, "You didn't mention marital status."

"Marriage is an ancient and unpleasant memory. You."

"Never. Never felt like being tied down—at least not in that sense." Her green eyes twinkled.

"Guess that leaves only one burning question," Jeff said. "My place or yours?"

"Which is closest?"

They adjourned to his room, shedding clothes before the door was closed. She had a body the sight of which might make some men shrivel in shock and awe. And she was uninhibited, innovative and very enthusiastic. Jeff tried to give as good as he got. He couldn't remember having a better time.

Much later, as they spooned on the bed they had destroyed, she murmured something about an early flight as he started to doze.

"Me, too. Need a ride?"

"I think I just had one! But, yes, thanks."

―――――――

Jeff awoke in the dark. The bed was empty. He made his way to the bathroom. The door was ajar and the light was on. Once his eyes adjusted to the glare, he saw a message scrawled in lipstick on the mirror: "Jeff—Fun! Lobby at

7? Alex."

All that, he thought, and a flair for the dramatic!

Alex was waiting in the lobby looking fresh and little worse for wear. She handed him a cup of coffee.

"Hope black's okay."

Jeff checked out and requested his car.

He wasn't that familiar with the L.A. area so asked the GPS to get them to LAX. In a Latin-tinged voice, the GPS *chica* directed him to the 710 north. But, before nearing the 105, she warned of bumper-to-bumper and rerouted them on Alondra west through Compton to pick up the 110.

Compton was unlovely. Barred windows. Graffiti encrusted. Idly, Jon watched a light plane making an approach to a local airport.

He was about to ask Alex if he could see her again when there was a bone-jarring jolt. It was as if the car had fallen into a hole and then bounced up again.

"What the hell? Have I hit something?"

Then it happened again. This time the car was thrown violently to the right. The tires bounced against the curb.

Alex screamed, "Earthquake!"

Jeff saw utility poles toppling with live wires whiplashing everywhere. In all his years of studying earthquakes, this was his first actual experience with one.

"Stay in the car. The tires will insulate us."

Another tremendous jolt. The car rocked to-and-fro on its suspension.

They heard an explosion. In his rear-view mirror, he could see fire and a plume of smoke a block behind them. Probably a gas main.

Another jolt. Some of the pavement was starting to crack and buckle.

"Why doesn't it stop?" She gripped Jeff's arm as the car

continued to rock as if it were a boat.

Another explosion, this one to their right.

"We've got to get out of here," he said, calmly as he could. "We can't drive or walk very far. We're going to have to try to fly."

"Fly! Are you kidding?"

"I saw an airport nearby. I'm a pilot," he said. What he didn't tell her was that he'd let his license lapse about 10 years earlier and hadn't flown since. "We've got to make a run for the airport and get ourselves off the ground."

And they did—down the street to the airport's nearest entrance. The ground continued to shake, twice so violently they were thrown to their knees. As they neared the gate, a car shot out at high speed, barely dodged a downed utility pole, and continued erratically down the street. Two young men were in the car. He hoped they were who he thought they were.

They ran across the parking lot, power lines no longer a danger. In the distance they heard more explosions. And sirens. Hard to believe, Jeff thought, but the city's finest are already starting to respond.

On the other side of the flight business office, he saw what he'd hoped to see. There were about a dozen aircraft neatly parked on the flight line. But there was one pulled right up to the office, both its doors ajar. It was the plane he saw landing. The two in the car were probably teacher and student. They'd landed in an earthquake.

The plane was an old Archer 180, very similar to the Warrior he'd trained in and rented periodically while still current.

"That, I hope, is our ticket out of here," Jeff shouted, pulling her toward the plane. He took her behind the right wing. "Climb up and get in."

He scrambled around the Piper, ducked his head, contorting to enter the cockpit door.

"*Yes,*" he exulted. The key was still in the ignition. The condition of the cockpit spoke of a hasty retreat, maps and paperwork in disarray. Two headsets, one on the floor, the other between the seats, were still plugged in.

From the condition of both interior and exterior, it was obviously a trainer. The vinyl dash was cracked, the carpet frayed. He wasn't concerned. The FAA requires 100-hour inspections for rentals, so the plane was probably okay mechanically.

No time for preflight. He flipped on the master and fuel pump, pushed the mixture to rich, cracked open the throttle, ignored the primer, checked to ensure the carb heat was off and turned the key. The hot engine sprang instantly to life. He put his feet on the brakes, revved the engine to 2,000 rpm. It sounded good.

He checked the fuel gauges—right full, left half. The two hadn't been up very long.

He began to taxi while handing Alex her headsets. The avionics, navigation lights and strobe had been left on. He told her through the intercom to flip the lever on her door to lock it and buckle up.

She complied, her face drained of color. The ground continued to dance. A couple of jolts were severe enough to cause the wings to flap like a bird's.

Jeff checked the wind sock. Unfortunately he was going to have to take off with a tailwind. The field had side-by-side runways—07-25 right and left. The wind, though variable, was primarily out of the west. He taxied to the nearest of the parallel runways. There wasn't time to taxi all the way to the east end to take off into the wind.

Christ, I hope this *is* like riding a bicycle.

He put in 20-degrees of flap to provide additional lift to keep the roll as short as possible. He didn't remember if flaps were a good idea in a tailwind takeoff. He made a fast turn onto the runway, almost on two of the three wheels of the tricycle gear. He lined up on the run and pushed the throttle forward. The plane accelerated smoothly, but the ride was bumpy. The runway was cracking and buckling. That, plus the lack of lift with the tailwind, would make for a long take-off roll.

The plane slewed from side to side on the damaged runway. Jeff had difficulty keeping it centered. He'd used up two-thirds of the relatively short strip, but was barely at rotate speed. He slowly pulled back on the yoke and raised the nose. The stall horn blared immediately. He lowered the nose to increase speed and tried again. This time he was able to kiss the tortured Earth goodbye.

He gained altitude slowly, allowing the plane to increase speed. The air was turbulent. He hoped Alex wasn't prone to air sickness. The plane was rocked by updrafts.

"Okay," Jeff said, almost to himself, "where the hell are we going?" He looked at Alex. "How 'bout Vegas? We need to get ourselves to a major airport."

She was too shell-shocked to respond.

"I think that's our best bet. I don't know how extensive the quake is, but I doubt it's affected Vegas on the other side of the San Gabriels. The San Andreas Fault runs along the west side of the mountains."

He had turned north and they flew over downtown L.A. near the junctions of the 10 and 110. He didn't know the skyline well, but it looked as if a couple of skyscrapers had collapsed—based on the fires, smoke and debris he could see. There was also a strange white cloud floating above downtown. It looked like a blizzard. In fact, it was. A blizzard of office paper blown skyward from the wreckage by fierce heat-driven updrafts.

The intersection of the two major thoroughfares was a jumble of twisted concrete and rebar. Toy cars littered the ground. A few sections of roadway were still standing on their concrete pillars. Stranded motorists were probably praying the next tremor wouldn't also hurl them into the void.

To the north Jeff saw a strange sight. It looked like two huge cartoon eyes on a hillside gazing southwest at the destruction of downtown. It took him a moment to realize he was looking at what was left standing of the famed

"Hollywood" sign in the Hollywood Hills.

The air was very rough and choppy until he hit about 5,000 feet. Then it began to smooth out a little. He looked over at Alex. She seemed transfixed by the disfigured landscape below.

Jeff scanned the cockpit. In his door's side pocket was an L.A. sectional aeronautical chart, well creased with use. He unfolded the large, highly detailed and cumbersome map. He could see it overlapped to include Las Vegas near the California-Nevada border. It took him a few seconds to get the map oriented and remember enough to decipher the dense, cryptic to the untrained eye, information it contained.

"Alex," he said. "I need your help. I have to work with this map for a while. Would you watch for other aircraft? After all this, we don't need a mid-air collision."

There was little likelihood of traffic. The commercials all would have been diverted. Privates were probably down by now or out of the area. It was mainly to give her something to do.

It appeared they'd need to exit the L.A. basin through *El Cajon* Pass and then on to Vegas. He knew he didn't want to land at McCarran International. It would be extremely busy handling traffic diverted from major L.A. area airports. And, although he doubted it would matter at this stage in the game, he *was* flying a stolen plane without a license and without a flight plan on file.

He noticed somebody had drawn a red circle on the map around the pass and scrawled: "h. winds and turb." He'd done some mountain flying and knew that passes could be dangerous. They tended to funnel winds, speeding them up like a venturi tube. With following winds out of the west, the pass could pose a real problem.

He looked for small, suitable uncontrolled fields in the Vegas area at which to land, and, just across the border, found the whimsically named Sky Ranch—32L—near Sandy Valley. It was right on the flight path, just southwest of Vegas.

The panel-mounted GPS was on. It was one with which he wasn't familiar. But, essentially, they all work about the same. He hit "reset" then "go to" and typed in "32L." The field had a paved 3,200-foot strip and was about 200 air miles from their location. He made note of the Unicom and Automated Weather Observing Station frequencies. He selected the field, called up the moving map on the GPS and turned northeast to pick up the course.

Next worry, fuel. He remembered the Archer had 48 gallons in two tanks. A full and half-full tank were more than enough for the 200-mile run to the Nevada field.

He checked his watch and couldn't believe it was only 9 a.m. The hour or so since the first jolt seemed like a day. The sun, still low over the mountains to the east, was having difficulty penetrating the yellow, smoky pall that hung over the area.

He checked his engine gauges and everything was in the green. He leveled out at 5,000 feet and reduced power to about 75 percent to hit the recommended cruising speed. Jeff calculated their ETA at about 11 a.m.

Now he needed to check the route on the moving map. It confirmed they'd be flying through *El Cajon* between the San Gabriel and San Bernardino Mountains. The top of the pass was about 4,200 feet. A major landmark to the left was the 10,000-foot Mt. San Antonio, more commonly known as Mt. Baldy.

He remembered the Archer had a ceiling of about 13,000 feet. To try to avoid trouble he decided to fly over the pass at 8,000 feet and not through it.

Jeff took time to view the devastation below. The low-wing configuration made sight-seeing a little difficult, but the destruction was evident looking ahead or behind. They were flying over a wind farm, the towers and their wind turbines toppled randomly like pick-up sticks. A few leaned at crazy angles, held up by turbine blades embedded in the ground.

Jeff saw Alex looking at the huge field of fallen wind generators. "Those towers probably stood over 200 feet," he said.

He increased power and began to climb slowly as the mountains loomed in the windshield. The GPS had him jog east; then northeast again to line up with the pass. He could see Mt. Baldy to his left through the haze.

Always the scientist, Jeff observed the folds of the San Andreas Fault running as far as he could see left and right along the base of the mountains. The severity of the quake led him to wonder if this were the "Big One" anticipated for over 100 years.

He flashed back to an article he'd read a year or two earlier authored by a team from Stanford. It proposed the bizarre hypothesis that the weight of the nearly four feet of additional water resulting from the melt down of ice sheets and glaciers was deforming the Pacific tectonic plate, building pressure along the San Andreas. The authors proposed that this pressure could hasten the likelihood of a severe quake.

He had reviewed the paper in his capacity as a member of the editorial committee of the *Geologic Journal*. The *Journal* rejected the paper as too speculative. One reviewer even called it bad science fiction.

As far as he knew, the hypothesis had never been made public.

As he climbed toward the pass, there was increasing turbulence. Even at this altitude, the plane bounced like a yo-yo in the unstable air. At one point they dropped like a stone about 300 feet before recovering. Though belted in, Jeff's head hit the ceiling.

"You okay?" he asked. "I think my stomach's in my throat."

She nodded, tight lipped. They tightened their harnesses.

Once beyond the mountains, Jon descended to 5,000

feet. The air was relatively stable with good visibility. They passed Barstow on the left and, before crossing the Nevada border, clipped the northern edge of the huge Mojave National Preserve on the right.

As they approached the field, he began to get nervous. What was that line from the old Tom Petty tune? "Coming down is the hardest thing."

About 10 miles out, he dialed up the field's AWOS. The computer-generated voice told him the wind was 290° at eight, gusting to 17. He recalibrated the altimeter with the local barometric pressure, and made a mental map of the field and his point of entry to figure out what traffic pattern was appropriate. The runway was 03-21. That meant an 80° cross-wind landing on 21. Great. First landing in 10 years and it has to be cross wind.

He checked the placard on the panel for the plane's registration—N244DL.

"Sky Ranch area traffic. This is Archer 2-4-4-Delta-Lima. Eight-miles out, approaching from the southwest for full stop. Will pick up the downwind for 2-1. 4-Delta-Lima."

"Alex, you ready to put her down? Remember, any landing you walk away from is a good one." She wasn't amused.

The landing went better than expected. He flipped on the fuel pump, descended to the pattern altitude and, on entry, reduced power, added flaps and pulled up the nose to hit the appropriate speed on each leg of the pattern—downwind, base and final.

He remembered to crab into the cross wind as he approached. He over corrected, but got it back on the center line for touch down. After a couple of small bounces, they were on *terra firma*.

Alex looked at him with an expression somewhat akin to admiration.

"Great job," she said, relief apparent. "How long have you been flying?"

Jeff burst out laughing, a release from the stress of the last three hours.

Once recovered: "I let my license lapse 10 years ago. This is the first time I've flown since '35. I didn't want to worry you."

"No shit?"

They ordered a taxi for the half hour ride to Vegas. First stop was a mall to pick up a carry-on each, a change of clothing and toiletries. They also replaced their tablets, abandoned with the rest of their stuff on that quaking street in Compton.

Flights to their destinations weren't available until the next day, so they checked into a small hotel off the Strip for the night. They were famished and ordered from room service.

During dinner, Jeff turned on CNN. After watching for a few minutes, it became obvious the net knew very little about what had happened and what was going on. Viewers were assured efforts were being made to put reportorial "feet on the street," but that continued aftershocks, collapsing buildings, explosions and widespread fires made it too dangerous.

At one point, the continuous loop of early aerial footage and repetitious commentary was interrupted by a live report from an L.A. TV station that had been able to get back-up power working. A frazzled and obviously frightened young woman faced the camera. At the right edge of the screen, a dangling fluorescent fixture cast a hot-white glare on the jumbled set.

"Hello," she quavered. "If you're receiving this feed, I'm Paula Wyman, a reporter with KABC news. The station is pretty much of a wreck, but some of us were able to get the back-up generator started and one studio more or less operational. We're using a satcam for the feed. We are not able to transmit locally and our website is down.

"The quake hit around 8 a.m. and it just wouldn't stop. After the main quakes, big aftershocks continue to rock the area. No one at the station has been able to go out to look at the damage. None of us knows what's happened to family and friends. All communication is out."

As if to verify her story, the image shook and the light fixture oscillated. The reporter covered her head as some plaster and debris rained on the set. The tremor passed in a few seconds. She was shaking visibly.

"I don't know how much longer we can maintain the feed. I can't believe this is really happening. Some staff members have been killed or hurt. All we could do was drag the bodies to the cafeteria and use what limited medical supplies and knowledge we have to help the injured. I hope...."

The picture went black.

The anchor, who had been transfixed watching the feed on her monitor, looked up and struggled to gather her wits.

"This is probably the first live account to come out of Los Angeles to this point." She paused, trying to get her emotions in check. "Our hopes and prayers are with the survivors at KABC and the many thousands of injured throughout the area."

She stopped, obviously listening to instructions from the control room coming in her head set.

"In case you missed it, we're going to repeat the feed from KABC. Then I understand we will go live to Stanford University to interview a seismologist who may have some insights into what has happened in L.A."

After the KABC feed, the anchor returned and read from the teleprompter: "Dr. Thad Nichols, a seismologist at Stanford University in Palo Alto, now joins us live."

Jeff remembered the name. Nichols was primary author of the paper describing the water-weight hypothesis.

"Good evening, Dr. Nichols. Thanks for joining us on such short notice. I'm sure this earthquake has rocked the scientific world, too."

She was getting her form back. "What can you tell us about the severity of the quake?"

"We don't really know. The measurement scales available to us weren't able to read its magnitude. The best known, of course, is the Richter Scale, topping out at 10. It came into use in 1935 and, to date, the nearest an earthquake has come to the top of the Richter was the devastating 9.5 event in Chile in 1960. There have been a couple of 9.0s. But quakes of this magnitude, fortunately, are rare."

"Do you have any idea how far beyond the top of Richter Scale this quake might have been?"

"I'd hate to speculate. But let me give you an example of how powerful the 9.5 quake in Chile was. The Richter provides energy equivalents in TNT all along the scale. A 9.5 event creates energy equivalent to 2.7 gigatons of TNT. By comparison, the Hiroshima nuclear bomb produced an estimated 18 kilotons of energy. Simply put, that's 2.7 billion tons of TNT verses 18,000 tons of TNT. So the 9.5 was the equivalent of 150 million Hiroshima-sized bombs."

The anchor looked astonished. "Did you really say that the L.A. quake was stronger than—what was that—150 million Hiroshima bombs?"

"Yes, by and large. But you must remember that earthquake energy is not concentrated in one limited area as is that of a nuclear explosion. This quake's energy was distributed up and down the 800-mile San Andreas Fault and its subsidiaries. But the L.A. area seems to have gotten the brunt of it."

"Is there any way to estimate the death toll?"

"Not really. There are too many variables. Obviously, a major quake in an area of low population density will result in fewer deaths and injuries than in a densely populated megaplex like L.A. But early reports indicate the toll will be horrific, not only because of the severity of the quake and continued aftershocks, but because of the total destruction of infrastructure and basic services. Search and rescue operations will be difficult and certainly take more time than many trapped survivors have. Frankly, getting a metropolitan area with a population of 15 million operating at some basic subsistence level will take years.

"Since I haven't committed it to memory, I brought an abbreviated general description of damage and loss of life associated with a 9.0-plus quake."

He looked down and began to read: "Near or total destruction. Severe damage or collapse of all buildings. Heavy damage extending to distant locations. In heavily populated areas, tremendous loss of life. Permanent damage to the area's topography."

He looked up.

"Dr. Nichols, along those lines, our satellite imagery seems to indicate that several skyscrapers in downtown L.A. have collapsed. Do you have anything on that?"

"Yes, I'm sorry to report that the second tallest structure downtown has fallen. The 1,000-foot HSBC building, recently acquired in its merger with U.S. Bank, has been reduced to rubble. Another casualty is the third tallest building, the 850-foot Aon Center. It also appears many of the city's 30 or so other buildings above 500 feet have toppled, as have numerous smaller structures. But the city's tallest building, the Wilshire Grand Tower at 1,100 feet, is still standing.

"There may be a lesson in this," Nichols continued. "The former U.S. Bank Tower was built in 1989 to withstand a quake of 8.3 on the Richter. That was thought to be a safe margin. It survived the Northridge 6.4 quake in 1994 as did most other buildings in the area. Their steel-frame construction was thought to be the reason. Steel has good ductile strength and plasticity, allowing buildings to bend and sway, not break, in a severe quake.

"But a study of 100 buildings of various sizes following Northridge indicated that 75 percent had severe cracks and fissures in welded seams and joints. The report concluded that these and other buildings were in jeopardy when the next big quake hits.

"The Wilshire Tower, completed in 2017, on the other hand, beefed up welds and added another quake-fighting technique—base isolation for structural vibration control. That's probably what saved it. But, though standing, there's no telling at this point if the building is still structurally viable."

"Do you have any idea why this quake was so severe? I know everyone's been talking for decades about 'The Big One.' But this has got to be beyond anyone's worst nightmare."

Jeff could see the first break in Nichol's confident demeanor. I know what you're thinking. Do I tell them or don't I?

"I don't know how much detail or scientific gibberish your viewers want, so I'll keep it relatively simple. Earthquakes of this magnitude are caused by plate tectonic activity. The San Andreas Fault is the boundary of the Pacific Plate, very slowly moving essentially north, and the North American Plate, moving essentially south, grinding against each other. The quake resulted from of the two plates getting stuck, causing pressure to build along the fault. The quake was the release of that pressure."

The anchor looked thoughtful. "Then I assume this has been the cause of previous serious quakes along the fault, including the disastrous San Francisco quake early last century. When was it?"

"The date was 1906," he responded.

"So, if this has been going on all this time, why this monstrous quake now?"

She's gotcha, Jeff smiled. Nichols hesitated. Then took the plunge.

"Of course no one is certain. There are several

hypotheses including one developed by a team of which I'm a member. Our data seems to indicate that the weight of the additional water contributing to rising ocean levels has deformed the Pacific Plate very slightly, causing it to butt more strongly against the North American Plate. Laypersons view tectonic plates as huge monolithic structures. But often they're more like broken dinner plates. Various sections can be independent of each other.

"I know this sounds outrageous—until you do the math. The San Andreas System is about 800 miles long, most of it along the California coast. If you go west about 100 miles to include much of the continental shelf, that's 80,000 square miles. The ocean water level is now at about four feet above the historic benchmark. That means the eastern edge of the Pacific Plate is being weighed down by about *336 billion tons of additional water*. And each additional foot will add another *67 billion tons*. Is that weight sufficient to cause the plate deformation I just described? We believe it is. Can we prove it? At this point, no."

The anchor shook her head in apparent disbelief. "You mean to say that *the warming* is the cause of this earthquake?"

"*No*," Nichols shot back. "I said it's one of a number of possibilities. It will take a lot more research before anyone would presume to make a definitive statement. Actually, we may never know for sure."

She looked at Nichols for an instant, obviously uncertain where she could go from there. "Thanks, Dr. Nichols, for your insights. I hope you will be available to help us understand the scientific aspects of this unbelievable tragedy as our coverage continues."

There was no repeat of the previous evening. They showered and fell onto the California king too physically and emotionally exhausted to do more than cuddle. In the morning, after escorting Alex to her gate, Jeff asked if he could see her again.

Alex looked a little surprised.

"Are you sure? I'm afraid I really came on like a slut. Whatever can you think of me? She batted her eyelashes and looked down, demurely.

Jeff laughed. He knew no response was required.

———————

Jeff followed the news after his return to Stillwater with morbid, albeit scientific, fascination and a "there but for the grace of an old Archer go I."

It was a week before the aftershocks diminished appreciably. The destruction in L.A., Orange and Ventura Counties verged on total. It tapered off slowly south toward San Diego and north to Santa Barbara.

California and the Federal government worked to coordinate rescue efforts, deploying the National Guard, regular Army troops, the Navy and Coast Guard. There was no plan. How could there be? No one could ever have conceived of a calamity of these proportions. The military and the bureaucrats stepped on each other's toes, making contradictory statements and going off in different directions.

Meanwhile, the tens of thousands of survivors who could walked until they found rescuers with water, food and medical help. 'Copters with speakers overflew the carnage, directing people to aid centers and temporary camps hastily being set up on the beaches because it was easier to supply them from water than over land. Those needing immediate evacuation were taken out by boat. Transport ships from the San Diego Naval base, the largest naval facility on the West Coast and home port of the Pacific Fleet, were dispatched as quickly as possible north to the devastated area. Surviving Coast Guard vessels from bases in L.A., Long Beach and San Diego were also pressed into service.

The focus initially was on saving survivors. The daunting task of digging through millions of tons of rubble would have to wait until heavy equipment could get in, even though everyone knew time for those buried alive was running out.

Looting began well before the aftershocks subsided, but consisted primarily of people looking for water, food, clothing and medical supplies. Not much was left of big ticket consumer items, the usual target of looters in less catastrophic disasters. In any case, few survivors had homes left to outfit with new TVs or refrigerators.

The news media, of course, pulled out all the stops, trying to outdo one another with lurid and sensational coverage. After the second day, with help of the Feds, California pretty effectively shut them down. Fox News and National Guard choppers had collided over Central L.A., killing all on board. At that point news 'copters actually dominated the skies in the area. The FAA slapped a no-fly zone over the three counties.

The media screamed "First Amendment" and threatened to sue, knowing full well that the process would take too long to get them back in the game. So the major nets reluctantly agreed to pool coverage, both air and ground.

Of the many unforeseen consequences of the quake was its impact on insurance companies. Only about 15 percent of homes in California carried earthquake insurance, reflecting, Jeff thought, people's incredible ability to hide from scary realities. But most commercial buildings were covered. According to news reports, several insurance companies with very heavy exposure were already hinting at bankruptcy.

No one wanted to say it, but there were questions as to whether the area should ever be rebuilt. In an interview two weeks after the initial quake, Anita Fernandez, California's lieutenant governor, came close when she said:

"The long-term viability of the area can only be determined after extensive seismic and geologic study. Until such studies are completed and evaluated, permits for reconstruction of infrastructure, commercial and residential buildings will not be granted."

Later, in class discussions about the quake, Jeff pulled out one of his favorite quotes—from paleontologist Derek Ager:

"Though the theories of plate tectonics now provide us with a *modus operandi,* they still seem to me to be a periodic phenomenon. Nothing is world-wide, but everything is episodic. In other words, the history of any one part of the earth, like the life of soldier, consists of long periods of boredom and short periods of terror."

COUSTEAU CITY
UMM AL-QUWAIN
MAY 21, 2051

"Obviously man has to enter the sea. There is no choice in the matter. The human population is increasing so rapidly and land resources being depleted at such a rate, that we must take sustenance from the great cornucopia. The flesh and vegetables of the sea are vital."
—Jacques-Yves Cousteau, *The Silent World* (1981)

"A lot of people attack the sea; I make love to it."
—Jacques-Yves Cousteau

The large white van pulled up to the curb in front of Dubai Airport's International Terminal. It bore a red flag with white crescent and star. Underneath, in English and Arabic: Umm al-Quwain Marine Research Center.

In the short walk from the terminal to the van, Kent Whitaker began to sweat. A dry heat my ass, he thought. The two members of his crew—pushing a couple of cases of equipment—looked even less comfortable. The driver helped them manhandle the gear into the back.

Once moving, the driver announced in halting English that it would be about a 30-minute ride.

Whitaker, in his decades-long career reporting for the Environmental News Network (ENN), had never visited The Emirates. He'd been almost everywhere else. But this might be his last foray into the field. A desk job—executive editor—was waiting for him at network headquarters in Chicago. He thought it might be about time.

Through tinted windows he watched the tan-colored, heavily urbanized landscape roll past. The times, he knew, had not been kind to Dubai and Abu Dhabi. Soaring temperatures and increasing desertification had curbed tourism in what had become known as the Disneyworld of the Middle East—minus, of course, the focus on good, clean family fun.

Developers, in their undoubted wisdom, had chosen to build their gaudy, glitzy pleasure palaces at sea level, open to the Persian Gulf. Now they were ringed by seawalls, dikes, levies and berms in an effort to keep the gulf at bay.

The crashing of the oil market also hadn't helped. The region's primary source of income, next to tourism, was in steady decline as the world, albeit reluctantly, worked to kick its fossil fuel habit.

Wind off the gulf buffeted the slab-sided van. The atmosphere was slightly beige. A "shamal" had been blowing for several days, carrying fine dust particles from Iraq's deserts southeasterly across the gulf. Prior to landing, the pilot had given passengers a short tutorial. Shamals, once confined to spring and summer, had become increasingly common year around. The winds could reach 50 mph and disrupt air, sea and land transportation. The fine dust coated and penetrated everything.

The van pulled into a parking lot at the foot of a concrete pier. The large marina contained a sprinkling of yachts, several of them in the mega-category. There were also a couple of Umm-al-Quwain Marine Research Center vessels. Exiting the van, Kent noticed a two-story, chalky-white building sprawled along the waterfront, its red awnings lowered to shield windows from the intense sun. It was the research center's headquarters.

The driver was joined by a couple of muscled dock hands who helped move the equipment cases down the pier toward a waiting boat. A tall, darkly tanned man stood casually by a timberhead watching their progress. He walked over to meet them.

Extending a hand. "Jon Carver."

"Kent Whitaker. It's a pleasure...."

"Welcome to Umm al-Quwain. Sorry about the wind and dust. I presume you know about our shamals."

"The pilot provided a mini-lecture," Kent said. "No apologies necessary. I've seen worse."

Carver smiled. "Come on board. Last time I checked, the air conditioning was working."

Entering the cabin, they were joined by a strikingly handsome woman.

"Gentlemen, may I present my wife—Daliyah Bint Hanifa al-Mu'alla, head of UAQ's Marine Research Center and my co-conspirator on the project."

"Just Daliyah." She shook hands firmly with Kent and the crew.

"This is Warren Lester, my photographer. Jack Crowley handles lighting and sound."

"Please sit. May we offer iced tea, lemonade, beer or something stronger? Tea sounded good to all. "It's a short trip," she said. "We're only about eight miles out."

Kent estimated the vessel had about 50 feet of waterline. Booms and winches at the rear made it a working boat. As it pulled from the pier, the deep thrum of its engines spoke of lots of power. Clear of the marina, it accelerated swiftly, cutting through the moderate in-bound swells.

Jon looked at Kent. "I've seen lots of your work over the years and enjoyed it, although, considering some of the topics, 'enjoy' might not be the best word. I even remember what must have been one of your first reports—the demise of the Kilimanjaro ice sheet. When was that? Early '20s?"

"Thanks. I think it was '22."

"May I assume the three of you are divers?"

Kent looked a little embarrassed. "Warren and Jack are very accomplished underwater. Best I can claim is some snorkeling and a crash SCUBA course a few days ago. I suspect I know just enough to be dangerous."

"Not a problem. We have some pretty user-friendly ways to get around. Can you tell me exactly what you need from us?"

For the next few minutes, Kent outlined his rough plan for the shoot, stressing that he'd have to rely on Jon—and Daliyah—for guidance.

"We're planning a 30-minute special on the project. So we'll need lots of video of the facilities—inside and out—and interviews with you and others you'd recommend. As I see it, we'll focus on the project as a prototype for helping alleviate hunger and the fact that it's the first successful long-term facility for living and working underwater.

"And it now occurs to me that your relationship—he smiled at Daliyah—might also be a focus."

"Absolutely. If it weren't for Daliyah, none of this would have been possible." Her smile in response was dazzling.

Lucky son of a bitch, Kent thought.

———

The boat slowed. On the port side, Kent saw a square

tower bristling with antennae and dishes rising about 30 feet from the sea. As he watched, a large platform was lowered from an opening about 20 feet up the tower. It was attached to the tower and to a pillar of equal height about 75 feet west. It slowly descended in tracks. Farther west, jutting up from the sea bed, was a breakwater of interlocking steel plates.

The boat made a turn to starboard and slowly approached the platform—actually a dock—now at sea level. The breakwater had calmed the chop. Crew members threw out bumpers and tied off.

"Shall we?" Carver asked.

It was an easy step up. The dock was about 12-feet wide. The tower was larger, more massive than it had appeared. Looking south as they stood waiting for the cases to be brought up, Kent saw several enormous hydroponic gardens bobbing gently in the swell. Their plex roofs glinted in the strong sunlight. Near the tower was a large floating platform with a bullseye and a wind sock—a helipad.

"The tower probably seems like some contraption out of a bad sci-fi movie. Or, at best, a classic case of over-engineering. But it's actually a pretty simple way to provide a dry entrance to our village below, one that takes into account wave action and the continuously rising sea level."

As he spoke, the dock began smoothly rising toward the opening.

"This is the way in for staff or guests unable or uninterested in making a wet entrance. We also use it for freight. Many of the staff, however, simply free dive about 35 feet, entering the hub through the moon pool."

Yeah, Kent thought. Have they started growing gills?

The opening was wide, tall and framed by heavy gasketed doors. The party stepped onto a thick-rubber mat, the floor of the elevator.

"We'll descend about 50 feet," Carver said, "and enter through an airlock. The facility is pressurized at two atmospheres—about 30 PSI—to offset water pressure at this depth. You may need to clear your sinuses on entry the way divers do."

Kent remembered the technique from his basic training. Squeeze your nose and try to force air out of your ears. It had seemed to work.

Once through the airlock, Carver didn't give them much time to rubberneck. The central hub was at least two-stories high, its ceiling a clear dome providing almost 180-degrees of underwater view. A soft, rippling light bathed the building. A large oval moon pool, its surface black and perfectly still, was to their right. Tropical plants, some extending almost to the ceiling, were everywhere in evidence.

"You must be pretty beat after your trip, so we'll take you to your quarters. You can freshen up and relax until dinner. I think you'll find the menu interesting; all dishes were made primarily from ingredients produced here. You'll be amazed at how much one can do with kelp."

He and the crew were housed in adjoining rooms a short distance down one of the arms radiating from the hub. Kent had read the arms were constructed from recycled marine cargo containers. The rooms, accessed from a narrow outside hallway, were about six-feet wide, 15-feet long and had eight-foot ceilings.

Claustrophobes might take some comfort from the two by three-foot windows, one each in the ceiling and in the middle of the outside wall. There was a single bed with night table at one end, a small head with shower at the other. A footlocker, wardrobe and some shelving hugged the walls.

But it was the view that attracted his attention. Night was falling topside. In the underwater twilight he could see the neighboring arm stretching into the gathering gloom.

Its lighted windows glowed softly, attracting schools of fish. He kept his light off so he could watch the fish flitting in unison to and fro, black when silhouetted, as they passed in front of the windows. Mesmerizing.

Kent unpacked. He was glad he'd followed instructions and brought some warm clothing. The facility was cold and felt damp. He pulled a sweater on over his shirt. He assumed dinner wasn't formal.

He lay down and was nodding off when there was a knock at the door. Time, he thought, to try the kelp.

They were escorted back to the hub and to a small, second-level dining room. It was disconcerting to look up at what appeared to be a ceiling of water. At night the roof seemed to disappear.

Joining Carver and his wife was a tall, blonde woman. Carver introduced her as Dr. Nikki Carver, his daughter. The resemblance was striking.

"Nikki is our staff medico," Carver said. "Actually, she's much more than that. She practices in a very new field—human marine physiology. Specifically, that's the impact on humans of living and working underwater. She also sets our broken bones and dispenses pills as necessary.

They sat. Carver smiled broadly. "Before dinner, I believe we are going to have a show."

He spoke in Arabic to the waiter who walked to a wall and turned off the lights. As they faded, Carver pointed up.

As his eyes became accustomed to the dark, Kent saw flickers, then streaks, of neon-blue light in the sea-sky above. Soon the ceiling was awash with pulsating color. He looked at Daliyah as she gazed raptly upward at the display, her face bathed in the pale blue and flickering glow.

"I'm glad this happened tonight," she said. "It's not a

common occurrence. I like to think of this as our version of the Aurora Borealis."

"At the risk of dispelling the magic," Carver interjected, "the marine biologist in me is compelled to tell you that what you're seeing are microscopic *dinoflagellates* known as *bahia fosforescente*. They're bioluminescent, producing light when disturbed, in this case by a school of fish that's cruising among them having late dinner.

"And speaking of dinner...."

The first course was a savory miso soup with kelp. It was followed by a salad with fresh garden greens, tomatoes and cucumbers. The main course was broiled, garlic-seasoned jumbo shrimp with roasted zucchini and summer squash. The dinner rolls were slightly green, made, they were told, with kelp flour. Desert was chocolate cake, also made with kelp flour. Coffee and tea followed.

"For the sake of complete disclosure," Carver said, "some basic ingredients, seasonings and beverages were imported from the mainland. Otherwise...."

Kent and the crew were highly complimentary.

"But," Kent said, "I hope you're not going to tell us that kelp is also used to make your breakfast cereal."

"Not yet, but, in addition to being nutritious, we're finding it's very versatile. In fact, we sponsored a nationwide contest in Umm al-Quwain a couple of years ago, challenging Quwainers to develop recipes. We received hundreds. I think the chocolate cake was among the winners.

"Are your accommodations satisfactory?" Daliyah asked. "They're about the best we have to offer."

"Fine, thanks," Kent replied. Jack and Warren nodded in agreement.

"But I must ask about the cool temperatures. I'm glad you warned us to bring warm clothing."

"As you can imagine, we had very little to go on as we built Cousteau City. With few exceptions, humans have had little experience living for extended periods underwater. The most ambitious experiment took place about 90 years ago in the Red Sea, just across the Arabian Peninsula from where we're sitting. Of course I'm referring to Jacques Cousteau's Conshelf I, II and III."

Kent could tell he was dealing with an academic. This sounded like a lecture.

"Initially, Cousteau envisioned a growing need to put workers underwater for drilling and mining operations. He believed it would be far more efficient to have acclimated workers living on site rather than spending hours descending, then ascending slowly to depressurize. His Conshelf experiments—funded, in fact, by mining and petrochemical interests—were designed to prove feasibility.

"But Cousteau and his sponsors soon realized that improvements in manned and unmanned underwater vehicles and deep drilling techniques were eliminating the need for divers living at depth. So Cousteau moved on to what would become his real legacy—global underwater exploration and environmental causes.

"I know this is a long answer to a short question, but one of many things we've had to learn is how to control humidity and condensation. We maintain internal temperatures as close as possible to the external water temperature. If it's warmer inside the buildings—even if only by a few degrees—water vapor condenses on the cooler windows and walls. Believe me. Putting on some additional clothing is better than living in a swamp. We also run incoming surface air through dehumidifiers to dry it out as much as possible."

"Well," Daliyah interjected, "The hour grows late and we get up and to work early around here." Kent could sense she was adept at reining in her voluble husband when necessary. "Breakfast, and I promise no kelp cereal, is at 7 a.m. in the first-floor cafeteria. We can convene there and make plans for the day."

Kent pulled the covers up to his chin. The cool dampness would take some getting used to. He closed his eyes, but sleep wouldn't come. His usual bout of jet lag.

Instead, he stared at the window in the ceiling. He wondered what was going on out there in the stygian blackness. As his eyes became accustomed to the dark, he noticed the window wasn't completely black. Perhaps it was lights in hub or windows in the other arms; perhaps it was some slight bioluminescence.

He remembered the blue-indigo light illuminating Daliyah's face before dinner. Kent was not a man prone to envy, but he envied Carver, not just because of his wife's exotic beauty, but because the two shared a dream and were working together to make it a reality.

Kent and his wife of almost 20 years had divorced recently. It was not his choice. He still loved Jill, but she had found someone else.

He always thought they could survive his peripatetic career; she was also employed. But he was wrong. She apparently had needed more than he could or would give. The breaking point came when he was offered a state-side management position with the network, but opted, instead, to spend three weeks covering the evacuation of several large islands in the Philippines. On his return—suffering from dysentery—she admitted to having an ongoing affair and asked for a divorce.

Sleep's not happening he told himself. Wonder if anyone would mind if I wandered around for a while.

He walked into the softly lighted hub. It was about 75 yards across and had two levels. The arms radiated from the second level. Looking down, Kent saw the moon pool at the far side. He knew that the two atmospheres of pressure inside the building—matching outside water pressure—kept the water from spewing up like a geyser. Two medium-sized HOVs—human-operated subs—hung on cranes at the side of the pool. Lockers and storage compartments ringed the pool.

In the center of the hub was a lush tropical garden with a short, wandering walking path and a few benches. The remainder of the floor space was carved into various roofless functional areas. The purposes of most were easily discernable—cafeteria, clinic, small store, library, theatre, game room, offices.

Kent noticed a solitary figure sitting on a bench in the garden. He wondered what Carver's daughter was doing up at this hour.

"Mind if I join you?" Kent asked, as he approached the bench. "Looks like we're both up late." She moved over in response.

"Come here often?"

"I presume," she said with a smile, "that's not a pickup line."

He laughed. "No. I would have needed several drinks before I could come up with something that original."

"Yes, I do come here often. Unlike Jon, I'm a landlubber and need the occasional comfort of terrestrial flora. Jet lag?"

Kent nodded. "And what's your excuse?"

"Ruptured appendix. *No*, not mine. I had to remove one after dinner. Surgery isn't part of my job description. But, occasionally, I need to step outside my comfort zone. There was no time to get the guy to the hospital in UAQ. Fortunately, it's a fairly simple procedure, particularly if done early before infection spreads. I probably shouldn't confess this, but step-by-step illustrated instructions are available on line for docs to use in an emergency. I just had to follow along. And I think I even remembered to get all the retractors out before I closed him up."

"Congratulations. And don't be embarrassed by having

a crib sheet. That's not too different from what I do. Without a teleprompter, I sometimes couldn't utter a coherent thought on camera."

They sat for a moment.

"Tell me," Kent said. "How long have Jon and Daliyah been married?" Nikki told him about three years.

"They were married right here—almost where we're sitting—early in the construction. The wedding was small and caused quite a scandal. Daliyah's a member of UAQ's royal family, a first cousin of Sheikh Hadad, whom I think you'll meet. Not only did she marry an infidel, but she rejected the expected elaborate wedding. Daliyah has a mind of her own, a truly emancipated Arab woman.

"I'm very happy for Jon. Until Daliyah he'd lived a pretty lonely life. Now she's his whole world."

"Pardon me, but I have a hard time believing a guy like your dad would lead a lonely existence."

"Oh, there were plenty of casual relationships, but he had a problem with the 'Big C,' you know, Commitment. I guess that turned out to be just as well. When the right one came along, as they say, he was ready....

"Well, I think I've decompressed sufficiently to get some sleep," she said. "You may want to try to do the same."

They stood and she offered her hand. "It was nice to have the chance to talk."

There was no kelp in sight at breakfast. Kent and the crew, in addition to finding a variety of Middle-Eastern breakfast dishes at the buffet, were offered eggs fried, scrambled or poached. Carver explained that a couple of chicken coops were tucked away in one of the hydro-gardens.

The three opted for the traditional local dishes topped off with strong Arabic coffee.

Kent suggested to the couple that they spend the

morning doing background interviews on camera. They could then shoot appropriate interiors—interesting features of the facility they'd recommend. Tomorrow they would focus on exterior video.

Carver interjected that UAQ's ruler—Sheikh Hadad bin Rashid al-Mu'alla—would be on-site later in the day.

"He felt it was time for one of his regular visits. In any case, he'd rather be interviewed here than in his office. We'll need to accommodate his schedule."

Kent assured him they would be flexible.

"I had Warren scout around before breakfast for a couple of good locations for the interviews. I also took a walk last night and thought the garden would work well as a backdrop."

Warren suggested the moon pool, shooting from one side with the underwater vehicles in the background. He also rued the fact he didn't have a camera in hand at dinner the night before to catch the "light show."

"Any chance there'd be a repeat tonight?"

Carver shrugged. "Let's hope."

Kent sat the couple on the same bench where he and Nikki had their late-night conversation. The background was a jungle-like scene with fan palms, flowering vines and large, vivid bird-of-paradise blooms. Kent knew he could make a lot on air of the existence of this small tropical paradise under the Persian Gulf.

He had no problem getting them talking. For the next couple of hours, the two—primarily Carver—sketched the evolution of the idea and eventual realization of the aquafarming facility.

Jon outlined the advantages of undersea farming: a stable environment with consistent temperatures; freedom from the effects of disastrous weather conditions; availability of vast amounts of acreage on suitable areas of the world's continental shelves.

"Once thought to be an alien and hostile environment, more than 100 years of undersea exploration have shown that humans can live and work in the oceans. The technology was all in place. All that was needed was the incentive. And I think the warming provides humankind with the strongest possible reason to return to the sea—*survival.*

"Our approach to the rising sea thus far has been to try to defeat it. I think the rational among us realize it's a battle we can't win. What's that old saying? 'If you can't beat 'em, join 'em.' We need to embrace the watery world and learn to coexist."

Without prompting, Carver then moved on to the construction phase.

"We've been very pleased to see so many ideas that existed only on paper successfully executed. Has everything worked as planned? Of course not."

Carver laughed, obviously thinking about some of the adversities they'd had to overcome.

Kent sat back and let it roll. The perfect interviewee....

"For example, there was the hydro-platform that almost got away. We underestimated the cable strength required to moor the platforms to the bottom. The first major storm that came along, wave action snapped the cables as we reduced buoyancy to try to reel it down. We chased that partially submerged garden for most of a day until we were able to snag it, drag it back and secure it."

He went on—for the benefit of the interview—to detail the difficultly encountered dealing with humidity and condensation in the core buildings. He invoked the name of Cousteau and provided a historical sketch of early efforts at living and working underwater.

"Another significant problem hampered getting our second shrimp enclosure operating." Carver explained that, inadvertently, the mile-square "corral" was placed in what he called a "food-source shadow" cast by the first enclosure.

"We learned the hard way that currents carrying plankton and other microorganisms on which the shrimp feed tended to pass first through the original enclosure before reaching the second. Shrimp in the new enclosure, therefore, received insufficient nutrition. We had to move it."

After Carver related several other examples, Kent changed directions.

"Daliyah," he said, "married couples who work together often report it puts a strain on the relationship. What's it like working with this guy on a project as complex and intense as this one? I've known several couples, for example, who broke up while trying to do a relatively simple thing like building a house together."

"Working with Jon is not a problem. He takes direction very well." She smiled.

"Actually, we had long talks about this prior to our marriage. We decided to try a division of labor. Jon would handle construction, management of the facility and operational details. I'd focus on the marine science, personnel and so on. We've managed to stick to that division pretty well and respect each other's judgment. We also decided, in general terms, to keep work and marriage as separate as possible. Of course, we haven't always succeeded. But we've come this far. And the house is just about finished."

A staff member arrived and needed to speak with Carver. Kent signaled Warren to shut it down. They spoke quietly for a moment.

"We can expect the sheikh," Carver consulted his watch," shortly after lunch. I suggest you set up for his arrival at the moon pool. He always makes a wet entrance. He's a highly accomplished diver and this is his way of having some fun. Good video. Yes?"

Forewarned that the sheikh's 'copter had landed, Kent, Daliyah and Jon joined the camera crew at the moon pool. In a couple of minutes the sheikh's head broke water near the center of the pool. Obviously enjoying himself, he gave an exuberant shout and waved at his audience. He breast-stroked to the rim and pulled himself up and out. He was dark, compact, muscled, clean shaven and boyish-looking, though probably in his late 30s.

As he toweled off, Daliyah and Jon approached. There were the usual hugs and pecking of cheeks. The two men posed an interesting contrast; the blond Carver towering at least six inches over the swarthy sheikh. Carver said something and the three laughed good-naturedly. Kent sensed real affection.

The sheikh, wearing only a bathing suit, walked over and Carver handled the introduction, rattling off the long name and title. "Hadad is fine. Give me a few minutes to put on some clothes. We'll do the interview here?"

Kent nodded.

True to his word, Hadad quickly rejoined the group wearing jeans and a London School of Economics sweatshirt. Kent sat him on a high stool near the pool with the HOVs in the background. Jack hooked him up and did a sound check.

"What, no make-up?" Hadad quipped, white teeth flashing.

The interview went well. The sheikh was certainly Carver's equal as an extemporaneous speaker.

"It seems Jon and I were thinking along the same lines, but independently. It was Daliyah who brought us together. As director of UAQ's Marine Research Center, she was familiar with his work.

"UAQ is a very small country, smallest of the Emirates, and relatively poor. Our population is about 60,000. Our land is almost fully urbanized. With the exception of limited off-shore natural gas, we have not shared in the petroleum largesse enjoyed by some of the other Emirates.

"We have always been a seafaring people, taking much of what we need from the gulf—food for our own consumption, pearls for export. In better times, we could also rely to some extent on animal husbandry, small farms, date and citrus orchards. But the warming has desiccated our land, making traditional agriculture problematic. Tourism, another traditional source of revenue, has also dried up with the increasing heat and loss of our beautiful beaches to the rising waters.

"So I took a chance and bankrolled Jon's aquaculture project. While there's still more to do, the concept has been proven. Expansion plans include additional enclosures for sardines and mackerel. Annual output—and it will increase as we add capacity—is sufficient to reduce substantially the need to import increasingly expensive basic commodities. As a state-run facility, there is no profit motive. Prices are based strictly on the cost of production."

Kent interjected: "Do you ever see the day when the farm will be able to export some of its output, making it a profit center?"

"That's not on our radar. But other Emirates are watching the project with interest as are several countries in the Middle East and Asia. We've hosted a number of delegations and may end up exporting the concept, if not our products."

Interview concluded, Hadad joined the group for a tour of the facilities to shoot additional video. Included were typical staff quarters located in several of the arms. Carver explained that a crew of about 100 lives on-site, rotating every two weeks with another 100 workers returning from shore leaves.

"We'd considered dormitories, but thought staff would appreciate individual quarters. They're small, about six by 10-feet, and each arm has two shared heads with showers.

But, as you can see, they're reasonably comfortable.

"Daliyah and I, as the only married couple on-site, have larger accommodations. If we need to create more space, we go double-wide."

A look at several workshops and labs in another arm followed. Some of these, too, were double-wide. In one of the labs—labeled Marine Physiology—Nikki happened to be monitoring a guy working up a sweat on a treadmill. She explained that she had developed base-line data on a number of subjects and checked them regularly to chart any significant changes.

The lab also included a small hyperbaric chamber.

"Working at these depths, there's very little likelihood of developing the bends. But, we have had a couple of cases in which recreational wreck divers have had problems and been decompressed here. I'm also able to use it for various aspects of my research."

The tour concluded with video of food preparation in the kitchen, off-duty crew in the recreation room and a tour of the facility's guts—the small reactor, desal plant and ventilation system housed in the pedestal beneath the first floor on which the hub rested.

Finally, the party witnessed the launch of one of the HOVs on a routine inspection patrol. Warren's camera followed the mini-sub as it sank into the pool, disconnected from the crane and umbilical and slowly descended, its two-man crew clearly visible in the cabin's red-lighted interior.

Kent was early for dinner. Warren had brought a camera and was setting up, hoping for another display of bioluminescence.

Nikki was also early, nursing a drink. She looked up. "Come here often?"

It was flippant, even flirty. Kent wondered if there were

something real there. Dream on, he thought. I must have 20 years on her.

"Not often enough. May I join you?"

"Only if you apologize for not warning me about the visit to my lab. I would have liked to have put on a clean lab coat for the camera. And maybe some lipstick.

"I apologize." He sat. "The tour was pretty ad hoc, but you looked lovely and very professional. How's your patient?"

"Razin? He's fine, thanks. Already up and around."

There was an awkward silence. Kent was saved by the waiter who asked about a drink.

"Whatever Dr. Carver's having," he said.

"Are you always this trusting?"

"Only with people I trust."

"And how do you know you can trust me?"

"I figure anyone who can remove a ruptured appendix following instructions online is trustworthy."

She laughed. "You have pretty low standards...."

Time, Kent thought, to change the subject. "Tell me about the sheikh. Anything I haven't already picked up in the public record."

"I don't know him very well. I've been around for less than a year. You'd need to ask Jon for any inside information, although I'm not sure he'd say much. He and Hadad are very good friends, diving buddies.

"I do know Hadad was recently engaged to a lawyer he met in Abu Dhabi. I think the state wedding is scheduled early next year. He is, as they say, 'much beloved' by his people for his liberal ways and foresight. You can easily see he doesn't take himself too seriously; doesn't stand on formality."

At that point they were joined by the others. The sheikh was still wearing his alma mater's sweatshirt.

Dinner conversation focused primarily on the next day's outing to shoot exteriors. On leaving the moon pool, Carver recommended an ascent almost to the surface for an overview shot of the facility, followed by a short swim to look at kelp harvesting operations. Next a visit to one of the hydro-platforms. In the afternoon, a shrimp harvest was underway in Corral Two. The process, he said, probably would be most easily shot from the refrigerated ship into which the shrimp were being loaded, although some underwater video of the suctioning crew would also be possible.

"Finally, if there's time, I'd like to have you see the site at which we're constructing our underwater Olympic venue."

He laughed at their reaction.

"Some of the guys have developed new underwater games to pursue in their off hours. Things like spear-gun archery, a version of shuffleboard, aqua-sled races, an obstacle course for full-suited divers. I think there's more, but I can't keep track."

During the flan, Carver signaled for lights out and Warren got his wish. This time Kent watched the blue, flickering light bathe Nikki's face. She caught his look, stared back and smiled.

After everyone had dispersed following dinner, Kent walked to the park bench with high hopes.

She was waiting.

Kent left Nikki about 3 a.m. He tried not to slink down the dim corridors to his room. Consenting adults and all that, but he couldn't help wonder how Carver would react to their roll in the sack.

He showered off her fragrance and crawled in for what he hoped would be a few hours' sleep. He drifted off to thoughts of her strong, white limbs wrapped around him.

At 6:30 a.m., bowing to the insistent alarm, he dressed without much enthusiasm. Today was his day in the water. He knew he didn't have to accompany the crew. They were perfectly capable of rounding up good video without a third wheel along. But, what the hell? If you're ending your career in the field, you may as well go out with a bang, or, in this case, a splash. Ironic that your first major assignment was Kilimanjaro at 19,000-feet above sea level; your last at 35-feet below.

After a quick breakfast, the party moved to the pool. Nikki was nowhere to be seen. Hadad had joined them to say goodbye. He had to get back to business. He thanked Kent, the crew and said he looked forward to seeing the program.

"Remember, use only video of my good side."

Poolside, the expert divers suited up leaving Kent standing around feeling stupid. Carver came to the rescue, handing him a light neoprene suit to wear over his bathing trunks. "Slip into this and then we'll talk about the rest of your gear. Start with your feet and work upwards."

It felt like trying to stuff yourself into a sausage casing. When he'd worked it up to his thighs, Daliyah helped him get his arms in and zipped him up from the back. She handed him fins.

"And these are your weights." She began slipping them into pockets around his waist. "We'll adjust for final buoyancy once you're in the water. Here's your harness, regulator and mask. The gear's different from the others for reasons we'll explain."

Warren and Jack signaled they were ready. Everyone sat on the edge of the pool and put on fins. Kent followed suit. Helpers carried out steel air tanks, strapped them on the divers' buoyancy vests, attached and tested regulators.

Meanwhile, a guy disconnected a hose from the side of the pool, brought it to Kent, attached it to the regulator on the back of the harness and had Kent slip it on. He fitted the mask to his face and asked him to breathe normally.

"Okay?"

Kent gave him thumbs up. His helper waggled a finger under his nose.

"Remember, you say 'okay' with circled thumb and forefinger. 'Thumbs up' means, 'I need to ascend.'

"This is called SNUBA—Snorkeling Underwater Breathing Apparatus. The line's attached to a small solar-powered air compressor floating on the surface. It goes where you go. We've improved the technology so we can dive to about 40 feet. Once you get used to it, you'll find it very comfortable and maneuverable."

Kent gave a half-hearted 'okay.'" He felt like an adult relegated to the kid's card table at Thanksgiving.

First stop, topside for an establishing shot. Good visibility allowed Warren's wide lens to image most of Cousteau City 30-40 feet below. For what he couldn't get, he slowly panned.

Kent noticed that his compressor automatically reeled in line as he ascended. As he dove with the rest in a northerly direction, it played out line and followed dutifully behind. It was *a lot* more comfortable than the SCUBA gear with which he had struggled. He felt more like a fish than an alien interloper.

The huge kelp field came up quickly. Initially they swam over rows and rows of recently cut stumps. Ahead they could see a harvester moving slowly, floating just above the bottom, mowing down rows of towering plants that grew almost to the surface.

Two divers were in attendance. Kent saw they were using SNUBA, probably to extend their dive times. The machine, in many ways resembling a corn harvester, was remotely controlled. The cut stalks were sucked into a large trailing tube that went to the surface where a kelp slurry, minced by sharp gratings in the tube, was spread to a depth of six inches in rectangular compartments in barges. The kelp bales dried in the sun and the barges later were pushed ashore by tending tugs.

To maximize their time, a launch ferried them to the nearest hydro-platform. Kent simply disconnected from the compressor. Warren had the launch slowly circle the huge platform while Jack recorded Carver's running description. Viewers would learn that each platform was about four-acres in size and had its own desal plant to provide fresh water. The sodium and chloride pulled from the salt water was captured and sold ashore. Some of the sodium was kept to be recycled as a component in fertilizer used in the hydroponic solution.

"We grow year-around, so produce thousands of tons of vegetables annually on each of the four platforms now in operation. The units stay on the surface as much as possible, but can be closed up and submerged below wave action in bad weather. At present we're focusing on varieties of lettuce, cabbage, tomatoes, cucumbers and squash like zucchini."

The air onboard smelled fresh, fecund. The rows were tight; the plants encouraged to grow vertically to maximize the real estate. Clucking noises led the party to chicken coops at one end of the platform.

Lunch was waiting back on the launch. Daliyah asked how he liked SNUBA.

"I can see how it could become addicting," he said.

While they ate, the launch moved some distance east where a small cargo vessel was anchored inside a shrimp enclosure.

"Each of the two enclosures," Carver told the camera, "is a mile square. In these relatively warm waters, with more than adequate nutrition and no predation, the jumbos grow quickly. We have an annual harvest from each corral of about 1,000 tons."

A crew member dropped the corral's fine-meshed barrier to provide entrance, and, when in position, Warren shot the large tube snaking up from beneath the surface to the rusty ship's deck. They could hear the noise of large pumps used for suction.

The three waited on the launch while the camera crew went onboard to shoot shrimp being blown into the hold. Then, rerigged, the two went down to capture images of the harvesting action.

"It takes about two days," Carver said. "Incidentally, our guys have been watching too many American westerns in our theatre. For fun they've started calling themselves 'fishboys.' They've gone as far as to wear the costume, even on shore. Cowboy hats are on sale in our little store. We've managed to dissuade them from toting six-guns and wearing spurs."

They had to forgo visiting the "Olympic" field. It was getting late. Kent and crew had to pack for the trip back to the mainland for a flight in the morning. An early farewell dinner was planned.

Kent did the wet entrance with the rest of the divers and felt pretty good about himself, even if he'd been diving with kid's stuff. He hurried to his room to pack.

He arrived early for dinner, hoping Nikki would have done the same. But he sat drinking by himself for about 10 minutes before the rest of the party arrived. Nikki studiously avoided eye contact.

Shit. I wonder what that means.

There was some decent champagne and a few toasts. Kent toasted the "fishboys," expressing hope they would always ride the watery range. At least that got a little smile from Nikki. The dinner entrée was roasted mackerel with garlic and paprika.

As dinner broke up, Nikki looked at Kent and nodded slightly in the direction of the park. They went separate ways and arrived almost simultaneously. She was clearly embarrassed.

"Sorry about the cloak and dagger stuff, but Daliyah's already suspicious. A woman's sixth sense, I suppose."

"Well, it's not as if we've done anything two consenting adults shouldn't do. Or is there a special set of rules here in Cousteau City?"

"Sort of. It's like a small Muslim town. Women, especially unmarried women, are expected to behave in certain ways. As an infidel from the decadent West—and Jon's daughter—I know I'm cut some slack. But I do work with these people and need to retain their respect."

"Listen," Kent said, checking his watch, "I don't have a lot of time. But I'd really like to see you again. Do you ever get to the States?"

"No, I really have no reason to go back. Maybe you'll get another assignment in the Middle East."

"Probably not going to happen. This is my last hurrah. I'm taking a management position at headquarters in Chicago when I return—a reward, I guess, for almost 30 years of globetrotting. Could we meet halfway for a few days, say London?"

She looked thoughtful. "Well, I'm delivering a paper at a medical conference in Glasgow in a few months...."

"I'll be there."

She looked dubious.

"Please send me details. Gotta run. Is a hug okay or will you be stoned?"

They hugged demurely. With that they separated.

Jon and Daliyah rode up with them in the elevator. The farewells were warm. Kent told them it was a great story and complimented them on their work. "We'll probably be in production for a couple of weeks. I'll let you know when it's scheduled to run."

They watched and waved as the boat pulled away from

the dock.

Warren had kept a camera out and wanted the boat to circle the area for a while. Sunset was close and Kent wondered if a shamal weren't brewing. The sun, fat and red, was sinking into a haze on the horizon. It promised to be quite a show.

Warren asked to have the boat positioned on the east side of the tower, obviously angling for a silhouette of the lonely monolith. The sun began to dip into the gulf, painting sky and water an almost fluorescent orange. It was a magnificent shot. If nothing else, the report would be an artistic success.

As they headed toward shore, the sea wine dark, Kent watched the sunset fade over Iraq's now *unfertile* crescent, the source of thousands of tons of dust being blown regularly across the gulf. Over 5,000 years ago, the storied Tigris and Euphrates Rivers watered Mesopotamia, encouraging the development of the world's first agriculture and, with it, the eventual end of human hunting and gathering and the beginning of modern civilization.

It is also the area some Biblical scholars—besides dating the Earth at 6,000 years old and debating the number angels that could sit on the head of a pin—had decided is the site of the Garden of Eden. Kent wondered what Adam and Eve would think of it now.

Today, the two once life-giving rivers were little more than creeks. Downstream from their confluence, the Shatt-al-Arab delivers their muddy trickles to the gulf. Increasing temperatures and centuries of uncontrolled water draw-down have created a desert where once uncounted square miles of wheat waved in the wind.

How ironic, thought Kent, that lying under 35-feet of water only a few hundred miles from the site of the birth of agriculture—from the cradle of civilization—sits the prototype of what could help save humanity from its folly.

Only time would tell.

STARTING OVER
GREENLAND
JULY 20, 2059

*In the summer (985 A.D.) Eirik went to live in the land which he
had discovered, and which he called Greenland, "because," said he,
"men will desire much the more to go there if the land has a good
name."*
—*Eirik The Red's Saga*, John Sephton, translator, 1880

Rollie Gersten was having the best roller coaster ride of
his young life. With a bungee cord wrapped several times
around his waist and attached to the bow railing of the
containership, the 15-year-old stood on the deck and rode
up and down as it plunged from trough to trough, cold
wind-driven spume occasionally slapping him in the face.
It was midday, but the North Atlantic sky was dark with
low, lead-bellied clouds. The ocean, too, was dark—more
black than blue.

Rollie was cold. His too-large borrowed yellow slicker
wasn't keeping him dry. Rivulets of salt water rolled off the

ill-fitting hood and managed to drip down his neck. He didn't care. He vowed to stay out as long as he could—a much better option than returning to the reeking cabin below he shared with his family. His dad, mom and two younger sisters all were seasick—very seasick. They did their best to coordinate emergency trips to the head, but often had to resort to the buckets.

He didn't know why he had been spared.

Well, Rollie—he said to himself as the ship sliced into an oncoming wall of water—you're not in Kansas anymore! This hardly compares to the roller coaster at the county fair in Hays.

Rollie looked back at the bridge wondering if Thor Thorvaldson was still at the helm. Thorvaldson, third mate of the *Northern Star*, was a huge red-bearded Dane of indeterminate age. He had befriended Rollie soon after the Gerstens came on board—probably because of his irrepressible curiosity, enthusiasm and energy. On his off hours, he had shown him the ship from stem to stern and introduced him to the crew.

Last night, when the family was in particularly bad shape, Thor had rescued Rollie and taken him to the mess for dinner and a movie. The movie was one he had never heard of—*Water World*. Thor said it had been released in the 1990s and was a big flop.

As he watched, Rollie saw that the film was about a world almost totally inundated by melted ice sheets and glaciers. The hero, piloting an ingeniously-designed trimaran, was searching for a map that would lead him to dry land. He was being pursued by a motley bunch of criminals in an old oil tanker.

Thor said he and the crew had watched it more times than he could remember—for laughs. One scene seemed to be a particular favorite. The hero harpooned a rickety plane launched from the tanker to try to bomb his boat. The line got wrapped around the mast and the plane was forced to circle as the line reeled it in closer and closer.

The crew cheered loudly and threw popcorn at the screen when the line broke and the plane spun into the sea. He laughed along but didn't think it was quite as funny as they did.

Rollie wondered when Thor would reel *him* in. He'd said he'd have to end his ride if things got too rough. A few minutes later, a crew member arrived to unhook and escort him safely to the mess to dry off and warm up with hot chocolate.

———————

The klaxon awoke him soon after he went to bed. He'd opened a porthole near his bunk to get some fresh air into the cabin. Thor had explained after an earlier alarm that the horn was used to alert the crew that an iceberg was in the vicinity. The ship's radar allowed them to give most bergs a wide berth, but, occasionally, they would come upon a flattop that radar had difficulty detecting. The klaxon warned of a sudden shift in course.

Thor had assured him there was no real danger. The ship had other means to detect their presence. He said he couldn't remember the last time a ship on this North Atlantic route had collided with one.

But what if we did hit one? Rollie wondered. Would we quickly plunge to the bottom like the *Titanic?* It would be entirely his fault because he was the one responsible for the family's exodus to Greenland.

Actually, the decision to leave the dusty, dun-colored plains of Kansas to start over in Greenland had been made by his parents. But it was he who had made the initial suggestion.

Ms. Harrington, who taught geography and other social sciences, had put pieces of paper with the names of countries of the world into a hat and walked it up and down the aisles. Each of the 13 ninth graders in the class picked a country that would be the subject of their term papers. Rollie came up with Greenland.

At that point all he knew about Greenland was that its rapidly melting ice sheet had, to date, contributed about six feet to the rising ocean level worldwide. It wasn't Greenland's fault, but it was not a very popular country. Boy, he thought, am I going to get shit for this.

Still, as he always did, Rollie threw himself into the research. What he found was intriguing.

Greenland is the largest non-continental island in the world. It had been argued that it should be considered a continent. However, since it's part of the North American tectonic plate, the island never achieved that status. Though officially part of North America, the country has always been more aligned with Europe. It had been a Danish colony from 1721 to 1953 when it became an autonomous territory. In 2034 it obtained complete independence. Greenland's economy had grown to the point that it was no longer as dependent on support from Denmark, which, in earlier times, had supplied about half of its revenues.

Though it has a huge land mass, the island has the smallest population of any country in the world—fewer than 100,000 in the most recent census. The small population, of course, resulted primarily from limited real estate. Over 80 percent of the land mass had been covered by a sheet of ice—almost two miles thick in some places.

But the warming changed all that. Since last century, the ice sheet had been rapidly shrinking as thousands of square miles of ice slid or simply melted and poured into the surrounding ocean, uncovering virgin land never trod by human feet or turned by a plow. That, plus Greenland's warming climate, is what got Rollie's attention and shifted his research to focus on its agriculture.

Before the warming, farming had been of little importance—primarily growing potatoes and raising sheep. But, in the past 70 years, the growing season had increased by seven weeks, allowing the addition of new crops—apples, strawberries, broccoli, cauliflower, cabbage, carrots, beets and other root vegetables. With up to 20 hours of daylight in the summer, some areas, particularly in the south, now grew winter wheat and fodder to feed the increasing sheep, dairy and beef cattle herds. Reindeer, supervised by Laplander immigrants, were also thriving.

Always curious, Rollie wondered who was farming all that new territory. Are there enough Greenlanders?

Further research answered his question. Greenland was actively seeking experienced farmers from abroad in order to become an agricultural products exporter and to help it become as self-sufficient as possible in the face of its increasing population. Not only had the warming opened up new real estate for agriculture, it had turned the country into one of the world's new mining frontiers as the retreating ice sheet uncovered precious metals.

The country also benefitted from the opening in the '20s of the Transpolar Sea Route, the Arctic shipping lane running from the Atlantic to the Pacific across the center of the Arctic Ocean made possible by the melting of arctic ice. International funding contributed to expanding the port in the capital, Nuuk, to service or break cargoes for vessels navigating one leg of the route along Greenland's west coast.

I wonder? Rollie mused.

He knew his family, like so many farm families on the Plains, was in serious trouble. The 2,000 acres the Gerstens had farmed through several generations had simply dried up. The aquifer providing water for its center-pivot irrigation system was almost depleted. The Gerstens hadn't produced a decent wheat, corn or soy bean crop in years.

They'd experimented with dry farming techniques, attempting to grow vegetables. But, in the ever-increasing heat, the soil retained insufficient moisture content. For a time his dad had run a feedlot on the farm to fatten area beef before farmers shipped to market. But the increasing cost of feed and falling beef prices scuttled the project. Both his parents now worked low-paying jobs in Hays to support the family at a subsistence level.

He went to Greenland's governmental site and picked Ministry of Interior. From there he drilled down to the Department of Agriculture. Dominating its home page was an offer that sounded too good to be true. Qualified farmer emigrants were being offered up to 1,000 acres of land for free. Transportation was provided. And the deal included no interest, long-term loans for buildings and equipment. The first payments weren't due for five years.

Rollie could hardly contain himself. He vowed to tell his dad that evening. It was his night to cook dinner, so, as he cleaned the chicken and sliced vegetables for a stir-fry, he planned his speech.

During dinner, he was so agitated his mom asked if he were all right. As his sisters cleaned up, Rollie approached his dad and asked if they could talk.

"Sure, but if it's about sex, I've already told you all I know."

Rollie blushed and quickly forgot his main points.

"Greenland wants farmers," was all he could get out.

Patiently, his dad pulled the story out of him. He was used to what he called Rollie's "enthusiasms."

The two, and his mom, spent the rest of the evening going through all the material on the Greenland site.

"Well, Greenland certainly *does* seem to want farmers," was his dad's summary.

Several long family meetings followed in days to come.

The property sold quickly, but, of course, for only a fraction of what it had been worth. The regional utility had contacted the Gerstens about a year earlier during its search for a site for a wind farm. At 2,300 feet, the property happened to have the highest elevation in a very flat Ellis County, making it a good location for the utility to capture the winds blowing across the Plains.

The family initially declined, hoping to hang on. But then the Greenland opportunity came knocking.

The sale provided what his dad called a "grub stake" to help them get started. He also sold all their equipment at auction and raised a little more cash.

The agreement with Greenland allowed them to ship a half a container of personal property. Initially, his mother worried that wouldn't be enough space. But it turned out to be more than sufficient.

Except for a few family heirlooms, the furniture, in pretty rough shape, would be left behind. Dad had thought he'd ship his power tools, but electrical service in Greenland was different and would require that the tools be rewired. So he packed up the best of his hand tools.

Clothing, too, was an issue. Kansas winters were cold, but no match for Greenland's frigid Polar Night, 3-4 hours of sunlight from November through January. And, while the climate had warmed substantially, its long summer days of Midnight Sun were nothing like the searing heat of America's midsection. So they packed the best of their warm clothes, knowing they would probably have to rethink their wardrobes after arrival.

Family photos and a couple of boxes of personal items for each family member rounded out the shipment.

The one thing Rollie was sad to leave behind was his trusty bike. He and his old Raleigh were rarely separated. For years he'd pedaled it all over the countryside. The bike had even given him his nickname. "Rollie" was Ronald. But, instead of "Ronnie," his friends had taken to calling him "Rollie."

As the departure date neared, Jens Tobiassen, the family's relocation facilitator, let them know that travel plans had to be changed. The Gerstens were to pick up a Greenland Air flight in New York, but the airline had just gone on what was likely to be a protracted strike. The agreement had required they use the country's airline for their transportation. Instead they were booked on a Greenlandic-registered containership that also had facilities for a limited number of passengers. The ship was scheduled to leave two days later than their flight.

Rather than sit around their Newark Airport area hotel waiting for the ship to sail, dad suggested they take a day to visit Manhattan. It was the first chance, and probably the last, any of them would have to see this storied city.

The next morning they caught a huge hovercraft at a floating dock in Jersey City and crossed the Hudson over the long-abandoned Holland Tunnel. The noisy three-decked ferry was packed with workers headed for jobs in Manhattan, still the most densely populated borough of New York City, its economic and administrative center and the city's historic birthplace.

Hoverferries had become the preferred mode of transportation for Manhattan-bound workers from the surrounding boroughs. The rising ocean, now at eight feet above last century's benchmark, had inundated about 15 percent of the island's real estate and flooded its tunnels and subway system. Only a couple of its well-known bridges—the George Washington and Brooklyn—were still in operation. For these, on and off ramps had to be extended far into the city over flooded streets below.

After disembarking at a floating dock on the West Side, the family boarded a tour boat bound for the Statue of Liberty, the financial district and United Nations Headquarters.

A decade earlier Lady Liberty had been disassembled and then put back together on a newly constructed base 20-feet higher than its previous perch in the Hudson River. The guide reminded them that the project was funded by corporate and private contributions from all over the country.

The famous financial district had not fared as well. Its relatively low elevation put it underwater above Wall Street and the Stock Exchange. And its location at the south end of the island meant it took the worst pounding when hurricanes blew in from the Atlantic. But, rather than give up what was still considered the world's primary financial center, as they became inundated, building lobbies were moved to their second or third floors and interconnected by a network of skybridges with moving walkways—some traveling at up to 20 miles-per-hour.

As the tour boat motored slowly over the sunken Battery Park and the failed Manhattan seawall, the guide pointed out the yellow water taxis skimming from building to building above the submerged streets.

Rollie thought the United Nations was the saddest sight he'd seen all day. The building, once a symbol of hope for the world, sat abandoned in water above its foundation, its hundreds of flagpoles bereft of the colorful symbols of member nations. He didn't need to hear the guide's explanation. The UN was unable to keep up with the warming-related turmoil in the world—the increasing violence and outright warfare over disappearing resources. Its efforts to provide humanitarian aid also were swamped by the magnitude of the problem. And member nations simply stopped paying dues as they turned inward to deal with their own increasingly precarious financial and political situations.

The rest of the day was a little more upbeat. They left the tour boat at Midtown and took a land taxi to Central Park to visit the zoo, paddle around The Lake, eat hot dogs from street vendors and take in as many of the marvels of The Metropolitan Museum of Art as time permitted. They finished the day at sunset on the viewing deck of the Empire State Building.

Rollie strongly suspected Greenland would be nothing at all like this.

―――――――

Thor invited Rollie to join him on the bridge as they prepared to dock at Nuuk's huge container port. Captain Per Ingebrand was at the helm. The deck was eerie, illuminated as it was with red light to improve night vision. Ingebrand periodically checked the ghostly green GPS as it painted the ship's progress toward the port and its birth.

Though after midnight, the horizon glowed with the soft light of the Midnight Sun. In summer, Southern Greenland had as many as 18 hours of daylight. According to a chart Thor showed him, the sun had set this day—July 21—at 11 p.m. and would rise again at 3 a.m. Nuuk, their destination, had a few hours of semi-darkness each night.

Rollie looked out from his high perch at the containers below, neatly stacked four or five deep in perfect rows. He could see the lights of the container port floating on the horizon. In the soft glow of the Midnight Sun, he got his first glimpse of Greenland. Nuuk, the capital, a city of about 30,000, is located on the southwestern side of the island. Dad said they'd spend a little time in Nuuk before homesteading their farm near the town of Narsaq in the country's main agricultural region in the south.

Below, the 20 or so other passengers were preparing to disembark. A couple of families were also fellow emigrés, soon to relocate to their new farms. The Gerstens had met them only briefly because of their seasickness. But all had vowed to stay in touch.

In anticipation of his trip to the bridge, Rollie repacked his two suitcases earlier. He'd left his parents and sisters sitting on their bunks, suitcases close at hand. They were no longer quite as pale, but clearly were ready to get off the boat as soon as possible.

As they neared the coast, Rollie saw *Sermitsiaq*, the

4,000-foot mountain that looms over the city. With fog at its base, it appeared to float like an apparition backlighted by the not-quite-dark sky.

The sun was just appearing in the east as *Northern Star's* passengers filed down the gangplank. Members of the crew helped with luggage. Rollie was amazed by the hustle and bustle of the port at this early hour. Thor had told him it operated 24/7 to serve traffic on the Trans Polar Route. Huge cranes loaded and unloaded the massive ships, swinging containers like toy blocks. Haulers zipped by pulling stacks of containers that were being transshipped. Across the harbor, ships were being refueled, resupplied and, in some cases, refitted.

As he walked into his new world, Rollie fingered Thor's parting gift bulging in his pocket—the tip of a Narwhal tusk incised with a drawing of a three-masted whaling ship. Thor had told him that if he ever wanted to go to sea, he'd be happy to vouch for him.

Jens Tobiassen, the relocation coordinator for the incoming farm families, stood on the dock. He seemed quite comfortable in the early morning chill wearing only a heavy cable-knit sweater. He also seemed surprisingly pleasant for someone who had gotten up so early to meet his foreign charges.

"*Godmorgen og velkommen,*" he said with a big smile. Then, in almost accentless English, "Good Morning and Welcome." Their host told the three families they were being transported to a hotel in Old Nuuk. A big breakfast would be followed by a day of rest and orientation.

He herded them to small Chinese electric vans waiting on the roadway.

As they left the frantic activity of the port, city streets seemed relatively quiet. When driving through several residential districts, Rollie noticed two things. The old-looking wooden houses were painted in bright colors—red, blue, yellow, green. And there were no trees. Even in dry old Kansas we have trees, Rollie mused. He supposed the houses were a rainbow of color to compensate for the dreary landscape.

The sign on their destination said "Hotel Hans Egede." He was later to learn that Egede was a Danish missionary who founded Nuuk in 1728. His church was close to the hotel

---

The two rooms were like heaven compared to the shipboard accommodations. After reviving themselves in hot showers—using all the water they wanted—the Gerstens reported to a private dining room. There Tobiassen invited them to fill their plates at a traditional Greenland buffet.

For the benefit of the newcomers, many of the dozens of selections were labeled. There was big pot of *Suaasat,* a soup of reindeer meat with onions and potatoes, identified as the national dish. There was also strawberry soup; pastries filled with cheese, jam, custard, cinnamon; rhubarb pie and blueberries; hot meat pies made with sausage; pickled herring, small raw shrimp, cod in a thick cream sauce. And on it went.

Rollie and his mom exchanged glances. She arched one eyebrow, her usual signal indicating surprise. He wondered if there were any cornflakes, but went ahead and filled his plate, vowing to try almost everything. They hadn't eaten a lot of fish in Kansas—just frozen fish sticks. And reindeer certainly was in short supply. But he was willing to give everything a try.

His sisters were picky eaters, but, having fully recovered from seasickness, were famished. They stuck with the more familiar fare, but he caught his younger sister, Rachel, holding her nose as she contemplated the pickled herring on her plate.

After breakfast, Tobiassen strongly suggested they return to their rooms to rest. He said the first of their orientation sessions would start at 3 p.m.

The Gerstens were last to arrive. The other two families were already seated. There were tentative smiles and waves as they sat down. Tobiassen entered promptly at 3 p.m. and went to a small podium. Actually, he stood in front of the podium, probably feeling it was too formal for the occasion.

After another welcome and questions about the accommodations and breakfast, he suggested the families take a minute to introduce themselves.

"I understand the crossing was rough and that many of you spent most of it in your cabins."

There was the usual awkward moment until someone decided to be first to speak.

Rollie's dad stood rather reluctantly and cleared his throat. He knew, for most farmers, public speaking didn't come easily.

"We're the Gerstens from near Hays, Kansas. This is Jane, my wife, Rollie, Michelle or Mickey and Rachel." He paused to consider what to say next. "We farmed about 2,000 acres—mainly wheat, corn and soybeans. But Kansas has pretty well dried up, so we're glad to be here and to have this opportunity."

John Beresford stood and introduced his wife, Emily. They had one son who was in college and would join them after he graduated. They'd raised dairy cattle in Nebraska until they lost the farm in foreclosure.

The third family—the Thorntons from near Wichita—consisted of two boisterous young sons and a teenage daughter. Rollie could clearly see that she—her name was Melanie—would rather be any place else but here. For her, thought Rollie, this is going to be a tough transition.

Tobiassen continued. "I know you've read the materials and are fully aware of the terms of our agreement, so I won't repeat any of that. If you do have questions, feel free to ask after the session.

"What I'd like to talk about is the kind of welcome you can expect from many Greenlanders—especially those in the farming community. It will not—how do you say it? It will not be with *open arms*. Many farmers strongly object to the government's plan to provide free land and support for foreign farmers. Why not, they ask, give us the additional land and resources to make it productive? The government's answer has been that there are not enough farmers to take advantage of the new lands and that farmers from abroad will also bring new ideas to help increase our productivity."

He looked around the room to assess the reaction to what he'd said. Dad sat stone faced. He had wondered what kind of reception they would have. Now his fears were confirmed.

"Greenlanders are—he struggled for a word—a *closed* people. We have always been on our own up here at the top of the world. We have been accustomed to taking care of ourselves. Until recently, there's been very little immigration. The warming has changed all that as our melting ice uncovered new lands for farming and new mineral resources to exploit. We are not used to foreigners, so the transition for Greenlanders may be every bit as difficult as yours.

"In addition, we are well aware that Greenland, as a country, is not well loved. The melting of our ice cap has been a major contributor to the ever-rising sea level. It's not our fault, of course, but we feel unfairly blamed."

Jim Thornton stood, his large hands gripping the chair in front of him.

"Don't mean to interrupt, but what are we supposed to do about this? We're not talking about the potential for violence, are we?"

"No, no violence. But you can expect—what's that phrase? 'The cold shoulder.'

"So, what can you do?" Tobiassen asked rhetorically.

"Since my job now is helping families like yours settle here, I've done a little research. I have found that immigrants always have problems assimilating, no matter what country we're talking about. It's natural. They come to a totally unfamiliar place with a different language, different customs. And they are often met with suspicion or hostility from the host population because they are different and may threaten the *status quo* in any number of ways.

"Often it's not until the second or even third generations that they begin to be absorbed into the host population.

"The question is: How do we speed up the process?

"One of the best ways is for immigrants to learn the host language. Another is to respect or, better, to participate in aspects of the host culture. Instead, most first generation immigrants cluster together, continue to speak their own language and try to maintain their ethnic or cultural identities. This only increases the gap between the two groups.

"To help with language, your children will study Danish intensively in school. As you know, we have established a special school for English speakers in Narsaq. The school opened last year and we have two bilingual teachers on the staff. They teach all subjects, but focus about half of each school day on language study. Students who become sufficiently proficient in Danish will transfer to our public school system.

"Children are encouraged to bring the language home to help their parents learn. It would help if an effort is made to speak Danish around the home as much as possible. There are also on-line courses available for adults.

"Relating to Greenlandic culture may be much easier

than learning the language. Our countries are very similar in many ways. We celebrate Christmas, the New Year and Easter much as you do. We also have an Independence Day celebration a lot like your 4th of July—although our independence dates only to 2034. We have festivals throughout the year to observe our history and culture. Community gatherings with music, dancing, story-telling and food are commonplace—especially during the long Polar Nights. In our short summer, we frantically take advantage of the long days and warmer temperatures to engage in sports and outdoor activities.

"Get involved. It may be awkward at first. But the effort will be noticed and appreciated. Slowly any walls will come down."

He stopped and looked around the room.

"Good. Everyone's still awake. But I see a few drooping eyelids.

"Just one more thought about assimilation and I'll send you off for a good night's sleep.

"As farmers from a technologically advanced country, you might find some of our methods old-fashioned. But please understand that conditions here are very different from what you've been accustomed to. This is a rocky island, the soil is thin, the weather harsh. Over the years we have learned to cope with these shortcomings. But, as our growing season steadily increases, we can now experiment with new crops and animal products. This is where we need your help. Often the best way to lead is by example. Use new practices on your farms. Your fellow farmers are interested in improvement. If they witness increases in productivity, they will adopt new techniques. In short, lead by showing, not telling.

"Our goal is not only to feed Greenland, but, by using new lands given us by the warming, to help to feed a hungry world. In this case, bad can lead to good. Our melting ice cap has contributed to the rising oceans, but it has also provided vast new real estate for farming. Ironic, isn't it?

"Okay, tomorrow morning we'll tour Nuuk and, in the afternoon, we'll fly you north to see the very active Jacobshavin Glacier. And then on Narsaq, flying over the southern tip of that bad, bad ice cap you've heard so much about. I think you will be amazed."

Before bed around 9 p.m., the Gerstens, as instructed, closed the drapes in their rooms against the bright daylight. They knew they would awaken to a world that had not really experienced night.

The morning was misty with light rain. A small bus was waiting. Tobiassen told them their primary destination was the National Greenland Museum, but that he'd point out interesting sights along the way.

The first of these was the Hans Egede House, the oldest structure in Nuuk, dating to 1728. Egede, known as the "Apostle of Greenland," launched the first Danish mission to the island. The house is used today for official government receptions. Their route also took them past Nuuk Cathedral, a bright-red wooden Lutheran church built in 1849.

"I don't want you to think the Nuuk is only about churches," Tobiassen said, as he pointed out a modern shopping center, hotel and entertainment complex in the downtown area.

Rollie was fascinated by what he saw at the National Museum. Exhibits and displays covered the 4,500 years of the island's cultural history—from its oldest inhabitants, the Inuit, and the failed colonization by the Vikings around 1,000 AD; to the Danish colonial period and modern times.

Rollie and his dad were particularly interested in displays of ancient iron farming implements, seal-skin kayaks and dog sleds. But the sight that affected him most was of four mummified remains of an Inuit family dated to 1475. They were almost perfectly preserved. A baby boy, its round face surrounded by fur, seemed to stare at Rollie—across almost 700 years.

On the way to the airport, he ventured to ask a question.

"What ever happened to the Inuit? Are they on a reservation or something?"

Tobiassen laughed.

"That's a good question, Rollie, although I've never had it asked quite that way before. Look around you at the people on the streets. Many have Inuit ancestry. Over the centuries, Inuit and Danes intermarried. There are also many pure Inuit, but they prefer to live in the far North, trying to maintain their old ways. That's become increasingly difficult because of the melting ice and the impact of the warming on the Artic animals on which they have depended."

———————

The 16-passenger jet rose steeply, pushing passengers back into their seats. Once they'd leveled off and throttled back, Tobiassen explained through wireless earphones that they were heading north up Greenland's west coast to view the glacier. They maintained an altitude of about 10,000 feet so it would be relatively easy to discern features of the landscape.

Passengers on the left side could see the waters of the Labrador Sea that separate Greenland from Canada. Its indigo blue was punctuated with recently calved, dazzling-white icebergs on their leisurely journeys south, eventually to add their millions of tons of fresh water to the slowly rising oceans. Right-side passengers were treated to the view of a rocky landscape leading to ice-topped coastal mountains to the east.

After less than an hour in the air, their host warned that

the glacier was a few miles ahead.

"The Jacobshavn is one of the largest and fastest moving of the more than 200 outlet glaciers in Greenland," Tobiassen said. "It drains about 6.5 percent of the entire ice sheet and calves more than 10 percent of the icebergs. Some years it has been clocked moving at more than 20-feet per day."

The plane climbed to provide a wider view. The glacier looked like a bright-white river flowing between two black, rocky shores.

"Some 35 billion tons of icebergs calve off and pass out of the *fjord* every year. Icebergs are sometimes up to half a mile in height—too tall to float down the channel. They stick on the bottom of its shallower areas, sometimes for years, until they are broken up by the force of the glacier and icebergs further up the *fjord*."

After circling a couple of times, the plane broke off on a southeast heading.

"We're now on our way to Narsaq near the extreme southern tip of the country—the largest town nearest to your new farms. Below us is the famous, or should I say, infamous ice sheet that covers most of our midsection. Even after many decades of melting, its dimensions are still impressive—approximately 1,200 miles long and 450 miles wide. Its highest point—called The Summit—is about 8,000 feet above sea level.

"What may be even more interesting is what we can't see under the surface. The weight of trillions of tons of ice over the past 120,000 years has actually deformed the bedrock beneath creating a huge bowl that's below sea level and throwing up the mountains that ring it. Should the ice ever completely melt, Greenland could be left with an enormous fresh water lake in its interior.

"And, though you can't see it, we're now flying over the world's longest canyon. Ice-penetrating radar years ago discovered the canyon running north and south for approximately 450 miles. It averages six miles in width and is as deep as 2,600 feet. Not surprisingly, it has become known as Greenland's Grand Canyon.

"We're going to descend to 5,000 feet so I can try to point out some interesting features of the ice cap. Just ahead is a large fresh water lake created by the melt. These lakes thaw and refreeze depending on the time of year. Often cracks in lake beds appear that quickly drain the water all the way to the base of the ice sheet. This water lubricates the bedrock below and encourages slippage of the formation toward the sea."

Rollie was amazed by the color of the lake. To say it was emerald green didn't do it justice. The water was so clear that the sun reflected an impossible-to-name color up from the icy lake bed.

"You'll have to look carefully for these," Tobiassen said. "See if you can spot what appear to be round, black holes in the ice. I think there's one coming up on the right. They're called 'moulins' and are, in fact, holes that form and drain melt water from lakes like the one we just saw. Some carry water hundreds of feet vertically down to bedrock where it may accelerate the speed of glacial movement or encourage calving. Others feed subterranean rivers that honeycomb the ice sheet."

The plane began to descend and banked left. Ahead was the bright blue North Atlantic.

"We'll be landing in Narsaq in a few minutes. If you'll look below you'll see what appears to be a ribbon of highway. It's actually a causeway—a road on pillars—that's under construction from Nuuk to Narsaq. There are very few roads in Greenland between our cities because the terrain is so rough and we must contend with rivers of water pouring off the ice sheet. Several of these rushing rivers can be seen as we approach Narsaq. Inner-city transportation is primarily by boat or plane."

Narsaq was unlike any city Rollie had ever seen. The hillocky green landscape rose slowly from a black, jumbled seacoast toward ice-covered mountains to the north. The hillsides were covered with remnants of spring flowers in white, yellow, orange and purple.

Several powerful glacial rivers flowed close to the city, slashing their ways to the sea. Their rumblings could be heard day and night throughout the community.

It was July, but Narsaq's small deep-water port still contained "slob ice," remnants of ice brought by tides in from the open ocean. Huddled around the port were Narsaq's several industries—a dairy processor converting milk to butter and several varieties of cheese, a meat-packing plant preparing beef, mutton and reindeer products, a vegetable and fruit processing plant, wool warehouses. All products were for local consumption, national and world export.

The waterfront also had a relatively new fish processing plant catering to the burgeoning cod fishery. Rollie learned that the warming waters of North Atlantic were driving cod farther and farther north into the arms of Greenland's expanding fishing fleet.

Fortunately, prevailing winds from the northwest usually blew most of the stench from these facilities—particularly the slaughter house and fish processing plant—out to sea.

Residential areas were a lot like those in Nuuk—small wood-frame homes in bright colors. There'd been much recent new construction to accommodate the growing population. Many of the newer homes were made of concrete block, reflecting the high cost of wood for construction. They, too, added to the kaleidoscope of color.

Unlike Nuuk, however, there were a few small trees here and there—pine and spruce—carefully tended by homeowners who prized them every bit as much as gardeners in warmer climes prized roses or bougainvillea.

Most homes also had small vegetable gardens. Some had apple trees.

The Gerstens were assigned to a small, older home— bright blue—rent-free for two years until the family's financial future was more settled. While neat and clean, Rollie's mom was upset because there were only two bedrooms. He happily volunteered to sleep on a day bed in the living room. He didn't sleep much and looked forward to reading late, working at the kitchen table on projects and being close to the refrigerator for his inevitable bed-time snack.

The Gersten's 1,000 acres were located about 15 miles northeast of Narsaq in a valley finally vacated by a glacier some ten years earlier. To the north were the rugged rim mountains that had spawned the glacier. The tips of their craggy peaks were frosted with snow, even in July. But the local agricultural agent had assured Rollie's dad there'd be no more glacial activity in the valley.

The two stood by a cairn of rocks that marked the southeast corner of their new farm. Stuck in the cairn was a wooden sign with the number "103." Rollie wondered if that meant theirs was the 103rd farm given to immigrant farmers or if there were some other numbering scheme.

The wind blowing down the valley was cool and carried the fecund smell of wet earth. In a briefing earlier they'd been told that the ice sheet had covered and protected the rich soil of a verdant tundra that existed on the huge island 2.7 million years prior to it being entombed in ice. The retreating glaciers didn't scour the soil from the land because it was frozen and heavily compacted by the weight of the ice.

The two looked at the land and tried to imagine their farm. After analyzing the markets and costs to produce the various agricultural products the land would support,

Rollie's dad decided it best to diversify by growing strawberries, planting a large apple orchard and raising hay to support a dairy herd. This would make it a year-around operation, ensuring steady cash flow and also providing a hedge against market fluctuations or any of the numerous other complications that plague farmers.

The first chore that waited was clearing the land of remaining stones and boulders. Most farms Rollie had seen were rimmed with fences made with stones cleared from the fields. The process, while time consuming, would be made easier with the use of an unusual piece of equipment they'd seen elsewhere around Narsaq. The hybrid John Deere vehicle—in its familiar green and yellow livery—was a combination front loader and backhoe that could also be fitted with a blade up front and rigged to drag a plow, disc harrow or bailer for making hay. It short, it could do anything the Gerstens needed. A loaner from the local agricultural cooperative was scheduled for delivery the next week so they could begin clearing.

The decision to be dairy farmers led to another decision, one not very popular with Rollie's mom. A dairy herd required almost around the clock attention, particularly during the long Polar Night. This meant providing, in addition to a barn with milking equipment, housing for those who would tend the cows. Dad proposed that the barn also contain living quarters.

"This," he said, "is not unusual. Historically many farm families lived with their animals. But I'm not suggesting that we move into the barn. I want us to take advantage of this free house for the two years it's being offered. Instead, I'll live out there as necessary with a hired hand until we start generating some cash and can build our family home."

He said it was also important that the kids stay in town for as long as possible to be close to school and friends.

The foreigner's school, as most locals called it, was about a 10-minute walk from the house. The small, rather rundown two-story building appeared to have been a warehouse. But the insides had been nicely renovated and felt friendly. It was also well equipped with modern computers, internal networking and holographic projection equipment.

Its 16 students were divided into elementary and secondary groups based on age and prior academic achievement. Each of two fresh-faced, bi-lingual and enthusiastic young women teachers—recent graduates Rollie imagined—interacted primarily with one of the two groups. But, particularly when it came to language instruction in the afternoons, the two would come together.

And, for academics, it was expected that the older kids would help tutor the younger, something Rollie enjoyed—except when attempting to work with his siblings.

Rollie had studied Spanish in Hays for three years and demonstrated a facility with language. Danish, though a completely different language, also seemed to come relatively easily. But, of course, he worked hard at it. By the end of the first term—deep into Polar Night—Rollie was offered the chance to team up with a student from the public high school who had made similar progress with English. It was a new program designed to help newcomers transition to public school.

Thus it was that Rollie met Sophie.

Their first meeting was at a coffee shop after school. Rollie had no idea what to expect, so he practiced greetings and vocabulary for topics he imagined they'd discuss. The idea was for Rollie to speak Danish and Sophie to respond in English. Then the two would critique each other.

He sat with a cup of mocha reading through some verb

conjugations when became aware he wasn't alone. He looked up and gulped—something he hated to do because it made his rather large Adam's apple bob. Rollie, now 16, had developed a very healthy interest in girls. And this was some girl! Fair skinned, long white-blond hair and eyes as blue as ice melt.

"Hi. You are Rollie." She made the question a statement. "I am Sophie."

He rose awkwardly, bumping the table and almost spilling his drink. Suddenly Danish was the farthest thing from his mind.

"*Hej, jeg er* Rollie!" he finally managed to get out. This is not going at all well, he thought.

During the rest of the meeting, Rollie learned that Sophie was a junior, that her father was a sheep farmer, that she liked studying "the English" and that she hoped to become a flight attendant for Greenland Air so she could see the world.

Rollie managed to convey the Gersten's plans to grow strawberries, have an apple orchard and run a dairy herd. Sophie wanted to know where he was from. The only way he could explain was to draw a rough sketch of the U.S. on a napkin and to mark Hays with a star in the middle of the country.

They quickly got over the initial shyness and laughed a lot about how they mangaled their new languages.

Before leaving, Sophie let him know that secondary students from his school were invited to a dance the next weekend. She gave him formal invitations that could be handed out.

"I hope you can be coming," she said with a smile.

———————

Mickey, at her mother's insistence, gave Rollie a short tutorial on the latest dance steps. After a few minutes, she told him he was impossible and would probably make a fool of himself. He thanked her for the vote of confidence and continued to practice.

The dance was held in the school gymnasium, music echoing loudly off all the hard surfaces. It was comforting for Rollie to see that some things truly are universal. Most of the girls sat on one side of the room; the boys loitered on the other looking a bit sheepish.

Sophie was stunning in a short pale blue dress. She looked encouragingly at Rollie. Okay, he thought, I've braved the North Atlantic. Surely I can do this. When the next song he believed he could handle began blaring, he crossed the invisible gender great divide and offered Sophie his hand.

After they danced, Rollie was escorting Sophie to her seat when, suddenly, a red-faced guy half a head taller, forced his way between them.

"My girl," he said in guttural English. His breath smelled of alcohol.

Before Rollie could react, he shoved him backwards with both hands. A confederate had knelt behind him and Rollie went down hard on his back. Laughter erupted from the crowd gathered to watch the American take a fall.

The laughter stopped almost immediately when Rollie executed a perfect kick-up and was suddenly standing on his feet, instinctively adopting a fighting stance.

Whoa, thought Rollie. Is this for real?

Rollie had studied Karate for a couple of years, one of his "enthusiasms," at a small *dojo* in a nearly empty strip mall in Hays. He was well on his way to a black belt when family finances required that he quit. The *sensei* took it pretty hard. Not only was he his best pupil, but the remaining students were probably not enough to keep him in business.

Okay, now what do I do? His opponent—who either wasn't very bright or was very drunk or both—reacted slowly to Rollie's miraculous recovery. He was obviously outmatched, so Rollie didn't want to take advantage. Let's not escalate. Let's just return in kind.

"*Nej, min pige!*" "No, my girl!" Rollie said in perfect Danish. This got the expected reaction. They guy lumbered forward, cocking his right hand for a punch. Rollie easily side stepped, dropped to the floor and employed a kick sweep to knock him off his feet. The big guy fell hard with an "ooomph."

At that point, chaperons finally arrived. Since Rollie was standing over his opponent, he appeared to be the aggressor. Quick interviews with a few of the onlookers made clear what had happened. But both Rollie and the guy—whose name was Olaf—were required to leave the dance. Sophie walked with him as he was escorted to the door.

"My hero!" she said, followed by her tinkling laugh.

———————

Following a language session, Rollie and Sophie sat bundled up on his back porch watching the Aurora Borealis. They'd occasionally work at his house after school. Her mother would come to town from their farm to pick her up. Rollie had never been invited to the Svensson's because, as Sophie had once haltingly explained, her father was very "against foreign farmers." Her mother knew she was working with Rollie, but the two had kept it from him.

The aurora, almost a nightly feature of Polar Night skies, was especially luminous as a result of recent intense solar flare activity. Crimson and chartreuse banners undulated slowly across almost the entire expanse of sky, hazing over what would otherwise have been the usual dramatic display of the heavens.

Rollie watched the aurora bathe Sophie's face in its almost unearthly hues. He couldn't resist. Without giving it any thought, he leaned over and kissed her on the cheek.

She froze, and then, "Rollie, what you are doing?"

They were working on her syntax.

Surprised both by what he'd done and her reaction, he managed to get out: "*Nå, det var bare et kys.*" "Well, it was just a kiss."

"Just kiss? Mother tell me about the kiss. First the kiss, then the sex!"

"*Bare sex.*" "Just sex," Rollie said.

"What means 'just sex.' Is more than the sex?"

Rollie thought he'd better switch to English.

"No, I mean you don't need to call sex 'the sex.' There is no need for 'the.'"

"Okay. Sex, sex. Some girlfriends have sex. They do not like it. Boyfriends stupid and not know what they doing. I do not want sex, Rollie. I want to wait for married and have sex with the man I love."

Rollie must have looked perplexed.

"Sorry, Rollie. But I am not throwing you out."

"Dumping me," Rollie corrected.

"What means dumping?"

"It means not wanting to be with someone anymore."

"No Rollie. Not dumping. I want us to be friends like now. Good friends, *Gode venner!*"

Rollie was about to respond, when the back door opened and his mother stuck her head into the cold.

"Rollie, please tell Sophie that her father is here to pick her up and that he seems very upset."

He conveyed the message as best he could in both languages. A flicker of concern crossed her face.

In the living room his dad and Svensson stared silently at each other. Svensson looked angrily at Sophie. He spoke too quickly for Rollie to get much, but it was clear she was being berated for being there. One thing he heard for certain: "*Du vil ikke længere se denne dreng!*" "You will no longer see this boy!"

Svensson then turned to his dad and, in thickly accented English, said: "Yankee go home!"

His dad approached Svensson and looked him in the

eyes. In the best Danish he could muster, "*Dette ER vores hjem!*" "This IS our home!"

Svensson turned, took Sophie by the shoulder and marched her out the front door. As they walked down the snowy path to his truck, she turned, looked back at Rollie and gave him a dazzling smile.

Somehow he knew he'd be seeing her again.

CPSIA information can be obtained
at www.ICGtesting.com
Printed in the USA
LVOW10s1847010817
543422LV00003B/539/P